ravage

A DEVIANTS NOVEL

ALSO BY JEFF SAMPSON

VESPER
A DEVIANTS NOVEL

HAVOC
A DEVIANTS NOVEL

ravage

A DEVIANTS NOVEL

JEFF SAMPSON

Balzer + Bray
An Imprint of HarperCollins*Publishers*

Balzer + Bray is an imprint of HarperCollins Publishers.

Ravage: A Deviants Novel
Copyright © 2013 by Jeff Sampson
www.epicreads.com

Library of Congress Cataloging-in-Publication Data
Sampson, Jeff.
  Ravage : a Deviants novel / Jeff Sampson. — 1st ed.
    p.   cm. — (Deviants)
  Summary: "Sick of being at the mercy of adult conspiracies, Emily Webb forms a plan with the Deviants: They will destroy BioZenith."—Provided by publisher.
  ISBN 978-0-06-199280-3 (hardcover bdg. : alk. paper)
  [1. Werewolves—Fiction. 2. Friendship—Fiction. 3. Genetic engineering—Fiction. 4. Spirit possession—Fiction. 5. Science fiction.] I. Title.
PZ7.S164Rav 2013   2012028328
[Fic]—dc23   CIP
                                                                                                  AC

Typography by Jennifer Rozbruch
13 14 15 16   CG/RRDH   10 9 8 7 6 5 4 3 2 1
❖
First Edition

The Vesper Company

Michael Handler
President

"Envisioning the brightest stars, to lead our way."

I found the last of the stuff you wrote for
them in the big guy's office. Looks like
he already read it, because the pages are
crumpled. It's all here, just like you asked.

—EC

One Vesper Way | Volmond, WA 98723
Tel: (425) 555-7647 | Fax: (425) 555-8923

1

MAYBE THERE'S A SEWER ENTRANCE

It was well after business hours, but BioZenith was alive with activity.

Behind the tall barbed-wire fence, the two-building facility was lit up with floodlights. Sleek black vans filled the parking lot, like giant beetles surrounded by patrolling ants that were security personnel. Not just in the parking lot, either—I could see guys clad in mercenary uniforms on the roof and behind the office windows. A few strolled through the second-story walkway connecting the two buildings. All carried automatic rifles.

And to think, all this because of geeky old me.

For a supposed bioengineering firm dedicated to developing new and better crops, they certainly seemed to have found a reserve of cash to up their protection. But what else would you do after being raided multiple times by a team of werewolf-slash-superhuman hybrids you'd secretly created sixteen years earlier?

"So it doesn't look like we'll be getting in there easily anytime soon," Spencer said beside me.

I glanced over at him and grinned. "You getting that idea too, huh?"

The two of us crouched behind a concrete sign at the building across the street from BioZenith, dressed in our now standard nighttime uniforms: black sweatshirts, sweats, and easily kicked off sneakers. It was still early evening, around seven, but it was already dark outside. The fall air was cold and crisp, and leaves pooled around our feet in slimy, wet piles. I hugged my arms around myself—I should have worn a jacket. But I didn't want to risk ruining one if I needed to go all Wolftime Emily.

It was Thursday night. Five days had passed since I had last confronted a lead BioZenith scientist, one of the men responsible for making Spencer and me—and two others, Dalton and Tracie—into werewolf-type . . . *things*. I'd watched as strange, shadowy beings dragged Dalton, that scientist's son, through a portal into another dimension. I'd had to wrench my best friend, Megan, away from another shadow being who'd tried to enter her body. And I'd had to do it all while fighting against some incredibly bitchy teleki-netic cheerleaders.

Yeah, my life has rapidly become different from other people's.

Not four weeks ago I'd been a shy, geeky girl who spent her free time watching bad horror movies or joining groups online to chat about all my nerdy interests. This new life as a superpowered deviant came quickly and suddenly, a cha-otic storm of events. Sometimes it was cool—I mean, the self-confidence, the new friends, and the enhanced senses are awesome. But with them came a lot of problems that made my life stressful and frightening, especially consider-ing I'm hard-coded to be the leader of this pack, the alpha.

For the past five days, I'd been plotting a way to try to get Dalton back. And that's why I was across the street from BioZenith, with Spencer, trying to see how I was going to get back inside in light of the events of the previous week-end.

A nudge in my side. "Hey," Spencer whispered. "You there?"

"Hmm?" I blinked, then looked away from the would-be fortress that was BioZenith and back at my partner in teenage crime. "Oh yeah. Sorry. Just got caught up in my thoughts."

"Can't blame you." Spencer sighed and waved a hand

at the scene in front of us. "There's no way we can get in there tonight. Is there? I mean, if this was a video game I'd go all stealth and choke everyone until they passed out. But I'm guessing these guys have better AI. And those guns are a lot more real."

I grunted a laugh. "No kidding. Maybe there's a sewer entrance conveniently leading to an unguarded room inside."

Spencer chuckled. "There probably is. And it's probably filled with giant mutant rats!"

A heavy breeze rose up, and I shivered. Spencer's big brown eyes narrowed in concern and he crouch-walked closer to me.

"You're cold," he said. "Here." Gingerly, he placed an arm around my shoulder. When I didn't resist, he pulled me in close to his side.

I let out a calming breath and closed my eyes, inhaling his familiar scent—that musk of his that my wolf brain told me made him my "mate." A programmed pheromone put in place by our creators, though he didn't know that. It had bothered me at first, the idea that I was preordained by our secretly scientist-*parents*—my formerly long-lost mother, and both his mom and dad—to be attracted to Spencer. For a while I was torn between being near him and letting his presence calm my frayed nerves, or being disgusted at myself for needing such a crutch to get through my day.

But I'd spent enough time with Spencer to know now that I genuinely liked him. Not because someone told me to, but because he was smart and funny and adorably nerdy. I don't know if I would have noticed him much if circumstances hadn't brought us together—he was short and cute rather than big and manly hot, like the types of guys I used to think I was into. But all that mattered was that we were together now.

Well, more or less. We hadn't kissed or anything. Even having superpowers by night doesn't mean that by day I'm not still learning how to handle all the usual teenage stuff.

We sat there, for how long I didn't know, silent as we listened to the rustling of the trees behind the industrial buildings and watched the guards patrol.

Then: glaring bright lights, illuminating us as though it was the middle of the day. I pulled away from Spencer, adrenaline pumping, ready to fight or flee, whatever I needed to do.

But the lights passed and I realized it was just the headlights of a car going down the street, past BioZenith and disappearing into the distance. No one had seen us. We were safe.

"Yeah, okay," I said, running my hands back through my hair. "Okay. I'm fine. But I don't think we're doing any good hanging outside here. Want to go home?"

Spencer nodded at me. Making sure no one was looking in our direction, we made our way behind the building we were standing in front of until we reached the trees.

Groaning, Spencer stood to his full height, then stretched his back. "Crouching for an hour is not comfortable."

"Not even a little bit," I agreed as I cracked my neck.

I was disappointed. Getting out of the house after spending so long being paranoid in my bedroom was a relief. But it felt worthless. I'd meant to get inside BioZenith and find some way to Dalton, but instead I'd accomplished nothing.

"Hey, Em Dub," Spencer said, facing me as he walked backward into the trees. "I've been practicing."

I raised my eyebrows. "Practicing?"

"You know," he said. "Going hybrid."

I nodded appreciatively. Well, if we weren't invading BioZenith, at least we could have a training session.

One more wrinkle to this whole tale that I didn't mention above: Initially when this started, I'd go from my normal daytime self to a wild version of me I called "Nighttime Emily." She was the one with the powers, the superstrength, the fearlessness. Each night I became her longer and longer until eventually she herself turned into "Werewolf Emily."

I hadn't been in control of these shifts at first. But during the fight to save Megan and Dalton, I figured out once and for all how to reconcile the three parts of myself and access the powers I needed, when I needed them.

I became full hybrid.

In fact, accessing my new vision had become such second nature that I barely turned it off. I mostly only wore my glasses at home now, just to keep up appearances with my dad, stepmom, and stepsister.

Anyway, I realized if I could go hybrid, Spencer and Tracie probably could, too. Tracie had completely ignored all my attempts at contact since she wanted nothing to do with this werewolf stuff. But I emailed her instructions anyway. Spencer, obviously, was much more into it.

"All right, big shot." I crossed my arms and looked Spencer up and down. "Show me. Go Nighttime."

With a knowing smile, Spencer rolled his sleeves up to his elbows, then stood straight. The change was subtle, but I knew where to look. His shoulders rolled back as his posture straightened. His eyes narrowed slightly, focusing. His exposed forearms became taut with muscle, forcing some of his veins to bulge.

Looking him in the eye, I thought, *Go Nighttime*. And I was fully her.

I leaped.

Spencer was ready for me as I brought my fist toward his face. He blocked, then punched at my gut with his free hand. I leaped back, narrowly avoiding the blow.

We stood four feet from each other, stances wide, circling. Leaves and twigs crunched beneath our feet as we wound easily past the trees.

"Nice," I said. "Can you do this?"

In a flash my fingernails pulled free of my cuticles, growing into dark, sharp claws. Biting his lip, Spencer flexed his fingers. I could see his own nails darken, but they didn't grow.

With him distracted, I took the opening. I leaped forward and grabbed his ankles, then pulled his feet out from under him.

"Whoa!" he cried, arms flailing as he fell flat on his back in the dirt.

Throwing his legs back behind my waist, I slapped my hands on the ground on either side of his shoulder and put my face directly in front of his, towering over him, a wolf over her prey.

"Gotcha," I whispered.

For a long moment we looked into each other's eyes, our heavy breaths coming out in frozen clouds. His eyes were hungry; I knew mine must look like I wanted to ravage him. I was Nighttime Me, my inhibitions stripped away. I wanted to use my claws to shred his sweatshirt, tear off his sweatpants, and eat him alive—starting with his lips.

In the back of my head, Daytime Emily thought, *Whoa there. Too fast. Too fast!*

I let Nighttime recede, save for the vision. My fingernails returned to normal. Heart thudding, I pushed myself up from the awkward position I was in—basically, lying almost on top of Spencer—then cleared my throat.

"Um, yeah," I said. "Good job! Go team."

He grinned up at me sheepishly, and I could tell he'd let his own Nighttime self recede as well. I offered him a hand and he took it, and once back on his feet he brushed the dirt and leaves off his backside.

"I'll, uh, need to work on that claw thing," he said. "It's very Wolverine."

"Definitely," I said.

We stood there for a moment, hands in our pockets, neither one of us looking at the other full on. My pulse was still racing, and I could still smell his scent, still see his face and lips so close. . . .

"So think we should head home?" I asked. "We can figure out where to go from here with BioZenith tomorrow."

"Yeah, BioZenith," he said. "Sounds cool."

We trudged through the woods to the side street where Spencer had parked his mom's minivan. By the time we were in the car with the heat blasting, our nerves had calmed and we were back to talking like normal—about movies, games,

TV, school. Anything but the fact that in addition to all the new sensations that came with being all hybrid powered, I was suddenly developing an appetite for boys. Well, one in particular.

Spencer dropped me off in front of my house, and he watched me until I reached the front door. I waved at him, and we met each other's eyes once more, and I couldn't help but smile.

Craziness or no, I couldn't say my new life was all bad.

Before I could open the door, my phone chirped in my pocket. I pulled it free and saw I had a text message. The glowing screen read CASEY DELGADO.

Casey was one of the aforementioned telekinetic cheerleaders. Only she wasn't at all bitchy, that I'd seen anyway. In fact, after Dalton was taken she came to me and told me she wanted to try brokering some peace between us wolves and the cheerleaders—her two sisters and Dalton's girlfriend, Nikki.

8:37 PM: Hi, Emily! Still no luck with the girls ☹. Amy just doesn't want anything to do with this. She's sort of stubborn. But I'll keep trying. Any luck with Dalton?

I sighed. Of course Amy—the most outspoken and aggressive of the Delgado triplets—would be causing trouble still.

Tapping in a response, I opened the front door and

walked into the foyer. To my left was our dining room, and I could tell out of the corner of my eye that my dad was sitting at the table.

8:38 PM: Yeah, please keep trying. No luck with Dalton yet either. I'll try and find you at school tomorrow if you can get away from the others.

"Hey, Dad," I said, still focused on the phone as I read over the message, then pressed send.

"Hey, Leelee," he said.

His voice sounded strained. Off.

Shoving the phone in my pocket, I turned. My mouth was open to say something, but I immediately forgot what.

Sitting at the table next to my dad was another man. Tall, broad-shouldered. Red hair streaked with gray. Cruel features—or at least they looked cruel to me since I was already well acquainted with the person to whom they belonged.

"Hello, Emily," said Dalton's father. "We've got a lot to talk about."

YOU KNEW

"What . . ." I said, unable to finish my sentence. I shook my head and sputtered out, "What is *he* doing here?"

Mr. McKinney looked to my dad, as though expecting him to answer. My dad said nothing. He looked down at the table, his glasses askew, what little hair he had left was disheveled. His eyes were rimmed red. Had he been *crying*? My dad?

"Dad?" I asked, my voice rising in pitch. I hated the way I sounded—nervous and afraid. I couldn't help it. The knife that had been dangling over my head all week was held up by a thin thread, and I couldn't help but think Mr. McKinney was there with a pair of scissors ready to make the fatal snip.

My dad cleared his throat. "Leelee," he rasped out. "I didn't mean for . . ." He trailed off. I could see his hands, clasped in front of him on the table, tremble.

Mr. McKinney waved his hand at the chair across from him, the one nearest to where I stood. "Why don't you take a seat, Emily?"

"Why should I?" I asked.

His lip raised, almost as if he was going to snarl at me. "Because you have lots of questions. And I've got the answers. Sit."

The last word was not a request. I stood there for another moment, just to show that I no longer jumped on command—that Emily died weeks ago after I had to help kill a man in self-defense. Only when I saw the impatience flare in his eyes did I slowly pull the chair from the table, letting the legs screech across the wood floor, and sit down.

"Dad, where's Katherine and Dawn?" I asked. The house was quiet, but that didn't mean my stepmom and stepsister weren't around.

"At a movie," my dad said simply. He still wouldn't look up.

The kitchen behind Mr. McKinney was dark save for the green glow from electronic appliances. The lights were dimmed in the dining room and the living room. Everything was quiet, dark. Almost as if Mr. McKinney had set the place up to feel creepy and desolate.

I wouldn't necessarily put it past him.

"So how's Dalton?" I asked, breaking our silent stand-off. "I hear he had to go back to the hospital. Poor guy."

Mr. McKinney's eyes narrowed. "Let's not play games, Emily. We know all about your recent escapades. You were activated, and you and your friends have been using your abilities to wreak a little terror."

I shot a look at my dad. Why would Mr. McKinney say this in front of him?

"I don't know what you're talking about," I said.

Mr. McKinney leaned back in his chair. "Sure you do, Emily. You think we haven't been watching you? You think it's a coincidence you were able to get into our facilities so easily, and now you can't?" Leaning forward again, he placed both arms on the table. "Did you get a good look at the facility tonight?"

My chest seized. Watching me? They couldn't have. We'd have seen them. We'd have known.

Turning to my dad, I whispered, "Daddy. Please tell me what's going on and why Mr. McKinney is here."

My dad took in a shaky breath and finally looked up at me. His cheeks had gone gray. "It's okay, Leelee. I . . . I know about HAVOC. I know that you're a werewolf."

For a moment, it felt as though I'd huffed paint fumes.

The room went woozy, my head spun. My stomach lurched, queasy. I felt like I might throw up.

My dad knew.

All this time I'd thought I was alone. All this time I was trying to figure out how to handle my new reality, to keep my family safe, to find a way to keep *everyone* I knew safe from shadowmen and portals and men with guns.

I couldn't speak. I mean, I knew my mother was involved with BioZenith. I knew she was the project lead on HAVOC and was the one who'd made me the way I was.

But I never knew my mother. She was an abstract figure my whole life, just a name and a photograph, no one I truly loved. This was my *dad*. The man who raised me alone. The one who'd fed me a steady pop-geek diet that was a big part of who I was.

The one who protected me from the world. Until now.

A hand on my hand. I looked at my dad's pleading eyes as he reached over to grip me. His eyes were pleading, begging me to forgive him.

I yanked my hand away. "You knew," I whispered.

"Leelee, not at first," he said. "I swear I wouldn't have let you go through all this alone if I'd known everything that was happening."

My eyes burned with tears, but I refused to let them fall, to let Mr. McKinney see me crying for my daddy.

"You knew!" I shouted. My voice echoed through the house, and my dad flinched.

"You let her experiment on your own child?" I said, shaking my head at him. "You let your wife put chemicals into her baby? You let her make me into a freak? Hard-code who I'm supposed to be? Why would you do that?"

My fingers gripped the edge of the table so hard I could feel the polished wood splintering. Nighttime's strength. In my anger, she was slipping more and more to the forefront of my brain.

My dad only shook his head.

Mr. McKinney cleared his throat and stood up. He placed a hand on my dad's shoulder and said, "Greg, why don't you take a break and let Emily and me speak alone? I'm sure she'll be ready to hear what you have to say when she calms down."

"I *am* calm," I lied through gritted teeth.

The two adults ignored me. Eyes on the floor, my dad stood and nodded absently. He shuffled past me into the foyer, then into the living room and disappeared.

I didn't know if I would ever be able to look at him the same way again.

"Just a clarification," Mr. McKinney said as he sat down again. "We never did any sort of procedure on babies. That sort of late-term engineering never would have worked.

Your father merely donated his genetic material to his lovely, devoted wife so that she could create you in a test tube and enhance you before implantation into her own womb. She's quite dedicated to her science." He let out a small laugh. "In fact, it might interest you to know there were multiple Emilys. You were just one of the two who lived long enough to be born."

"Two?" I asked.

"The other would be the recently deceased Emily Cooke," he said. "Don't worry, no relation to you. Caroline and the Cookes were in a bit of a competition to see who could produce and implant the first viable human-animal vesper, and the winner got to keep the name Emily, as both ladies wanted it." He waved his hands in front of him. "And wouldn't you know, it ended up a tie."

"A competition," I said flatly. "Great."

This is what I should have wanted—my own big scene of exposition where the baddie lays out why he did what he did. Hell, I was supposed to spend my evening reading the BioZ files on my computer anyway.

But all I could think of was my dad, ashen faced and remorseful, admitting he knew about me and had done nothing to help.

"I'm sure you have a lot of questions for me, Emily," Mr. McKinney said. "I've spoken with the other parents involved, and we all agreed that after what happened to Dalton, we can't sit back and observe anymore."

"You couldn't have thought of that when Dr. Elliott decided to take a gun and start hunting us?" I spat.

Mr. McKinney sighed. "Well, Emily, I hate to admit it, but we were as blindsided by that as you were. You weren't supposed to be activated. The project was considered on hold indefinitely due to certain inherent dangers. Dr. Elliott, however, took it upon himself to use our systems to remotely activate your genetic mutations so that he could identify which children were vespers and then eliminate them. By the time we figured out what was happening, he was already dead."

I loosened my grip on the table and took in a breath. There were indentations on the tabletop where I'd clenched my fingers.

"Do you know why Dr. Elliott wanted to kill us? And how come he couldn't identify us without, uh, activating us?"

Mr. McKinney crossed his arms and put his chin to his chest, thinking. Finally he said, "We have our theories about why Gunther did what he did. But nothing concrete. As for your identities, we kept them top secret. Only those directly involved in the project knew who the parents and children were. I was actually impressed with your friend Spencer—I had no idea he'd be so capable as to break into my private system."

I smirked at him. "That's Spencer for you." Going stern again, I asked, "So after the shootings, rather than tell us what was going on, you wanted to just watch us?"

"Of course!" Mr. McKinney said. "This was our only opportunity to see how the modifications would work without any interference. The personality changes, the way the wolf genetics manifested themselves, the eventual melding of the three states that you achieved . . ." He shook his head. "Fascinating."

"Yeah," I said. "How about 'messed up'? You don't exactly seem broken up that your standing back and 'observing' led to us almost getting shot in the BioZenith labs and, oh yeah, your son being taken through a portal by shadowmen."

Mr. McKinney let out a sound that was halfway between a groan and a sigh. Leaning over his chair, he grabbed something off the floor, then placed it on the table: a black leather satchel. Reaching inside, he produced a touch-screen tablet. Ignoring me, he silently powered on the device, pressed a few buttons, and then slid it across the table. It skidded to a stop in front of me.

"Of course I'm concerned about my son," Mr. McKinney said, his voice cold. "You have no idea how much I care for my boy. But I have the good fortune of knowing exactly where he is."

"The other dimension," I said. "The one where the shadowmen came from."

He snorted. "*Shadowmen*. I suppose that's one way to describe them. Trust me when I say we are very familiar with them. Especially those at BioZenith who have been on the other side."

"My mother," I said. "And Tracie's father."

He nodded. "Very good. See, how would we ever know that you could have learned so much on your own if we'd interfered?"

I leaned forward and opened my eyes wide. "I just don't even know. Us silly old teenagers actually looking for answers when we turn into mythical creatures, it's crazy talk."

The man rolled his eyes and flicked his hand. "Sarcasm. Wonderful. Why don't you go ahead and watch the video I pulled up, hmm?"

Reaching forward, I grabbed the thin tablet and slid it toward me. Angling my head over it to block the glare from the dim light, I pressed the play symbol on the black screen.

Distortions were all I could see at first, veering from scrambled lines like a bad TV signal to oily smears like the surface of a soap bubble. After a few seconds of this, a face came into view. It was shaded in gray and the features bordered on indistinct, but enough was there for me to recognize the face from the old photographs we had lying around the house.

My mother. And she didn't look a day over thirty—when she should have been nearing fifty. Maybe time worked differently there. That's how it is for, like, Narnia, anyway.

The woman smiled. "Hello, Emily. I can't speak long as our connection can only be held open for a short time. I wish I could see you and speak to you in person, to see for myself the woman you've become." Her smile faltered and her eyes drooped. "I never wanted to leave you or your father, but my work took me here, and I've been here so long that the radiation that keeps the Akhakhu from crossing through the portals has affected me as well. I know you must feel so many things, but know that you can trust Harrison—Mr. McKinney—and that we can help you. Maybe soon I can . . . I can even speak to you in person."

A muffled voice sounded, and she glanced to the side. Speaking quickly, she said, "And don't blame your father, he—"

The screen went black.

I stared at it for a moment. Processing.

So that was my mother. The woman who literally created me. The woman who sat in meetings discussing how to use her own body as an incubator for some otherworldly experiment, who abandoned me in favor of her science, who'd messed with every part of who I was without letting me grow up to be . . . whatever it was I would have been.

I expected her to seem cold, detached. Evil, I guess. But she didn't look evil. In fact, she sort of looked like an older version of me.

I didn't know what to feel.

Mr. McKinney stood, grabbed his satchel from the table, and walked to stand next to me. He picked up the tablet and cleared his throat.

"There's much more that we should discuss," he said. "But we should do it with everyone. You and the rest of your 'pack' will meet with us, yes? You can convince them to come despite their feelings toward their parents."

"Yeah," I said. "Why not." Looking up, I asked, "I found everyone, didn't I? All the wolves?"

He nodded. "Emily Cooke, Spencer Holt, Tracie Townsend, my son, and yourself."

"Good," I said. "Then email me the time and place and we'll be there."

He smiled at me, a toothy shark's grin. "I'll do that right away."

I sat at my chair, staring across the dining table into the dark kitchen until I heard the front door open and shut behind me. Then I slowly lifted myself up, walked through the living room, and headed upstairs to my room.

Sitting at my computer, I brought up the files we'd stolen from BioZenith and Mr. McKinney's computer. Clicking through, I zeroed in on those files specifically about Project HAVOC: Human-Animal Vespers, Original Crossbreeds. I didn't trust Mr. McKinney any more than I did from the first moment I met him, and I could have sworn I saw something during my initial read-through of all these science papers. . . .

Then I found it. The list of the "vespers" that made it to term:

Vesper 1: Emily Webb

Vesper 2: Emily Cooke

Vesper 3: Dalton McKinney

Vesper 4: Tracie Townsend

Vesper 5: Spencer Holt

Vesper 0: REDACTED

That would be six vespers, not five like he'd said.

Mr. McKinney had lied to me.

I scanned through every one of the HAVOC files I could find, reading through the fancy science jargon as fast as I could. It took half an hour, but I finally found a name buried in an innocuous-looking file about some Secret Santa gift exchange from 1996.

And amidst the talk of gift-spending limits and discussion of the appropriateness of having the holiday party at a local bar instead of in the offices, under a list of newborn babies who everyone was going to pitch in and buy gifts for, I saw the name of someone I knew but hadn't seen in almost eight years.

Vesper 0's name was Evan Cooke.

At first I thought it was a typo, that someone meant to type Emily Cooke. Then I remembered the little towheaded boy who was the other Emily's sidekick when we were all in elementary school. I hadn't known him—or, many people— all that well, but I did know that he was Emily's cousin.

And for some reason we weren't supposed to know he existed.

I set about searching the internet for an email, some way to contact him. The usual places—Facebook and Twitter— weren't bringing anything up, so I went back to the older, defunct social sites. Midway through searching those, there came a knock at my door.

"Leelee?" my dad asked softly through the door. "Can we talk?"

I stopped typing and tore my eyes from the screen. My fingers trembled over the keyboard. I opened my mouth to say something, but no words came out.

My dad and I used to talk about everything. Before junior high, he was literally my best friend—the highlights of my day were coming home, blabbering on about school, and then curling up to watch TV with him.

My friend Megan became my confidante once puberty hit, and slowly we'd grown distant. But I always thought, if I really needed to, I could confide in my dad again. Spill all my secrets and have him hold me and assure me he still loved me.

I'd felt so intensely guilty, hiding my new life from him. I thought I was protecting him. But he was the one hiding things from me, and a whole hell of a lot longer than three weeks.

It turned out I didn't really know my dad like I thought I did.

A sigh from the other side of the door. "I only just found out this evening you've been changing," his voice said, muffled. "I never wanted this for you. I only agreed to it because . . . I was young. Your mother was—your mother *is*—so smart and she said this would make our baby perfect. And you are. And they offered us so much money. . . . I'm so sorry, Leelee."

I didn't know how to respond. What, I wouldn't have been good enough as a normal baby? Possibly messing me up for life was worth a cash payout? I know he didn't mean it that way, but that was all I could think, and I knew spitting those words at him would hurt him deeply.

So I didn't say anything at all.

Silence as I waited for him to speak again. He never did. At long last, I heard my dad's footsteps walk away.

Swallowing the sob in my throat, I forced myself to focus on the task at hand.

Evan Cooke's existence had caught Mr. McKinney in a lie. Before we had our little child-parent get-together between my pack and BioZenith, I planned to talk to this secret vesper and see what he had to say.

I'M PERSISTENT. SUE ME.

My night consisted of repeatedly dozing off momentarily before snapping wide awake again, my brain a flurry of thoughts about my crazy sci-fi life. There was more than a little tossing and turning, and by five a.m. the sheets were basically torn off my bed and my stuffed toy dog Fin was tossed on the floor.

I figured it was as good a time as any to officially wake up.

I jumped to my computer and opened my email. There was a new message, and my heart leaped in excitement—until I saw it was from Mr. McKinney.

Friday, Sept. 24, 2010—4:54 a.m. PST

From: Harrison.McKinney

To: missleeleewebb

Emily—

I consulted with the others last evening. We think it's best to convene as soon as possible, so we propose tomorrow at 1 p.m. We will have a lunch in our cafeteria— our private chef George Bonet is a master—and then give a private tour of the facility, during which we can share all that we know with one another. Please confirm ASAP.

—Harrison McKinney

What a treat. I'd already had an unofficial tour of BioZenith, and let me tell you, it's not exactly a trip through the Nestlé museum. Who wouldn't want to eat a big lunch and then go view the giant, mutated fetuses BioZenith keeps around in vats? It sounded *super appetizing.*

I grabbed my phone and flipped it open to text Spencer.

5:07 AM: Hey, you up?

Nothing for a few minutes. Then:

5:09 AM: no

5:10 AM: OMG you can text in your sleep? You have skills!

5:10 AM: mmhmm Im cool like that. wut u need?

5:11 AM: Crazy stuff went down last night after you dropped me off. We should talk right away. Can you come get me?

5:11 AM: its dark out that means sleep time

I grinned. Poor Spencer.

5:12 AM: All right, go back to bed. I'll see you at school later.

5:12 AM: k

I swiveled in my desk chair, unsure what to do with myself. I refreshed my in-box, but there was still no email response from Evan Cooke. Or Tracie or any of the cheerleaders, for that matter. What, was I the only one who was up before dawn? What teenager doesn't just jump out of bed at like five a.m. ready to run to school? I mean, *really*.

Finally I decided to just go to school insanely early. It's not like I wanted to eat breakfast across the table from my dad, anyway. I still didn't know what to think or feel. How much had he known about me, and when did he find out I was turning into a wolf? In the video my mom told me not to blame him for anything, but how couldn't I when he was obviously involved in making me the way I was?

The further along all this werewolf-hybrid-other-dimension stuff went, the more I learned that you can't trust anybody. But I thought at the very least I could trust my parents.

I pulled on a pair of jeans, a sweater, and a jacket, then walked quietly downstairs to put on my shoes and collect my bag, both of which I'd left by the front door. No one was awake yet. I opened the front door, then stopped to look back at the living room, the foyer with my dad's computer desks, the dining room. It all seemed smaller somehow.

A chill, damp wind rushed over me. I zipped up my jacket, put my bag over my shoulder, and left the house.

The early-morning trek to school was a hazy, misty blue, as though the world was in that bleary time halfway between asleep and awake. It must have rained overnight, because the leaves were wet and plastered to the street like festive fall wallpaper, and grass squelched beneath my shoes as I took shortcuts through various front yards.

It was around six by the time I made it to school. There were already cars in the teachers' parking lot, and I could see some walking through the buildings carrying stacks of papers in one hand and steaming thermoses in the other. There were even some other kids here, mostly the athletes who came early to get in a workout before school.

My eyes went to the track that ran around the baseball and football fields as I walked over the gravel auxiliary parking lot where the late-arriving students usually parked. I half hoped to see a tall, broad-shouldered, fresh-faced, red-haired boy out there sprinting to keep in shape during football season. But of course Dalton was gone.

Stolen by the shadowmen.

I cringed as the memory of Dalton, naked and scared out of his mind as he was dragged by shadowy beings through a rip in the universe, flashed through my thoughts. I tried not to imagine what could be happening to him over there, what those shadowy *things* could possibly be doing to him. It was a relief to know Mr. McKinney knew—or thought—Dalton was alive, at least. But that didn't mean he was okay.

You know, I was never the girl who had many motherly instincts. I preferred to use my dolls and stuffed animals to re-create epic movie action scenes rather than dressing them up and putting them in toy strollers to play Mommy. Maybe because I didn't have a mom growing up to copycat, I don't know.

But since this change, alpha instincts had risen within me, telling me to keep my pack close, to protect them. Programming, yeah. Just like the pheromones that made Spencer so alluring. But like with Spencer, I'd come to embrace this part of me. Even if it meant I now carried around a hollowness inside where Dalton would be.

At least maybe I could find him, save him. My mother apparently was surviving just fine in the shadowmen dimension, and Mr. McKinney didn't seem terribly concerned. Still, after the way the shadowmen had stalked us, had dragged Dalton away while he was paralyzed with fear . . .

Well, I had vowed to rescue him. And I intended to keep my promise.

It was the least I could do after already losing one of my pack, Emily Cooke, forever.

Absentmindedly I walked over the damp grass to sit on the bleachers. The metal seats were like ice beneath my thighs. Hands shoved deep in my pockets, I set my bag between my knees and watched the runners as they paced themselves. A month ago I would have thought they were crazy, both for being up so ridiculously early and for finding jogging an enjoyable activity. But the wolf side of me loved to run, found it exhilarating, and that joy had become a part of me now, too.

It took a moment, but then I realized I recognized someone on the track. She was in an expensive-looking yellow jogging suit, her black hair pulled back into a ponytail, her expression stern and focused.

Tracie Townsend.

Class president. Fellow werewolf. Formerly super chipper, almost annoyingly so . . . but ever since the changes began, she had started to think she was going crazy.

I hadn't seen her in days—the girl had become an expert at outmaneuvering me in the halls. She was like a ninja or something, able to meld with the shadows while I walked by, oblivious.

There was no way she was going to be able to hide wearing bright canary yellow, especially not against the backdrop of gray that was the early morning sky.

Leaving my bag on the bleachers, I stood and jumped nimbly from metal step to metal step, barely making a sound. I hit the ground and immediately started to jog, reaching the track just as Tracie came near. I matched her stride and ran next to her. She was so in the zone, she didn't even notice.

"Good morning!" I said, forcing my most upbeat of voices.

She started, but did not slow down. Glancing in my direction, she let out an exasperated sigh.

"I told you, Emily, not interested."

I shrugged. "I'm persistent. Sue me."

"Maybe I will!" she said. "You've been blowing up my phone and in-box for days. I hope you know I set your emails to automatically go to spam."

In front of us, one of the joggers stopped to tie his shoe. We rounded him in unison, not missing a beat.

"That's too bad," I said. "Spencer and I figured out how to control our powers so that we can access the best parts without any of the side effects." I tilted my head. "Mostly. It's a process."

Tracie looked at me side-eyed as she pumped her arms

to the rhythmic beat of our sneakers hitting dirt.

"Really?" she asked. Before I could she respond, she shook her head and added, "Actually, no, stop it. You told me things would be fine at the party last week and you were wrong. I'm done listening to you. I just want my life to be as normal as possible during the day."

She upped her speed and pulled ahead of me. Sweat beaded at her brow and began to drip from the tip of her nose.

Nighttime, looks like you get to come out and play, I thought. I could feel her—my—growing excitement as my arms and legs surged with strength. In seconds I went all Flash and effortlessly zoomed ahead of Tracie. Spinning on my heel, I jogged backward so that I could face her.

Grinning, I said, "So, just FYI, I am in no way an athlete. But notice my speed. Guess which part of me that came from?"

Tracie stopped running, stomped her foot, and put her hands on her hips. "You're going to run in front of me? Really?"

I stopped as well, then sauntered to stand directly in front of her. "Really."

"Watch it!"

Tracie and I both looked behind her to see two football players barreling toward us. We stepped out of the way just in time for them to hustle past.

"Sorry!" Tracie called out after them. "Good luck at the game tonight!"

They responded with disinterested grunts.

"Here," I said, gently placing a hand on her arm. "Let's go to the bleachers. There's some stuff you should know."

Tracie closed her eyes. She placed her hands out in front of her, palms toward the sky, and then raised her arms up as she took in a long, deep breath. Then, aiming her palms down, she let her breath come out in an exaggerated whoosh as she pushed her hands toward the ground. She did this a few times while I, and a few joggers who ran past us, stared at her.

Finally, Tracie opened her eyes. "Cleansing breaths," she explained off my look. "You were throwing me out of balance. I needed to put myself back in order."

"Oh," I said with a knowing nod. "Like yoga or something."

She gave me a withering look. "Yeah, something like that. Anyway, fine, let's get this over with. I have a lot on my plate and I don't need you stalking me through the halls all day. Again."

I grinned. "Excellent."

The two of us walked side by side back to the bleachers. Tracie grabbed a yellow gym bag that matched her tracksuit, then followed me up the steps to where I'd set my bag. We sat down on the cold metal seats and she pulled out a little container of moist towelettes. She proceeded to wipe the sweat off her face.

"You have five minutes," she said as she discarded the towelettes in a pocket of her bag, then produced another one to scrub at her hands. "Then I have to go shower so I can be at the student council morning meeting before I do announcements."

"Five minutes is all I need."

I spat it out as fast as I could, all that had happened since last I saw her—the real reason for Dalton's disappearance, what happened to Megan, the extra security at BioZenith, and how Spencer and I had been training to control our shifts. By the time I got to Mr. McKinney showing up at my house last night and everything that he'd revealed, I had her full attention.

"They want us to come to BioZenith tomorrow?" she asked. "And you're saying my mother knew that I'm like this?" She looked away from me, her eyes glazing over as she studied the line of evergreen trees beyond the sports fields. "I mean, I guess she must have. They would have had to . . . implant me." Her hand flew to her mouth and she gasped, "Oh God. I . . . Oh God."

I put my hand on her back and rubbed it comfortingly. She didn't pull away.

"I know," I said, my voice softening. "I just found out my own dad knew, too. I don't know if we can trust them. In fact, I'm pretty sure they're keeping a lot from us. I already figured out there's one more werewolf like us. Emily Cooke's cousin. I sent him an email but haven't heard back yet."

Tracie shook her head slowly. "My mother . . ." she said, completely ignoring what I'd said about Evan. "And they've been watching us. . . ."

I squirmed in my seat. I'd been saving the biggest revelation for last, and I wasn't sure how she'd take it.

"Tracie, there's one more thing," I said. "My mother and your father aren't dead. They were the scientists involved with the project, the ones who made us. And they're both alive in the dimension where those shadowmen come from."

Tracie closed her eyes once more. She breathed in, out. Then, strangely enough, she laughed.

"Of course," she said. "Why not? Of course he'd be alive. What's one more thing to completely throw off track everything I've worked for?" She snapped her head to look me dead on. "Do you know how hard I've worked for the past eight years to get where I am? My mother is an *artist*, so she thinks she can live in the clouds. If it wasn't for me, our bills would never get paid on time and our refrigerator would be filled with spoiled food. All while she flakes and spends her day painting or writing stories, living off the money my dad left for us." She let out an exasperated sigh. "The only way I'm going to get away from this city is to excel at everything, and the only way to do that is to be organized. But for the past month this stupid curse has done nothing but throw my life into turmoil."

"I understand," I said.

"Do you?" she snapped, her eyes wide and accusing. "Do you really, Emily? What were your goals before all this? Any?"

I didn't respond.

"Because I have many. And now I'm awake half the night as a"—she lowered her voice—"werewolf." Louder, she continued, "And when I'm not . . . *that* . . . my evening is spent in a state of paranoia where the world doesn't look right, inconveniently during prime homework time. Did you know I got a B-plus on a calculus assignment last week? A B-plus in *math*, Emily, which is the most rule-oriented subject in existence, and which is supposed to be my specialty. How does that make me look?"

"Not good?" I guessed.

She rolled her eyes. "Understatement."

I got up, then swiveled around to sit backward on the bleacher below Tracie so that I could look up at her.

"I get it, I do," I said. "My problems aren't the same, but trust me: My life has been insanity lately. I think at the very least Spencer and I can help you control the shifts so that you can go back to being yourself at night."

The girl fell silent, lips pursed. Her eyes scanned me as she considered all I'd said.

"You promise that you can help me get this thing organized?" she asked me, her tone hopeful. "This isn't just some ploy to lure me into another absurd *Mission Impossible* plot?"

"I promise," I said. I placed one hand on my heart and the other in the air—and as she watched, I forced both hands to transform so that they were covered in fur and my fingernails stretched into claws.

Tracie's eyes went wide. Her hands shot forward and she grabbed mine, lowering them so no one could see. I laughed.

"All right, I believe you," she said. With a start, she pulled away from me, reached into her bag, and pulled out her phone. "Oh damn, it's late. I need to shower. Text me when you want me to meet later. I can't stand another night of this."

I stood and climbed back over to where my own backpack lay. "Don't forget to take me off your spam filter."

With a roll of her eyes, she held up her phone to show that she had my contact page open. "Already done. I know how to keep my stuff organized."

"Awesome."

Her belongings gathered, Tracie offered me—for the first time—a weak smile. Then she flounced down the bleacher stairs to head toward the girls' locker room.

I couldn't help but grin to myself. It had taken some time, but Tracie was finally coming into the fold.

Now all I needed to do was make peace with the cheerleaders. They were the outliers in all this, the wild cards. Not created by BioZenith, but by some other company related to it somehow. They were intended to guard us, though Casey at least didn't know entirely why.

All I knew was that they trusted BioZenith and its employees as little as I did. Which meant before we met with the parents there tomorrow, I needed them on my side.

HOW DO YOU JUST SHUT
YOURSELF OFF?

"You look crazy exhausted."

Spencer met my grin with an expression that was not the least bit amused.

"That's probably because I got woken up by a text in the middle of the night," he said as he walked toward me. "But that's just a wild guess."

It was almost time for the first bell to ring, and I'd been waiting under the covered walkway outside the front entrance of school for Spencer to arrive. We were surrounded by at least a hundred other students all milling about, their laughter and chatter an incomprehensible buzz that echoed beneath the metal roof above us.

When Spencer reached me, I instinctively pulled him

into a hug, not caring what anyone thought. Which is, you know, progress—a month ago I'd have died of embarrassment before showing anyone any sort of public affection. For all the problems these changes had brought me, I had to admit they had done wonders for my confidence.

It didn't hurt that despite some of her faults, Nighttime Me had confidence to spare.

We held each other for a brief moment, the both of us inhaling our respective scents. Then, reluctantly, I pulled away—even with my lack of experience I knew that a too-long hug was just awkward.

"So what happened last night?" he asked, his exhaustion erased by a chipper grin. I almost blushed realizing it was me that had made him so happy.

I grabbed his arm and pulled him to an empty bench. We sat down and, leaning in close, I went over all that had happened with Mr. McKinney the night before and with Tracie that morning.

"Whoa," he said simply when I was done. "I mean, I knew my parents must have had something to do with that after what we found in those files, but . . ." He shook his head.

"At least Tracie is finally with us," I said. "All we need now is the cheerleaders. Too bad they still think I'm an evil skank and won't give me the time of day, even with Casey trying to convince them to talk." I shook my head. "Man, as much as I'm glad sometimes that Nighttime came along, I could have lived without all the stuff she pulled at parties pissing off every other kid at school."

Biting his lip, Spencer looked over the crowd. Catching sight of someone, his face broadened into a full smile. "You know what, I have an idea. There's a football game tonight, right?"

"It's a Friday in the fall, so yeah," I said.

Without warning, Spencer jumped to his feet. "Wait here," he said. "I'll be right back."

With that, he darted through the crowd. It took a moment, but I finally recognized who he was heading for— Mikey Harris, the tall, attractive, super-popular ringleader of the cool kids who I once tossed across a room while drunk.

It was a whole big thing.

Spencer and Mikey clasped hands and gave each other a quick bro hug before Spencer began talking animatedly, waving his hands while Mikey looked down at him, amused. I couldn't make out what they were discussing, but it sure looked interesting.

I let my eyes wander across the crowd. It had begun to thin as kids started to go into the school to hit up their lockers before heading to homeroom. As the crowd in front of me parted, I saw another person who had been avoiding me all week.

Megan. My best friend.

She stood outside of the walkway, leaning against a gnarled tree that had shed most of its leaves. Her skin and waist-long hair were so pale, her clothes so pitch-black, it almost seemed as though she'd stumbled out of an old black-and-white film and found herself in a world of color.

I tried to meet her eye, but her gaze was distant, her expression unreadable. She stood so still it was as if she was a wax figure of Megan instead of the girl herself.

There was something off about her. I knew she'd had her heart broken, thinking I'd abandoned her for new friends. I knew how horrible it was, what she'd gone through in the woods. But she didn't seem depressed or sad, not exactly.

Instead there was a strange aura about her. I blinked my eyes, thinking maybe my Nighttime vision was slipping back to daytime. But it was still there: a hazy, superimposed image of herself hovering in the air that had gone blurry around the edges.

Part of me wanted to stand up and walk over to her, just as I had Tracie, and make things right. We were best friends all through elementary and junior high, back before Megan was broken down by some super-bitchy girls. She'd been happy then. Trusting. A lot like a female Spencer—goofy

44

and funny and charming, the slightly more outgoing version of me.

Since high school started she'd been dour. She'd been hurt and closed herself off, and so I became her sole friend, just like she'd been mine. Then the werewolf stuff happened, I pulled away from her, and in her desperation to keep our friendship from collapsing she found out what I was. She begged me to change her into a werewolf too so that we could have powers and be part of a pack together. Of course I couldn't make it happen. In the real world you can't become a werewolf from a bite, you have to be born that way.

Despite my rescuing her from Dalton when he almost devoured her and despite my pulling her free from the shadowman who tried to invade her body, she refused to see me at the hospital. She didn't return my calls or emails.

As much as it hurt, I guess this meant we'd grown apart. That we were no longer friends. And no matter how much craziness overwhelmed my day and how many new pack members I found, it still hurt not to be able to talk to her about all the silly, geeky stuff we'd shared for so long.

Before I could go to Megan, a tall, skinny, incredibly hot guy with black hair came up to her—Patrick, the foreign exchange student from London who I'd gathered she'd recruited as a new friend. She gave him the briefest of smiles, coming to life for the first time since I'd seen her leaning against the tree. As they walked toward the school entrance, she took no notice of me—but Patrick did, his eyes flickering to me for just a moment.

When he saw me, he looked afraid.

And then they were gone, disappearing behind the milling crowd.

"All right, Em Dub, we're all set."

I blinked, then looked up to find Spencer had returned. "What?" I asked.

"I've set up a meeting with the cheerleaders that they can't get out of, tonight before the football game."

"How'd you do that?"

He grinned and spread his hands wide. "I'm going to be filling in for Mikey as Gary, the Carver High Cougar."

I opened my eyes wide and almost burst into a laugh. "The *mascot*?"

Sitting down next to me, he placed his arm around my shoulder. "Hey, I'm used to wearing fur by now. Wolf, cougar, same difference, right?"

I leaned into him and giggled. "Now this is a plan I can get behind. You're going to look just so gosh darn cute wearing the giant head."

"Hey now," he said, leaning into me as well. "I'm *always* gosh darn cute."

Our faces were close, so close that I could feel the warmth from his cheeks. I tilted my head, and he did the same, and we found ourselves meeting each other's eyes. Once again my heart began to pound like a tribal drum, my hands began to tremble. We both moved closer, just a fraction of an inch.

The first bell rang, and we both jumped.

Laughing at our nerves, we collected our bags and ran toward the front entrance so we wouldn't be late to homeroom. I reached my classroom first and waved at Spencer as he raced over the green linoleum to his.

One of these days I was going to just let Nighttime Emily take over completely to get over my nerves and actually kiss that boy.

Too bad I had to worry about that part of me only leaving it at a kiss.

You're right, that part of me whispered in the back of my mind. *I would devour that kid.*

Blushing and smiling at the same time, I slipped into my homeroom, just as the final bell rang.

I expected the day to calm down after my eventful morning. Just class after class, lunchtime, more classes, then home.

It started out that way. But then I began to notice Megan everywhere I went.

Between classes she'd be leaning against a locker, as still and emotionless as she'd been by the tree. In the classes we shared, she'd sit at the farthest desk from me, off in her own gray world. At lunch she and Patrick whispered between themselves while he cast glances in my direction.

Not once did Megan look at me.

I didn't know if she was giving me the silent treatment or what. It's not like she would be above doing something like that, I mean, this is Megan we're talking about.

But I couldn't help feeling there was something else going on. Something strange. Because Patrick seemed terrified of me, which made me wonder what Megan had told him. And even though Megan was always staring off into nothingness, it was almost as though I could feel her eyes boring into the back of my skull no matter where we were in position to each other.

By the end of the day, I'd had enough. I understood her anger at me, really I did. But come on, at least talk it through with me, right? Have one final fight before we sever for good? Acknowledge that I, y'know, *saved her frikkin' life*?

After school I was on the same bench where I'd sat that morning, waiting for Spencer to come out and give me a ride home. Somehow without my noticing, Megan appeared at the same tree I'd seen her at before school. Same position, same unreadable face. Almost as if she'd magically appeared there, waiting for me.

Taking a steeling breath, I stood, put my bag on my shoulder, and walked over to stand directly in front of her.

"Hey, Megan," I said.

For a moment she didn't move, didn't even flinch. Nothing to acknowledge that I was there.

Then, slowly, her eyes came into focus. I noticed the blue of her irises seemed paler somehow, almost gray. She blinked once, twice, then met my eyes.

"Emily," she said coolly.

I shifted feet uncomfortably. Behind me students screamed playfully and ran down the walkway toward the parking lot, but they seemed miles away, their voices distant echoes.

"It's been a while," I said. "How are you doing? I didn't get to see you at the hospital after . . . you know . . . after you were attacked."

She crossed her arms. "I know," she said. "I told them I didn't want to see you."

Ouch. The way she said it so flatly, so emotionless . . . how do you talk that way to your best friend of eight years? How do you just shut yourself off after all you'd been through together?

Despite my best effort to keep cool, I felt my vision go

blurry as tears formed. I didn't expect it to feel like this, like a punch to the gut. I mean, Megan had been mean and desperate and dismissive toward me, I shouldn't have cared so much after the way she treated me just for finding a few new friends.

But I still remembered the girl she had been just a few years ago, and the girl she was when we were alone together, and to have her talk to me like I was some insignificant stranger. . . .

I sniffed and wiped at my eyes with the back of my sleeves. "Allergies, sorry," I lied. Those growing tears wiped away, I went on. "I mean, I understand why you didn't want to see me, but I still worried, you know. I'm just glad to see you're good enough to be at school."

She rolled her eyes then looked past me. "I don't have super-healing powers like you werewolves, but you'd be surprised how well normal human bodies recover."

I took a step back, wondering if I should just go, give her more time. "Yeah . . ."

An abrupt giggle burst from her mouth, and I blinked in surprise. "Not that I'm exactly normal anymore," she said. I must have been giving her a strange look, because her expression went flat again and she waved her hand. "Oh, don't worry, I know now you were right about the whole werewolf-bite thing not doing anything. It doesn't matter, though. I don't want your powers anyway. I'm . . ." She grinned, though there was no joy behind the expression. "Better now."

"Better?" I asked.

Still grinning, she looked me directly in the eyes, but didn't elaborate.

Something wasn't right with her. This wasn't just post-traumatic stress. I remembered what happened the previous Saturday, the shadowman entering her body, the way it clung to her until I'd pulled Megan so far away that the being was forced to let go.

Could it have done something to her? Despite all I'd done to try to save her, had that creature still done something to her?

Or was it just easier to think she wasn't entirely herself than that she was actually better without me around?

I didn't get a chance to ask. At that moment, Patrick came to her side, looming above me. He swallowed as he looked me up and down, then grabbed Megan's arm and whispered in his British lilt, "Let's go, Megan."

Sadness at Megan treating me like a stranger gave way to anger at this whole stupid situation. It didn't have to be like this. Megan wasn't going to give me anything, so I rounded on Patrick.

Jumping forward, I jammed a finger into his chest.

"Ow!" he shouted. "What the hell?"

"So who are you, anyway?" I demanded. "You appear out of nowhere to live next to Spencer right when murders start happening; you read serial killer books; I see you at funerals for people you don't know, at the hospital to visit people you never met. And now you're hanging around Megan even though you wouldn't give her the time of day when you two first met. So what is your deal?"

I stepped closer and, wide-eyed, Patrick took a wild step back, almost tripping over his feet.

"W-what . . ." he stammered. "I haven't any idea what you're talking about."

Megan slipped between us, casual and smooth. "Don't worry about her, Patrick. She's just used to being the one keeping secrets." Smirking, she added, "I guess she doesn't like it when she's the one in the dark."

With that, she looped arms with him and the two of them walked toward the school entrance. I could only stare, confusion and rage coursing through me. Fists clenched at my side, I almost considered going full Nighttime to race forward, catch up to them, and demand answers.

"What was that about?"

I turned to find Spencer veering off the walkway to come stand next to me beneath the leafless tree.

"I don't know," I said.

Looking back at Megan and Patrick, I saw them greeting a thin man with wire glasses just outside the doors to school. I recognized him as Mr. Savage, some counselor guy who'd been sent to school to talk to us after Emily Cooke was murdered. Or at least, so he claimed. He'd tried to talk to me more than once, and I found him incredibly off-putting.

Megan, meanwhile, was grinning at him and chatting as though they were old friends.

Something strange was going on. On top of everything else, I was going to have to keep an eye on Megan, too.

"Should we follow them?" Spencer whispered to me.

I met his eyes and forced a smile. "Nah. Let's go home. You need to rest up for your big Cougar debut."

We walked over to the parking lot to his mom's minivan, making plans for how we'd approach the cheerleaders later. But I couldn't stop thinking about Megan.

And even though she'd long disappeared from view, I still couldn't help but feel like she was watching me.

I DO REMEMBER YOU

I've always been kind of a nut for organizing my things. I have files on my computer for each type of entertainment I own: DVDs, books, comics, video games. And in those files I have multiple lists for each: TV DVDs by series, movies by title, then movies by genre *and* title. There are separate lists for DVDs and Blu-rays, plus one combined list so I have my complete library in one place. Same for books, only it goes lists by author, lists by title, lists by series (organized by series name and another organized by author *then* series name), lists by genre. If I owned ebooks, I'd do the whole DVD/Blu-ray/combined list for books thing, too; I actually don't sort my books by hardcover and paperback, but man, I probably should, shouldn't I?

Uh, let's just sum it up and say that I like to keep my

things in order. And also that before all this werewolf business, I had a whole hell of a lot of free time.

Anyway, all this to say, after I got home from school to mercifully find the house empty, and after I checked my inbox to find it still empty save for spam, I pulled up a Word document that I'd created earlier in the week: "Things to Do."

1. Rescue Dalton
2. Get Tracie back
3. Befriend the cheerleaders
4. Make sure all of us are trained hybrid
5. Find out once and for all what the deal is with BZ

I typed an X next to 2, then a / next to 3, 4, and 5—half an X, since I felt like we were halfway there on those points. Progress!

Thinking for a moment, I then added:

6. Find Evan
7. Figure out how much Dad knows
8. Find out: What is the deal with Megan?

Great. More things to deal with. But writing them down was the first step to getting it all handled.

Shaking my head, I saved and closed the document. I

remembered the conversation Tracie and I had earlier about how she always needed to stay super organized. Maybe I'd tell her about my obsessive cataloging. We could totally bond.

The clock on my bedside table read 3:57. Still a few hours to go before Spencer was supposed to pick me up. I'd already texted Tracie to let her know when to expect us to arrive, and it was Friday, so I wasn't exactly feeling the need to do any homework. Homework is just another phrase for "work you frantically finish at eight p.m. Sunday night." Especially lately.

I spun in my desk chair, watching my room swirl around me. Invisible ants tingled over my skin and my leg kept shaking. Restless. Just a week ago I felt like I had no free time anymore, but now that I did, nothing that would have entertained me before felt exciting. I didn't want to read about someone having adventures, I wanted to be out on the streets, running full throttle.

Maybe that wasn't such a bad idea. Nothing strange about a girl going for a jog, right? It'd give me more time to think about the new additions to the list, as well as what I was going to say to the cheerleaders that night, and how we were going to deal with the face-off with our parents.

I spun my chair around to close my browser. Just as I was about to click the X in the corner, I saw a "(1)" next to the title of my in-box in the open tab. I had a new email.

I clicked the tab immediately to bring it to the front screen. At the top of my in-box was a message titled "RE: Hey."

It was from Evan Cooke.

Not wasting a minute, I clicked it open and scanned the message.

Friday, Sept. 24, 2010—4:01 p.m. PST
From: evandetta
To: missleeleeweb
Hi!
So I'm not sure how much we should write in emails. But I want you to know that I think I know what you're talking about and yes it happened to me too. I really, really hope this is for real, because things here have been insane and . . . well, I'm just going to hope you're real. Let me know when you're available to chat so we can talk in real time. I'm in the same time zone you are. Text me at 503-555-0858 anytime.
Evan

My heart raced and I couldn't keep the smile off my face. Another pack member. I'd found another pack member!

Deep inside, the wolf part of me howled, rejoicing.

Before I could hit reply or grab my phone to send a text, a chat window popped up on the side of the screen. At first I thought it was Megan—she was the only person I'd ever chatted with online, really, and I was used to the pop-up chime signaling a "wassup" from her.

But of course it wasn't her. Evan must have seen my little chat symbol change from AWAY to ONLINE.

Evan: Are you there?

My fingers hovering over the keyboard, I considered what to type. He seemed eager to chat, like Spencer and Dalton had been when I first confronted them with the fact of our werewolfness. But he seemed a little bit wary, too, and what if I said the wrong thing and scared him off like I almost did with Tracie?

Taking a breath, I decided to just go for it and hope for the best.

Emily: Hi! Yeah, I'm here. I'm so glad you emailed me.
Evan: Well, same here. I can't believe there's others like me out there.
Emily: Well, there are. And we probably have lots to talk about.

I waited for him to respond as quickly as he did the first time. The guy was obviously not a slow typist. But it was a full two minutes before the little chat box said that he was typing again.

Evan: Actually, do you have a webcam?
Emily: Yeah, I do. Why?
Evan: I want to make sure who I'm talking to is who you say you are. Just in case.

Wow, he was certainly paranoid. But why shouldn't he be? For all I knew, this was Mr. McKinney playacting as Evan Cooke. They already admitted they were watching us, though to what extent I didn't know.

Emily: Good idea. I'll hook it up.

A moment later, I had the little camera on my monitor aimed at my face and a square box featuring me in all my after-school flat-haired glory appeared above the chat window. A second later, my video box shrunk down to the corner and was replaced by the bigger, streaming image of a grown-up Evan Cooke.

Like his cousin, Evan was unreasonably attractive. Like, not just regular-people hot—unattainable movie-star hot.

He had dark blond hair cut short, a slender frame, angular yet narrow features, and eyes so crystal blue that they were gorgeous even all pixelated.

Those Cookes had some crazy-good genetics. Or maybe the Cooke scientists decided since they were making their kids into werewolf monstrosities, might as well give them the upper hand of being super good-looking as a consolation prize.

Seeing me, Evan smiled—his teeth were straight and white. Of course. I smiled back, hoping that the video quality hid my own lack of perfectly pearly whites.

"Can you hear me?" he said, his voice coming through my speakers clearly. His tone was soft and pleasant. For some reason, I felt right away like I could trust him.

"Yeah, I can hear you," I answered. "How about me?"

He nodded, and his smile faltered. Leaning back in his chair he ran his hands through the sides of his sandy hair.

"So you definitely are a teen girl, at least," he said. "That's good. I was worried that you might be my mom messing with me."

I tilted my head. "Your mom?" I asked. "Why would she fake an email?"

"Why wouldn't she?" he asked back. "She was the one who made me like this. She's been talking about how I'm 'special' for years and now that I'm changing and she's proven she wasn't schizophrenic all this time, she won't let me talk to anyone. I've been going crazy over here."

Okay. Whoa. So this was certainly different from how it was for the rest of us.

"We're probably going to need to start at the beginning," I said. "I mean, all of our parents kept this from us our entire lives."

"They did?" Evan asked. Then, whispering to himself, he said, "That would explain Emily."

"Your cousin?"

He blinked his big eyes, then looked back at the camera—at me. "Yeah, sorry, not you. It was just after my mom made us move that she started telling me about this 'special' stuff. She refused to let me talk to Emily after that for some reason, even though she and I were best friends since we were babies. She wouldn't . . ." He looked down at his desk. "She wouldn't even let me go to her funeral."

"I'm sorry," I said softly.

Shrugging, he looked back up. "That was when I started changing, so I was distracted anyway. Still. I would have liked to have been there."

God. How sad. I mean, I stupidly, selfishly felt bad about Emily Cooke because of all these instincts telling me she was part of my pack. I'd never really known her, though. Not like Evan. They'd been more than cousins—they'd been friends.

I wasn't exactly sure what to say. Coughing nervously, I decided to try and get back to business.

"So, I guess maybe I should lay out all that's been happening here," I said. "First, I should officially introduce myself. I'm Emily Webb, also known as the 'other Emily' to you and probably everyone you knew back when you went to school here. You probably remember me more like this."

Snatching my glasses off my desk, I put them on my face, then used one hand to hold my hair back in a ponytail.

Evan squinted at me as I did all this, as though struggling to remember, then laughed as I put on the finishing touches.

"I do remember you!" he said, suddenly excited. "Only your glasses were these hideous, thick, red-rimmed things, right?"

I couldn't help but laugh too. Letting my hair drop, I took off my glasses and said, "Yeah, that was me. I was totally fashionable as an eight-year-old."

"So, Emily Webb," Evan said, leaning forward on his elbows. "Tell me what's been up the past eight years. Though maybe jump to the past month or so."

Taking in a deep breath, I laid out the whole story. I'd been telling it so much lately that it was pretty rehearsed at that point. I noticed his eyes go wide when I talked about the werewolf transformations, but he stayed silent, listening until I reached today. It was only around the point I brought up the hybrid state that he began nodding knowingly.

"And that's everything that's happened until, oh, about an hour ago," I finished.

Letting out a low whistle, Evan leaned back in his chair and crossed his arms over his slender chest. For a moment he sat there, swiveling slightly back and forth, biting his lip and thinking.

Finally, he looked back at the camera and said, "So, I think you're right that all those people at BioZenith are lying to you."

"Why do you think that?" I asked.

"Because if they're anything like my mother, they're not just scientists," he said. "They're not just researching these shadowmen. They call them the Akhakhu. And they worship them."

It was my turn to go wide eyed. Talk about something I didn't see coming. My family was never really religious, but I knew people who were, and religion had always sort of interested me—the rituals and meanings and philosophy of it all.

But this felt different from that. First, I always kind of figured science and religion were directly opposed, so a bunch of scientists worshipping *anything* seemed strange. Beyond that, the shadowmen weren't holy or benevolent—

not at all. They were creatures from another universe that had stalked me and kidnapped one of my friends.

Who would worship beings like that?

"Okay," I said. "I think I'm ready to hear your story now."

Taking a deep breath, Evan began.

"This all started about eight years ago. Everything was perfectly normal when I was a kid. Emily and I were always together because our parents were always together. But that stopped after my dad left. That was when my mom started arguing with Emily's parents all the time.

"I didn't really know what was going on. I mean, my dad was gone and I didn't know why, and my mom was sometimes super clingy and sometimes really distant, and she was either always crying or always yelling. I remember her shouting at Emily's mother that she refused to keep her faith a secret. The last time I saw Emily, my mom kept saying she wouldn't let me be raised around my aunt and uncle. Only she called them a bunch of heretics who were denying their gods.

"Heavy stuff for a kid, but I remember it clearly because it was just so *strange*. My mom was never like that before, not ever. I don't know what went down between the four of them, but something must have. And next thing I know, my mom is piling our stuff into a van and we're driving overnight to a motel in Oregon. We stayed there for a few weeks before finally moving to a house in Portland. That's where I live now, by the way."

At that point he gestured his arms around his room, which looked to be half the size mine was. Though it was so neat that he probably had about the same amount of space.

Focusing the camera back on him, he continued, "Ever since then, my mother has insisted I was 'special' and that one day I would be chosen to lead our people to salvation, or some variation on that. I mean, nice thought and all, but I wasn't really raised religious before that and it just seemed like some creepy cult thing. You ever see that old movie *Carrie*? About the girl who killed people with her mind at the prom?"

"Of course."

"Some days my mom was like a half step away from locking me in a room and screaming about my dirty pillows, just like Carrie's mom. Especially if I ever asked if I could, like, write Emily a letter or something. She even monitored absolutely everything I did online so if I even came close to contacting Emily, she'd know. I guess at least she's given me some slack now that Emily . . . now that she's gone."

I shook my head. I couldn't imagine how trapped he must have felt. "That sounds rough. I'm surprised you seem so normal."

He barked a laugh, then winked. "I'm not exactly normal. But who is, right? I mean, I don't want to make it sound like it's the Manson family up in here; I got to go to school and have friends and she didn't drag me to sermons or anything. And her moods weren't constant, just every few weeks or so. Still, I wished I'd been able to talk to Emily about what we were doing in school or about boys we had crushes on or whatever."

Crushes on boys, huh? Apparently Spencer wouldn't have to be jealous of me spending time with the new guy like he'd been of Dalton. Even though Jealous Spencer was absolutely adorable.

"What happened when you started to change?" I asked.

"Actually," he said as he leaned in close to the cam once more, "that's something we should talk about. Because when you started talking about werewolves, I started thinking, 'This girl is lost in her own head, isn't she?' It wasn't until you got to the whole hybrid thing that it made sense."

"What do you mean?"

"I never turned into a werewolf. From day one, I was what you described as the hybrid, I guess. It did start only at night, but I can access it anytime now. I mean, my personality shifted a bit, but it just made me less shy. I was still me, only I had superpowers and could sprout claws if I needed to, and my vision could change depending on the situation."

Wow, now it was my turn to be Jealous Emily. Having the hybrid state without having to work at it sounded awesome.

And actually, maybe that was why he was Vesper 0 despite being last on the list of vespers in the HAVOC files. I'd noticed when I'd looked him up that he was younger than us by a few months. Maybe he was the more perfected form of their formula? Which meant his mom was right: He *was* special.

"It was all pretty great until I kept slipping between worlds," he finished.

I blinked.

Well, that was not something I expected.

"You okay?" he asked.

I shook my head, then stammered out, "I'm sorry, *what*? Slipping between worlds?"

He grinned. "I'm just full of surprises, huh? I saw the shadowmen too, just like you described them. Only when I wasn't completely focusing on staying whole, I'd sometimes sort of . . . slide to their dimension. It's the only way I can describe how it feels. It was scary as hell the first times, because it was always dark and alien, and because those shadowmen—the Akhakhu—at least the ones I've seen— look horrible. I mean, they're sort of human shaped, but it's like they've been bathing in radiation and their skin . . ." He visibly shuddered. "Boils. Lots of boils."

"But they look normal here," I said. "Well, as normal as shadows can be."

Evan shrugged. "Maybe we're only seeing their souls or something? I have no idea."

Pain lanced through my temples. I placed my hand on my forehead and massaged my fingers into my skin, my eyes closed.

Just when I thought I had a bead on things, I learn that there are other events and abilities happening that I have no idea about.

But if he could go between worlds at will, where Dalton was trapped, maybe . . .

"Oh God, Emily!" Evan's voice was so loud it made my speakers crackle.

I opened my eyes and looked at my monitor—and saw a shadowy figure just behind Evan, standing perfectly still.

I let out a startled cry. At the same time, Evan said, "Behind you!"

That's when I noticed, in the miniscreen in the corner of my monitor that showed the view from my camera: There was a shadowman behind me, too.

"You too!" I cried.

I spun my chair around and leaped to my feet, expecting the shadowman to grab me like it had grabbed Dalton, to start dragging me away.

But there was nothing there.

Immediately I spun to look at my monitor, just as Evan did the same. The shadowmen were no longer on either camera.

Chest heaving as he took deep breaths, Evan ran a hand through his hair and said, "Jeez!"

I leaned forward, putting both hands on my desk, willing my heart to pound slower. "No kidding."

Evan made a sound as though he was about to talk, but a distant slam sounded through my speakers instead.

"Crap," he muttered.

I looked at my monitor just in time to see Evan getting in close, his face taking up the entire screen. In a low, hushed voice, he quickly said, "Emily, there's lots more. But just remember not to trust any of the people involved in making us. No matter what they tell you, it's going to be a lie. This isn't about science for them anymore. It's about so much more. It's—"

With a pop and a crack from my speakers, the screen went blank.

"Evan?" I asked, staring into the camera. "Hey, what happened? Evan!"

Pulling my chair up behind me, I sat down once more and then closed the webcam window. Evan's name was in red on the chat program. He'd logged off.

I sat there for a long moment, tapping my fingernails against my desk, thinking.

For weeks now I'd been looking for answers. And in the past two days I'd been getting a flood of them . . . only they weren't enough to paint the whole picture, to put together the entire puzzle. And this puzzle was like one of those jigsaws where the image is of the same four marbles repeated over and over and the pieces are *really* small.

I was getting closer, I could feel it. And the sooner I could talk to Evan again, the more blanks I could fill in.

As long as he was okay. Grabbing my phone, I typed in the number he'd given in his email and sent a text: **Are you okay? Please let me know.** I figured his mom had just come home and he'd needed to log off in a hurry, but after those shadowmen . . .

Though I guess they weren't just "shadowmen" after all. I opened up my Things to Do file once more and added two new entries.

Find out: What are the Akhakhu?

Find out: *What do they want?*

I looked at my clock. It was after five p.m. Evan and I had been talking for more than an hour. Spencer would be by soon to pick me up.

Standing up, I stretched, then went to my window to

look outside. It was starting to get dark, and the streetlights were turning on one by one.

For a moment, I thought I saw the reflection of someone behind me in my bedroom window. I spun around again, just as I'd done at my desk—but still there was no one there, not even when I willed my vision to that of my wolf self, which was the only part of me that could see the shadowmen—Akhakhu, whatever—when they were around.

I didn't want to admit to myself that it hadn't been a shadowman I'd seen in the window though.

I could have sworn it was Megan.

6

OH MY GOD, YOU TWO ARE A THING

Spencer texted me not long after I'd finished chatting with Evan to let me know he'd be outside in a few minutes. Thankfully. Waiting any longer in my room would have been torture.

Well, maybe not torture, that's totally hyperbolic. But definitely annoying.

I put on my coat and raced downstairs. As soon as I hit the bottom step and slid on my socked feet into the living room, the front door opened. Placing a hand on the couch, I stopped myself and stood, frozen, as my dad and stepmom came in carrying groceries.

"Leelee," my dad said tepidly as he caught sight of me.

My stepmom, Katherine, was much more chipper. As

she set the bags she was carrying on the dining room table, she said, "Emily! I feel like I haven't seen you in days. Are you heading out again?"

"Um, yeah," I said, pointedly avoiding my dad's attempts to meet my eyes. "Spencer and I are going to the football game tonight."

Katherine raised her eyebrows at me over her large-lensed glasses. "Oh *really*," she said teasingly. "You two have been seeing a lot of each other lately. Has he kissed you yet?"

Despite the rush of anger and sadness I'd felt seeing my dad, I couldn't keep the embarrassed blush from heating up my cheeks. I kicked at the rug beneath the couch and said, "No, nothing like that, we're still just . . . hanging out."

Giving me a knowing look, Katherine smiled and said, "Mm-hmm." She came and gave me a quick hug—her giant sweatshirt with the embroidered fall leaves on it was super warm—then grabbed the bags she'd put on the dining room table and carried them into the kitchen.

As soon as she was out of view, I dropped the smile I was faking, lowered my head, and headed toward the door.

"Hey," my dad said softly, gently taking my arm in his hand. "I—"

Yanking my arm free, I snapped my head to look up directly in his eye. I could feel the stupid tears welling up again, but the anger was stronger—especially from the Nighttime side of me. I let Daytime slip away, and for just a moment I was free to be furiously righteous.

"I don't care," I said. "I don't want to hear anything you have to say right now. You can make your excuses tomorrow at BioZenith with all the other liars we called our parents."

Not waiting for a response, I shoved my feet into my shoes and, without bothering to tie them, stormed out the front door and down the front path to the street. Spencer was already there in the minivan, engine idling.

I could tell my dad was watching me from the door I'd left wide open behind me. As I let Nighttime's fearlessness recede so I could be more my usual self, I could see what his face must have looked like, and I felt an involuntary wince deep in my chest.

"Everything okay?" Spencer asked as I climbed into the minivan and slammed the door shut.

"No, but I'll be fine," I lied. "Let's go."

As we drove, I gave Spencer a quick update about Evan. We didn't have much time to discuss him, though, since we were soon at our first stop: Tracie's house.

It was a single-story rambler painted yellow with purple trim—probably thanks to her artist mom, though with the bold colors Tracie liked to wear maybe she picked out the paint. I wouldn't put it past her to update the paint job every few years to keep the house at competitive market price.

Unlike my house or Spencer's, Tracie's was separated from her neighbors' by dense trees on the sides and in the back. Last time I'd been here was when I'd chased Dalton into her backyard, and in the darkness and in the werewolfness of the situation, the place had seemed sort of sinister. In no small part due to seeing Tracie, in werewolf form, chained to her bedposts while a shadowman looked over her, and Dalton tried to bust down her window.

But by the fading daylight, the place was lovely, with a neatly tended garden and impeccable lawn. Everything organized and perfect, just like the girl who lived there.

True to form, she was ready and waiting on the porch the moment we parked on the street. I was surprised to see that she'd chosen a pair of jeans and a black sweater over one of her prim, paisley dresses. But I suppose most people were probably surprised to see me wearing similar clothes when I used to be all dowdy in oversize hoodies and crooked glasses.

Tracie climbed into the backseat, and I turned so we could talk. After she buckled her seat belt, she produced a notebook and a pink pen, then looked at me expectantly.

"Hi," I said and smiled. "Hope we didn't keep you waiting long."

She shrugged. "I was waiting on the porch for about forty-seven minutes, give or take, but I was just anxious to finally learn this hybrid thing."

"Forty-seven minutes?" Spencer asked as he pulled the minivan into the street and started driving toward school. "Just a guesstimate, right?" He grinned at her in the rear-view mirror.

Tracie rolled her eyes. "It's not like I went into seconds." To me, she asked, "So how do I do this? I've only got three hours until I'm covered in fur, and that might be a bit of a distraction at a football game."

"Ready to write?" I asked her.

She put pen to paper and nodded.

"Okay," I said. "Listen close. And we're probably going to need to practice."

I went over all that I'd figured out between Spencer and my training sessions. How it starts with focusing on the emotions I equate with each state. How to control my breathing and thoughts to hyper focus on what, exactly, I wanted to change. And the most important part: Making peace with the fact that these other forms weren't alien to me, but were a part of who I was.

At that, Tracie stopped writing and shot her head up to meet my eye.

"That insane person who I become," she said slowly, "is

not a part of who I am. The way the world looks when I'm her is unnatural."

"Maybe," I said. "Maybe she wouldn't exist at all if you hadn't been made this way. But she does exist, Tracie, and if you don't learn to accept that you may not be able to control this or access the parts of her that you need."

"All I need from her is the strength, the stamina, and the superior senses," she said. "I'm perfectly fine accepting that as a part of me."

Spencer cranked the wheel, turning us down a side street. As he did, he looked at Tracie once more through the rearview mirror.

"There must be something cool about your Nighttime self," he said. "I mean, I get super focused to the point where I can become obsessed with stupid minor things that distract me for hours, but that focus also lets me get things done that I'd never have finished before."

"And my Nighttime has no filter and is so reckless that she basically made me a pariah at school and also almost got me killed a lot," I added. "But sometimes I need to be a little fearless."

Tossing the notebook and pen on the seat next to her, Tracie crossed her arms and looked out the window at the rush of trees that we passed.

"I don't see the benefit of the world seeming to unravel

around me," she said, sullen.

"I dunno," Spencer said. "Remember how you were when we were inside BioZenith? How you were able to trick those flying robot spheres by going against their expectations? Being able to think like that could probably help you. If everything you always do is in a strict, logical pattern, then that just makes you predictable. And who wants that?"

With an annoyed sigh, she looked away from the street and met his eyes in the mirror. I expected her to get mad about basically being called boring, but Spencer offered her one of his warm, goofy smiles, and she couldn't keep the corners of her mouth from turning up into an answering grin—though she certainly tried.

"I suppose I could be kind and call my Nighttime self a creative thinker," she said. She waved her hand as though chasing away the thought. "But don't tell my mother I said that. She's been buying me art supplies for years even though I tell her I'm not interested. Luckily there are plenty of schools and children's groups to donate that stuff to."

Gravel crunched beneath the minivan's tires and I straightened in my seat to find that we were pulling into the parking lot on the side of the school closest to the football field. The field itself was lit up with floodlights, and the meager bleachers that acted as our stadium were filling up with parents and teens. I didn't see any players on the field yet, but they were probably still in the locker room getting ready.

"So what's the plan?" I asked Spencer.

"I'm going to go get into costume and then join the cheer-leaders in warming up the crowd when the game starts."

Tracie leaned forward between the two seats. "You're going to be Gary? What happened to Mikey? He's *always* Gary. I had to special order the suit for him since he's so tall, which had to go through all sorts of administrators. Spencer, it's going to droop all over you and get messed up!"

He shrugged, then unbuckled his belt. "Hey, it was the only way I could get close to Nikki and friends. They've been avoiding us ever since Saturday. I figure between me and Casey, I can get them behind the bleachers during the game so we can talk."

"So we should wait back there then?" I asked.

Spencer nodded, then glanced down at the dashboard clock. "Okay, I'm running late. I'd better get in there." Meeting my eyes, he said softly, "Catch you soon, Em Dub."

"Go bust some moves," I said as he opened the door and started to climb out. "I expect the best halftime show of my life."

With a wink, he said, "You better count on it." Then he slammed the door shut and raced across the parking lot toward the school.

Eyebrows raised, Tracie looked over at me. "Oh my God, you two are a *thing*, aren't you?" she said, then shook her head. "I'm going to have to hang around you two mooning all the time, aren't I?"

Unbuckling my seat belt, I said, "Hey, it'll be worth it to learn how to control your powers, won't it? Besides, it's not just the three of us anymore. We've also got Evan."

"Who?" she asked as she leaned into the backseat.

"Emily Cooke's cousin," I said. "Now how about we stop talking about my love life and practice going hybrid?"

YOU SOUND CRAZY

In the shadows behind the bleachers, Tracie and I sat cross-legged on the grass and practiced, um, breathing.

Well, I sat on the grass, anyway. She ran inside the school and came back with a blanket, which she folded up into a perfect, plush square. Where she found a blanket in school, I didn't know. Maybe class presidents had like a secret bedroom on campus or something.

Though our little training session had started out with me going into more detail on how I controlled my shifts, it wasn't long before Tracie was teaching me about her breathing regimens.

"It's all about the flow of oxygen in, and the flow of toxins out, in the correct ratios to support your goals," she said, her eyes closed as she raised her hands up and down as a visual aid. "If you're exercising, your body needs as much oxygen as possible. So you take a big breath in"—and she held her hands up for a count of four—"and out, but shorter, only a two count. For calming, I like to go in an equal ratio, and for a longer count on each."

I managed to mostly follow her directions, but it was easy to get distracted as more and more cars pulled into the parking lot, their headlights briefly blinding me before the engines were turned off and people trudged over the grass to climb into the bleachers on either side of the field. The noise level grew, and above me I could see the shadow of many a butt sitting on the cold metal benches. Snack-food debris and soda cups and cigarette butts rained down from above and collected on the dead, brittle grass directly beneath the bleachers.

"Oh," Tracie said. Then, shaking my arm she cried out, "Oh! Emily! I did it!"

Pulled from the delightful underside view of the football-viewing crowd, I was immediately caught up in Tracie's enthusiasm. It was hard not to—she'd never been excited around me. Progress!

"You did!" I cried back and clapped my hands. "Wait, what did you do?"

"I got the Nighttime eyesight," she said, breathless

despite her practiced inhales and exhales. "I can see super far. I can see those ants walking on that wall over there, in the dark. Look!"

She pointed to the brick wall of the nearest building, and I turned to look. All I saw was a distant, shadowy wall.

"Oh, well, I'm glad you can see far," I said as I turned back to her. "Spencer can too. I can't, though, since normally I need glasses. But at least I can see clearly when I get my Nighttime eyes."

She ignored me. "This is great," she said, flexing and unflexing her fingers, feeling her strength. "This is wonderful! I've never been able to appreciate this before now, since the world was so out of sorts. But this . . ." She shook her head. "No wonder you guys were so insistent I try this."

I couldn't help but grin. "Yeah, it can be pretty cool. Just wait till you figure out how to pull out the claws. You'll never have trouble getting the shrink-wrap off a DVD ever again."

Tracie laughed and put her hands on her cheeks in glee, looking for all the world like a little girl on Christmas morning. I hadn't seen her so lively or happy in *ages*, even if around school she always put on a front like everything was perfect.

Shuffling sounded above us, and the shadows cast down by the people in the bleachers shifted over our faces. I looked

83

up to see the crowd getting to their feet and start to cheer. Close but out of sight I heard female voices shouting rhythmic phrases: the cheerleaders.

"Hey, they're on." I jumped to my feet and wiped my backside to clear it of grass clippings. "Let's go watch."

Tracie leaped effortlessly to her feet as well, then giggled, clearly enjoying the strength coursing through her leg muscles. "Let's!" she said.

Side by side we rounded the bleachers, out of the shadows and into the glaringly bright floodlights that lit up the field as though it was the middle of the day. On the field directly in front of the bleachers, but behind the benches on which the coaches and extra players sat, was the cheerleading squad. Around a dozen strong, most of them had nothing to do with the genetically engineered superpowered teen shenanigans. All I cared about were the four that were front and center: Ruby-haired, porcelain-skinned Nikki Tate and the olive-skinned, black-haired triplets Amy, Brittany, and Casey Delgado.

It figured that the four cheerleaders with telekinetic powers would be the ones involved in most of the squad's wild tricks.

Oh, and tricks they did. The crowd hollered and applauded as the girls—and the few guys who acted as lifters—chanted "Watch out! We're here! We're ready to cheer!" while Nikki and Amy spiraled up into the air and landed nimbly with one foot in one of the triplets' hands, and the other in the hands of one of the guys. I could tell from the smirk on Amy's face that I was right about her jump having a little psychically influenced assistance.

But who am I to judge? I totally would have done the same thing.

As the cheerleaders finished their opening, a spate of laughter came from the far end of the bleachers, and some guys whistled and called, "Looking good, Spencer! Shake that thing!"

Almost involuntarily, I gripped Tracie's arm. "Here he comes," I said.

Tracie rolled her eyes at me. "Simmer down, you just saw him sixteen minutes ago."

I knew I was acting like a doofus as I grinned dorkily, watching Spencer run up in front of the cheerleaders. I mean, there was an impending meeting with a bunch of lying scientists and I couldn't trust my dad and Evan hadn't answered the text I'd sent a half hour before and I was about to confront the cheerleaders who hated me.

But seriously: He was adorable in that mascot outfit.

Tracie was right, the suit itself was built for a much taller guy, so the furry legs and arms and even the torso were all bunched up, making him look like one of those droopy puppies with all the wrinkles. And then there was the giant cartoon cougar head with its silly grin and narrowed eyes, which I guess was supposed to look sort of badass but just looked like something you'd see in a video game for five-year-olds.

Spencer had no problem getting into character. We're talking spastic dancing all over the field. The Dougie. A botched moonwalk. The sprinkler, people. THE SPRINKLER.

I about died laughing.

Luckily Tracie and the crowd found it as hilarious as I did, so I wasn't there cackling like a moron alone. I was legitimately disappointed when the football teams started to swarm onto the field, and Gary the Cougar had to come in front of the bleachers and take a bow. Even the cheerleaders applauded, all grins and pep.

As the teams ran by each other clapping hands, and someone on a loudspeaker began talking about the pledge of allegiance or something, Spencer removed his fake head to reveal his real one. Sweat-soaked hair was plastered to his forehead, and his cheeks were red. He spoke quietly to Casey, and then the two of them pulled Nikki, Amy, and Brittany away from the other cheerleaders.

"Come on," I said to Tracie. "Back behind the bleachers."

We only had to wait a few minutes for Spencer—minus

the head, but still wearing the oversize suit—to come around the back of the bleachers, followed by the four cheerleaders who knew our secret.

As the crowd roared their support for the home team, Nikki and the triplets came to stand in a line across from me, Spencer, and Tracie. Amy, defiant as always, crossed her arms and pursed her lips. Brittany fussed with her hair and seemed bored, while Casey clasped her hands in front of her waist. Nikki just looked exhausted.

"So," I said, then trailed off.

I could feel my nerves fraying, my confidence ebbing. Like I was going back to how I was a month ago, shy and nervous around the popular kids. I was tempted to pull up more of Nighttime, but I was afraid what the lack of a verbal filter would do. Hell, for all I knew I'd just end up in a wolf-on-telekinetic-cheerleader brawl.

"Well?" Amy snapped. "You and Casey and Spencer finally wore us down. We're here." She raised a hand and snapped her fingers. "Speak."

Wow, okay. Turned out I didn't need to go full Nighttime to face down snippy Amy after all. I was so tired of her crap.

I rolled my eyes. "Lovely," I said. "Anyway, Casey"—I nodded at her—"came to me last weekend after what went down in the woods and told me all about you guys. I know your parents told you to watch over all of us for some reason, and I know now that our own parents not only made me, Spencer, Tracie, and Dalton into what we are, but they've been observing us while we were hunted by a man with a gun and creepy shadow creatures, and they did nothing to stop it."

Brittany raised an eyebrow and let a ringlet of pitch-black hair fall from her fingers. "Shadow creatures?"

I nodded. "That's what took Dalton. We can only see them when we're in our wolf state—or, at least, have our wolf vision. They're from another dimension and want to possess us to cross over. Or something. I'm still not clear on all the details."

"You sound crazy," Amy said. "Like, you know you sound crazy, right?"

"Amy, listen to her," Casey said softly.

"No crazier than psychic powers," Spencer said with a shrug and a grin.

Amy opened her mouth to say more, but Nikki put a hand on her shoulder, then stepped forward.

"Do you know how Dalton is?" she asked. "Is he alive?"

I nodded. "Yes. And I plan to find a way to get him back. But I need your help."

Sighing, Amy turned from the group and began to pace behind her sisters and Nikki. "Oh, come on, are you really going to trust *her*?" she asked. "We already talked to Dalton's dad. You heard what he said about her being the one who made Dalton disappear."

They'd talked to Mr. McKinney? Well, I guess they must have. They were also there when Dalton was taken, but they hadn't said a thing all week even when the lie about Dalton going to see a specialist at a hospital out of state was being spread around. No wonder they'd been avoiding me—I could only imagine the stories Mr. McKinney had made up about who and what I am.

"Look," I said, "you can't trust Dalton's dad. Not my parents either, or Spencer's, or Tracie's, or Emily Cooke's. There's more going on than just science run amok. I talked to Evan Cooke, and he told me that there's some sort of weird cult surrounding these shadow people who took Dalton."

Brittany's eyes came alive. "Evan Cooke? Emily's cousin?"

"What does he have to do with anything?" Casey asked.

Tracie nudged me. "I almost forgot. I want to know, too."

I quickly laid out the story, summarizing what he'd told me over webcam. When I was done, Casey shook her head sadly.

"Poor guy," she whispered.

Brittany tucked her hair behind her ears. "Yeah, um, so . . . did he grow up hot or what?"

"Brittany!" Casey said. "Not important right now."

"I'm just wondering!" she said, raising her hands mock defensively.

Smirking, I said, "I wouldn't get my hopes up," I said. "He definitely grew up hot"—out of the corner of my eye I caught Spencer giving me a nervous glance—"but I got the impression he's not exactly looking to date girls."

"Damn." Brittany sighed. "The best boys are never straight."

"Oh my God!" Amy shouted. "No one cares who you're lusting for, Brittany. Just go for Mikey like I keep telling you. Seriously." Shaking her head, she focused on me. "So, we failed to protect him, Dalton got taken, and now you're some monster surrounded by a cult. What the hell are we supposed to do about it?"

She was answered by the crowd above us roaring in cheers and jumping to their feet. A voice over the speakers cried, "Touchdown Cougars!"

"We should be out there," Brittany said, craning her neck to try to see the field between the stomping feet on the bleachers. "We Will Rock You" began to play. The *stomp-stomp-clap* became deafening.

"No," Nikki said, low and forceful. "The others can

handle it. This is more important."

"Nik," Amy complained.

Nikki raised a hand. "Stop it, Amy. Just think: Why would Emily lie to us about any of this? And why did our parents make us watch them all this time? I want to know what's going on, too." Turning to me, she said, "So what exactly do you want from us?"

I looked at Tracie, who shrugged, then at Spencer, who nodded encouragingly.

"I'd like to call a truce, first of all," I said. "No more fights in front of parties. We almost got caught the last time."

Amy turned her lips down into an exaggerated pout. "Aw, but I loved making you fly."

Nikki elbowed her.

Ignoring her, I continued. "I don't know anything about your parents, or where they're from, or why they made you telekinetic. Or even how they did that. But the scientists at BioZenith—our parents—want me, Spencer, and Tracie to come there tomorrow so they can supposedly spill all their secrets. I don't trust them."

"You want us to go to that meeting with you?" Casey asked.

I shook my head as another roar rose up from the crowd.

"No. Well, sort of. I was just hoping you could come as

backup. Wait close enough to help us if we need it."

The four girls looked at one another, speaking wordlessly: Casey pleading with her eyes, Brittany questioning, Amy beginning to thaw, and Nikki nodding, taking charge.

Finally, they looked back at the three of us.

"All right," Nikki said. "We were told to watch and protect you anyway. And if you can learn more about why you're the way you are, maybe we will, too."

She offered me a tired smile. I was guessing she hadn't slept well in days. Seeing your boyfriend disappear into thin air would do that to you.

"Deal," I said, then offered my hand. Nikki stared at it for a moment, then reached forward to shake it.

"Hey, there you are," a voice called behind the cheerleaders.

We all looked to find one of the cheerleader guys standing there, a guy named Trevor.

Trevor jerked his thumb over his shoulder. "We're supposed to be cheering. You know, that's why you're wearing those matching sweaters and skirts?"

Shaking her head, Nikki said, "Yeah, of course." To the triplets, "Come on, let's get back out there." To me, in a hushed, conspiratorial voice that would in no way imply that I was a drug dealer, "Text me the details."

In practiced unison, the four cheerleaders spun on their heels and matched one another's strides. As they walked around the bleachers, Amy looked back over her shoulder and said, "You'd better not be getting us into trouble."

Plastering a smile on my face, I raised a hand and said, "Nice chatting with you too!"

"I've never seen Amy so pleasant," Tracie said once the cheerleaders were out of view.

Standing over us, Spencer put his hands on his costumed hips and grinned. "That went well, I think! See, I knew I could get them to talk to us."

"Shouldn't you be out there, Gary?" I asked. "The cheerleaders may be able to do backflips, but you're the real star."

"Oh yeah!" he said. "Better resume my duties. I'll see you guys in a bit. Have fun practicing." With a salute and a wink, he was off, half walking, half shuffling to avoid tripping over his feet and the fake tail he dragged in the dirt behind him.

Tracie and I spent the next hour continuing to practice going hybrid—she even managed to get a few of her fingernails to stretch into claws. Before I knew it, the crowd was cheering once more and the game was over, the Cougars victorious. I never pay attention to football unless it's on *Friday Night*

Lights, but the people in the bleachers certainly made it sound exciting.

Spencer showed up in his street clothes, still sweaty and smelling of boy musk, and after Tracie put the blanket back inside the school where she got it, the three of us walked to his minivan.

The parking lot was dark and mostly empty by then. The school bus for the visiting team was just pulling out, and some guys and girls were hanging out by cars, laughing and squealing over the team's victory. But those cars were on the other side of the gravel parking lot from where Spencer had parked. His van stood alone.

It wasn't until we got close that I saw the shadows of two people standing next to the van.

For a moment, I thought I was seeing more shadow-men—first over webcam, now here even though my eyes were from Nighttime and not the werewolf.

Then the shadowy figures came around the front of the van, into the streetlights. Before they disappeared behind the vehicle, I could clearly make out that both figures were tall and slender. One was female with long blond hair. The other, a guy with black hair.

Megan and Patrick.

Without saying a word, I broke into a run, leaving Spencer and Tracie behind me. My sneakers went from grass to gravel, and I almost slipped on the loose rocks as I skidded around the minivan to catch up to them.

Even though there was no place to hide, and even though I hadn't heard any car start and drive off, Megan and Patrick were gone.

I could have left it alone. Maybe I should have and just chalked it up to Megan turning into a weird creeper in light of all that had happened.

But I didn't want to think of her that way. And between the aura I sensed from her that morning, and her strange demeanor, and thinking I saw her in my bedroom window, and now this?

I couldn't save the mystery for another day.

Footsteps thudded on the gravel behind me. Spencer grabbed my arm, his expression worried. Tracie stopped beside him.

"What is it?" Spencer asked me. "Why did you just take off?"

With one last look at the empty lot beyond the minivan, I turned to meet his and Tracie's eyes.

"Do you guys mind if we make a stop before going home?" I asked. "I need to get to the bottom of something."

YOU THINK YOU KNOW A LOT, EMILY

Fifteen minutes later, we pulled up in front of Megan's house.

She lived only a few blocks from me, but that was where the houses got smaller and more run down. Not that I was rich or anything. My family did okay, even though my dad's construction work was inconsistent at best. I only now wonder if our ability to have such a nice house was funded by BioZenith. Yeah, no wonder my parents took that deal—mutate your child, never worry about finances again!

Anyway, Megan's house was usually quiet and dark, save for the times her brother's band—the Bubonic Teutonics—were getting all rock-tastic in the garage.

But that night, the whole place was lit up, cars were lined up on the street out front, and a bunch of college-aged people were standing on the front lawn and in the open garage, drinking cans of beer and partying it up.

Not exactly Megan's scene. But I didn't know where else to look for her. Maybe her brother or her parents—if they were there—would know.

Spencer, Tracie, and I climbed out of the van and wound past the cars in the driveway toward the garage. Tracie stuck close to me, doing her calming breathing exercises and constantly patting herself, as though feeling for something. Only then did I realize that it was past eight, the time when our personality changes came unbidden before we learned to control them. And Tracie had only learned how to go hybrid a few hours before.

I reached over and clenched her shoulder reassuringly. "You can do it," I whispered as the yellow lights of the garage washed over us.

She nodded but didn't say anything. Just breathed in, one, two, three, four, five. Then out.

Two girls sat at the drum set, one showing the other how to play while slurring the instructions. In the bed of a pickup truck on the other side of the garage, three guys and another girl lounged, telling loud stories, while a dog I'd never seen before walked between them, tail wagging, tongue lolling, waiting to get petted. The storytellers half-heartedly obliged.

"It's just, like, man," one of the guys drawled as he

tickled the dog under its chin. "You think you know a girl, and then she, like, she just cuts you off. Just severs. And it hurts so much, man. Like, in your chest. A chest hurt."

The others nodded knowingly. The guy next to him took a sip from his can and said, "That's rough, buddy."

The three of us walked past these unfamiliar people, nodding cordially and being ignored, then through the door into the house itself. There were more people milling here, too, most paired off and having deep conversations while looking into each other's glassy eyes. Mellow mood music swirled through the rooms.

No one seemed to take notice of us as we made our way to the living room. Which was fine by me. It was there that I found Megan's brother, Lucas, all beanpole body wrapped in shredded black clothes, his white-blond hair swept over half his face.

He was chatting with two people on the couch, whose backs were to me. I didn't want to be rude and interrupt, but when he ignored my insistent wave to get his attention, I walked straight up to the couch, placed my hands on the back, and loudly asked, "Hey, Lucas, have you seen Megan?"

Lucas snapped his attention to me, apparently startled by my sudden appearance. At the same time, the two people he'd been talking to craned their necks around to look up at me over the back of the couch.

I recognized them immediately.

"Jared?" I asked. But I wasn't surprised so much at his presence—being Lucas's band mate and all—as I was by the girl sitting next to him. "Dawn?!"

Jared—aka Deputy Jared, the clean-cut, totally hot, but totally Boy Scout–y police officer who'd helped me out after "discovering" the dead body of Dr. Gunther Elliott in Spencer's backyard, aka drummer of the Bubonic Teutonics—leaped to his feet, as though he'd been caught doing something bad.

Dawn, my stepsister, smiled and shook her head as she got to her feet at a normal person pace and stood beside Jared. She looked great, but that was nothing new—the girl was basically a Victoria's Secret model even when wearing an oversize shirt and face mask to bed. Today she was wearing some killer boots and a short skirt along with a tight, black Bubonic Teutonics T-shirt.

"Hey, Emily!" Jared said, forcing a smile and raising a hand in greeting. "Staying out of trouble?"

"Not really," Spencer said beside me. I nudged him and he laughed.

"Yeah, I'm fine," I said. I looked between him and Dawn, brow furrowed. "So, uh, I didn't know you two knew each other."

Dawn moved in close to Jared, her arm brushing his casually. "We haven't known each other that long," she said.

Then, turning her attention from me to Jared, she slapped his arm playfully and said, "Dude, you didn't tell me you knew my stepsister! Wait." Looking back at me, her expression went wary. "*How* do you know my stepsister?"

"We—" he started.

"Through Megan!" I shouted before he could answer. "Yeah, he's always over here practicing with Lucas, so we've, y'know. Crossed paths."

Dawn raised her eyebrows. "Interesting. So, Em, tell me, is this dude chill? Be honest."

I grinned and met Jared's eyes. "Jared is a perfect gentleman, an all-around good guy, and has done nothing but look out for the safety of us teenagers."

A trio of revelers came out of the kitchen, clinging to one another as they laughed and slurred their way toward the door. Dodging them, Lucas rounded the couch, then leaned against it directly in front of me and crossed his arms.

"Who are your friends?" he asked.

"Oh," I said. "This is Spencer."

Spencer waved, then nodded at Jared. "We met. Remember?"

Jared glanced at Dawn, then nodded back. "I wouldn't forget."

Gesturing toward Tracie I said, "This is Tracie Townsend. She's our class president."

"Welcome, Tracie!" Lucas said, sounding more lighthearted than he'd ever been. Well, around me, at least.

Tracie didn't acknowledge him. In fact, she wasn't acknowledging any of us. She stared off into the distance, her breaths shaky, her fists clenched.

"Is she okay?" Lucas asked, turning back to me.

The shift. It must have been happening, and she was fighting it, and here I was getting all jovial with a bunch of college kids.

Grabbing Tracie by the shoulders, I gently shoved her toward Spencer, then hissed at him, "Get her to the car. Stay with her." As he started to lead her out, I turned to Lucas, Jared, and Dawn and shrugged. "You remember her, Jared, she had a panic attack at last week's party, too. She's not good with crowds. She just needs some air."

Time was wasting. I needed to focus on the reason I'd made Spencer drive us there: Megan.

"So, Lucas," I said before anyone could try and spark a new conversation. "Is Megan around?"

In a low, serious voice, he said, "I'm not sure she wants to see you yet, Emily."

I waved my hand dismissively and forced a laugh. "Oh, that. No, don't worry about it, we were having a fight. But we made up at school earlier and she asked me here." I shrugged and tried to look innocent. "You know us chicks, always getting emotional about something."

"Yeah," Lucas said, his voice distant as he looked over

my head at some girls behind me in the kitchen. Apparently bored of talking with me, he said, "Should be in her room, guarding it from trespassers. Been there all night."

"Cool, thanks," I said.

He didn't seem to hear me, choosing instead to brush past me and go chat up the new object of his focus. I said my good-byes to Jared and Dawn, and they went back to cuddling on the couch.

As soon as I turned around, I dropped my smile. Weaving past the college kids in the wood-paneled hallway, I came to Megan's bedroom door and knocked.

No answer.

I'd hate it if someone burst into my room without my permission, but considering I'd just seen Megan at the school and we drove there faster than she and Patrick could possibly walk, I guessed she wasn't inside. I twisted the knob, slipped in, and shut the door behind me.

And was surprised to find Megan sitting at her computer, clicking away while reading the internet.

"Oh!" I said, startled even though it was, y'know, her room.

Megan retained her cool. In fact, it took her what felt like ages to even acknowledge I existed. Slowly she twisted her head to face me. She looked me up and down. Then looked back at her computer.

"What do you want?" she asked me.

Rolling my shoulders back, I tried to regain my composure. "Actually, I came here to ask you the same thing. I saw you and Patrick after the football game hanging out by Spencer's car. If you don't want anything to do with me, why were you there?"

"I wasn't," Megan said flatly, the blue glow of the monitor reflecting in her eyes. "I've been here all night."

Brow furrowed, I shook my head. "That's not possible. I *saw* you. In fact, I keep feeling you watching me all the time."

She scoffed. Shutting the browser window, she spun her chair around to face me. "I'm sorry, are you accusing me of stalking you? Like I'm that desperate to be friends? Ego much?"

Softly I said, "Actually, yeah, I do kind of think you're that desperate. You certainly were a week ago when you begged me to make you a werewolf."

She flicked her hand at me. "Please. I'm over it. I don't need you. I'm good. I'm *better* than good."

Sitting on the edge of her bed, I leaned forward on my knees and tried to catch her eyes. She looked anywhere but at me.

"Megan," I said. "I don't want you to hate me. And I know you don't want me to hate you. I know things are weird now. I know—"

"Oh, you know, you *know*." Getting to her feet, she

began to pace in front of me. "You think you know a lot, Emily. I know this about you, that's what I learned recently when you decided keeping secrets from me was a grand idea, that you're suddenly Encyclopedia Webb just because you can grow fur."

She stopped pacing, staring into the corner of her room away from me. When she spoke again, her voice was low, eerie.

"But there are lots of things you don't know, Emily. Lots and lots of things."

Slowly she turned to face me. A smile was plastered on her face, but her eyes were narrowed. Crazed. Even at her most surly I'd never seen her look like this. A chill ran over my arms and I shivered.

"Maybe I have been watching you," she said. Shrugging, "Or maybe I have much better things to do. Who knows?"

I stood and took a step toward her, but she raised a hand, stopping me.

"Megan," I said. "You're not acting like yourself. I'm worried that what happened in the woods did something to you."

She shrugged again. "Maybe if you worried a little less about yourself and more about your friends of eight years, I wouldn't have had anything happen to me in the woods at all."

"Megan . . ."

Pointing toward the door, she commanded, "Go."

I opened my mouth to protest and she dropped the fake smile. Practically roaring she repeated herself: *"Go!"*

I had nothing else to say. She wouldn't listen anyway. So I did as she asked and left the room. The partiers in the hall outside were a ruddy blur as I sped past them. My whole body felt hot. My arms trembled.

Seconds later I was outside, swallowed by cold night air. I walked to Spencer's minivan, opened the door, and said, "Hey, I'm going to walk home. Can you make sure Tracie gets home all right?"

Tracie was still in the backseat, focused on controlling her shift.

Spencer nodded. "Yeah, of course. Will you be okay?"

No.

"Yes," I said.

Though he was obviously concerned, Spencer did as I asked. I slammed the door shut and he drove away. I watched him go until his taillights disappeared around a corner. Then, I ran across the street into the woods.

Once I was out of sight, I shed my clothes. Splaying open my jacket, I shoved my sweater, my jeans, my shoes, and my underwear on top, then pulled it all together into a bundle. Shivering uncontrollably, dirt and twigs biting into my bare feet, I closed my eyes and focused on changing.

I didn't want to be my human self right then; not Daytime or Nighttime or the mix of the two that made up who I was now.

I wanted to be the wolf. To go on instinct and ignore the problems that kept arising even as I made plans to solve others. At least, for a little while.

Black and brown fur bristled over my arms, enveloping me in smooth warmth. My limbs elongated, whatever pain there should be distant and numb. My face followed, smashing and stretching into a snout, my teeth becoming sharpened fangs, my ears rising atop my head as they narrowed into points.

I grabbed the bundle of my clothes in one arm and held it close to my taut, muscular wolf-girl chest. Instincts took over then—the woods exploded into hundreds, thousands of smells and achingly loud noises that my ears twisted and turned to pick up.

Craning my head back, I closed my eyes and let out a long, loud howl. Out rushed anxiety and anger. In rushed freedom from stupid human worries.

Fully wolf, I dropped down and caught myself on my free, clawed hand. Then, pushing off with my powerful legs, I raced into the night.

ENVISIONING THE BRIGHTEST STARS, TO LEAD OUR WAY

I don't remember much about the rest of the night. What memories I can conjure up are mostly of chasing smells and fleeing human sounds and speeding through trees.

What I *can* remember is the feeling of complete, worry-free freedom. There were no people to make demands of me, no worried thoughts to consume me.

And thankfully, no shadowmen out watching me.

But it had to end eventually, and at some point in the middle of the night my wolf self made her way to the backyard of my house, where I reluctantly turned into a human again. Shedding my coat of fur was like jumping into the ocean, the cold air enveloping my exposed body and momentarily shocking me. Shivering uncontrollably, I slipped into my clothes.

It's funny how uninhibited being a werewolf had made me. Too bad my clothes couldn't transform along with me to make my story family friendly.

Fully dressed, I patted my jacket pockets to make sure my keys and phone were there. Both were—and when I pulled out my phone, I saw I had a text from Evan.

12:32 AM: I'm alive.

Attached was a photo he'd snapped of himself, his palm next to his face and the date written on it in marker. To prove it was him who'd sent it, apparently. Good idea—I'm not sure I'd have been able to sleep wondering if it had been his mother fake texting me.

I was tempted to call him back, but when I checked the time on my phone, my eyes went wide—it was after three a.m. I'd been a wolf for hours. I sent him a text instead.

Exhaustion rushed over me, and superstrength or no, the muscles in my legs ached. Sneaking in through the back door, I made my way silently up to my room, kicked off my shoes, and tore off my jacket. I set my alarm for nine a.m., then climbed fully clothed into bed and under my covers.

Seconds later, I was passed out.

My alarm screamed at me much too soon. Eyes snapping open, I smacked the off button and then lay in bed, staring at the ceiling.

Saturday. I had four hours until the big meeting at BioZenith.

I lay there for five minutes, then forced myself out of bed. I had work to do.

First off: Contact my team and make sure we were all ready. Texts went out to Spencer, Tracie, and Nikki, and one by one they all texted back to confirm our plans.

Spencer, Tracie, and I were all going to wear the stretchiest pants and shirts we owned so we could transform without worrying about the need to take off our clothes. Just in case.

Spencer had a small recording device he'd put together so we could play back what the parents told us later. He told me he rigged it up so it could call out—meaning we could have the cheerleaders listen in on someone's phone.

I was in total love with this guy's tech prowess, I have to say.

Tracie told me she'd spent the night practicing hybrid and, true to her A-type perfectionist self, thought she'd already mastered it. I could only hope she was right.

And Nikki agreed to all my plans. She and the triplets would hide in the minivan and listen in. If we needed help, they'd know it.

I felt like I was in some crazy heist movie and we were about to try and get the perfect score.

As twelve thirty rolled around, I took a shower and put

on fresh clothes: my stretched-out black sweater and the patched-up sweatpants that so often acted as my prowling gear. They'd kept me safe so far.

Wiping my hand across the steamed-up mirror, I looked myself in the eye and pulled my hair back into a ponytail. Then, I placed my hands on either side of the sink and leaned in close.

"You're ready for this," I said. "It's time to face our makers."

I had questions. They had lies.

I was going to make them give me answers.

"All right, ladies, time to duck down."

From the crowded backseat of the minivan, Brittany whined, "Ew, Spencer, you really need to vacuum in here."

"My mom always tells me the same thing," he said as he turned down the street that led into the industrial district. "But blame Mikey and the guys. I'm not the one who's eating back there."

Spencer had picked me up last after getting the cheerleaders and Tracie. They were crammed in the back, where they'd be waiting for our signal. Like us, they'd dressed all in black. Only their clothes were a lot nicer—and more expensive—than mine. I'm talking matching designer leather jackets and perfectly tailored yoga pants to go with their knit hats. They looked like a team of cat burglars.

I looked back over the front seat. "You comfortable back there?"

A chorus of nos.

"Not in the least," Tracie grumbled. She was crushed against the door while the others tried to arrange themselves.

"It's only until we're inside," I said as I looked back to the street. "Then just make sure none of the patrolling guards see you and we'll be good."

Spencer pulled to a stop at the giant fenced gate topped with barbed wire that was the entrance to the BioZenith facilities. To his left was a small guardhouse. He cranked open the window, then leaned out and grinned at the serious-looking man standing inside.

"Hi," Spencer said. "We're guests. We should be on a list or something."

"Your names," the guard barked.

"Spencer Holt, Emily Webb, and Tracie Townsend."

The guard looked down and pressed a touch screen on his desk. Nodding at Spencer, he pressed a button and the fenced gate started to slide open with a whir of gears and a clang of metal smacking metal.

As Spencer rolled up his window, I took in a deep breath and looked up at the two-story, two-building BioZenith facility in front of us. The place suddenly seemed much bigger than I remembered.

"Here we go," I whispered.

The parking lot was half full, and though there were a few guards walking around, none had guns. At least not the big rifles Spencer and I had seen them carry the other night when we'd scoped the place out.

Completely normal-looking people wearing business casual left the building in pairs and groups, laughing with each other before waving good-bye and heading to their cars. Through the windows I could see others at their desks, talking on phones or typing away on their computers. The building on the right—which had the main entrance—could have been any normal office building on the block.

Spencer pulled into a guest parking spot near the entrance, but not so close that anyone exiting the building would see the cheerleaders. Shutting off the car, he looked back and down at Nikki.

"Got your phone on?" he asked her.

Struggling from her position, she dug into her jacket pocket and produced a smartphone, tapped the screen a few times, then held it up for us to see. She'd loaded up some basic-looking app that I guess Spencer had sent her.

Grabbing a piece of his sweatshirt, Spencer held it close to his face and said, "Testing." His voice echoed out of the phone—he must have been grabbing the hidden microphone that was taped to his chest.

"It works," Nikki said simply.

"Great," Amy said beside her, wedged between the backset and the driver's seat. "Now can you guys go? This isn't comfortable."

"Yeah," I said, nodding to Tracie and Spencer. "We're ready."

As we opened the doors and jumped out, Casey called out, "Good luck!" I offered her a smile, then slammed the door closed.

Side by side, Spencer, Tracie, and I walked past the trees planted in little spots of green on the front walkway to the big glass entryway. We hefted open the doors and walked into the lobby, which had tan tile floors, an unoccupied receptionist desk next to the elevator bay, and a big section with plush couches and tables strewn with magazines.

That's where the parents were waiting for us.

They rose as we entered, and the three of us stopped.

There was an attractive blond couple with lined, somber faces that I recognized from Emily Cooke's funeral. Her parents.

Mr. McKinney, alone, standing in front of everyone with his arms crossed and a fake smile on his face.

A short white man with unkempt hair and a doughy, white woman, both in ill-fitting brown suits. Spencer's parents, the professors.

A black woman in a flowy, tropical-patterned dress, with hair pulled back by a kerchief and her hands and face overwhelmed by homemade earrings and bracelets and rings. Tracie's mom, the artist.

And there was my dad, still sitting, clutching and wrenching in his lap the fishing cap he sometimes wore to cover up his baldness.

My stepmom wasn't there. She probably didn't know about me, then. At least one adult in my life hadn't lied to me.

For a long moment, we all stood there staring at one another awkwardly. My dad wouldn't look at us, but Mr. McKinney, Spencer's parents, and Tracie's mom all offered smiles that we were unable to return. Mr. Cooke coughed, and the sound echoed through lobby, making the place feel all the more empty.

A ding rang out as an elevator reached the main floor. A pair of women walked out, talking and laughing loudly, clutches and jackets in hand. Catching sight of our group, they went silent, lowered their heads, and rushed out the front doors.

Mr. McKinney sighed, then walked up to us. "All right, might as well get started. You three are hungry, right? You're hungry. Come, we had our chef put together a great lunch."

Spencer and Tracie both looked to me and I shrugged. We stayed side by side as we followed Mr. McKinney past the seating area. Tracie's mom reached out to try and touch her arm, but Tracie pulled away. After that, the parents followed us in silence.

The cafeteria was through double doors behind the receptionist's desk. It was pretty big, about the same size as the school cafeteria, only much nicer. The tables were real wood, for one, and the seating was wooden chairs with plush upholstery. In lieu of windows on the back wall, giant photographs of flowers and grass and trees were displayed on screens that kept fading to show new scenery, like that boring screen-saver pack that always comes with new computers.

The three of us sat down on one side of a table while the parents went opposite—all of them. As we were served salads topped with rare duck and some sort of fancy root mash, Mr. McKinney talked.

And talked.

A lot of it was what he'd already told me at my house and that I'd already relayed to Spencer and Tracie: that they made us in test tubes, that they were observing us, that they want to *help* us now. Mr. McKinney dominated the conversation, but occasionally Mrs. Cooke would jump in, or Mr. Holt.

But it was nothing new. Nothing about what the shadowmen were really like—in fact, they never even mentioned the name "Akhakhu" that was all over the HAVOC files and that Evan had told me about.

Finally, Spencer interrupted and asked what was on

all our minds, "Okay, I get that you made us this way. But *why*? And how?"

The parents that I was guessing were the scientists in the group—Mr. McKinney, Mrs. Cooke, both Mr. and Mrs. Holt—looked at one another. The latter three seemed concerned, worried. Mr. McKinney, as usual, refused to act any way but in complete control. He was the one who answered.

"Let's start with the how," he said. "You are aware of the other dimension. Twenty years ago, the company that BioZenith was once a part of managed to breach into that world. That is when we first made contact with the other side. With the . . . shadowmen."

I'd been fidgeting with my duck, not having eaten anything. I wasn't going to trust any food they served me. At the mention of the shadowmen, I set the fork down and met Mr. McKinney's eye across the table.

"You mean the Akhakhu."

For a sliver of a second, Dalton's dad seemed flustered. Regaining his composure, he nodded and said, "Yes, the Akhakhu is what they called themselves. They are a race far more advanced than us. When we entered their world, we discovered them living in vast, technologically superior palaces. They didn't fear us, and in fact they were able to use their technology to communicate with us. We weren't the first other-dimensional beings to find the way there.

"They supplied us with technology that we could use to enhance our race, to improve the mistakes in our biology, to eradicate birth defects, to make us more than human." He laughed. "Well, not *us*, unfortunately. But our children. And theirs."

"So the technology they had was to mix humans and animals?" Tracie asked. "That's how they got ahead? That seems weird."

Spencer's mom leaned forward excitedly. "Oh no, it was so much more than that. They had all sorts of improvements! We could make it so someone could move things with their minds or—"

"Viv," Spencer's dad interrupted. She met his eye and he shook his head. Her enthusiastic smile faltered and she leaned back.

Clearing his throat, Mr. McKinney looked from Mrs. Holt back to me. "As Vivian was saying, there was more to their technology. But we at this branch of the corporation were given this particular bit of technology to experiment with. Your mother"—he nodded at me—"was the one who dubbed it HAVOC."

"'Human-Animal Vespers, Original Crossbreeds,'" I said. "Yeah, I saw that in the files. But what's a 'vesper' and why do the files refer to us that way?"

"'Envisioning the brightest stars, to lead our way,'"

Tracie's mom muttered, then popped a bit of salad in her mouth. The three of us teens all looked at her, and her hand fluttered to her chest, surprised. Swallowing the bite she'd just taken, she looked nervously over at Mr. McKinney, then said, "I always saw that on the letterhead. I thought it was nice."

"It was just a name for the kids who were enhanced," Mrs. Cooke said softly. "We didn't come up with it. It's what we were told to call you. All of you, all of the vespers, were viewed as the new, greater generation. The ones who would take humanity into the future." She let out a quick, rueful laugh.

Standing up, Mrs. Cooke dabbed her mouth with her napkin, then shoved back her chair. "I'm sorry, Harrison," she said to Mr. McKinney. "I don't see why we need to be here. We're no longer a part of this." Nodding cordially at us, she grabbed her husband's arm to get him to stand up and said to us, "Nice meeting you. I'm sorry about . . ." Shaking her head, she sighed. "Good luck to you."

Everyone went quiet and watched as the Cookes left the cafeteria, their footsteps echoing throughout the room before they disappeared through the double doors. The door hinges squeaked, then went silent.

Mr. McKinney cleared his throat. Looking at my dad and Tracie's mom next to him, he apologetically said, "You'll have to forgive them. They recently lost their daughter."

"Of course," my dad said. Trying to catch my eye, he added, "I don't even want to think about what that would be like."

I looked down at my uneaten food. It was cold by now.

"All right, so the tech stuff makes sense, I guess," Spencer said next to me. "I mean, I've been wondering how any of this is even possible, but alien science works for me. Just, why wolves? What's the point? You made it sound like there were all sorts of genetic engineering options, but you chose the werewolf program for your kids?"

Spencer's mom put her hand to her mouth. Her eyes glistened. "Oh, sweetie. My poor baby. It wasn't supposed to be werewolves at all. You poor thing."

Spencer rolled his eyes and, in a "you're embarrassing me!" tone said, "Mom!"

Hand still over her mouth, Mrs. Holt leaned into her husband.

"We wanted to give you the abilities we felt would make you the strongest," Mr. McKinney said. "We wanted to improve all of your senses without any of the drawbacks. But when we tested the five of you after your births, using the genetic markers we put in place so that we could activate you remotely, your shifts were erratic. Monstrous. You weren't meant to turn into half-human, half-wolf hybrids, but that's what you became. We couldn't bear seeing you when you . . . weren't yourselves. So we deactivated you, struck your names from our records so that only those who worked directly on the project would know who you were, and chose to let you live normal lives."

Except that wasn't the end of HAVOC. They messed up with us five. And I remembered Mr. McKinney mentioning other potential Emilys, little genetically mutated fetuses in glass vials that didn't make it. We were just the batch that got closest.

Until they made Evan.

I wanted to throw this fact in Mr. McKinney's face and expose his lie. But I didn't want to tip my hand just yet. I still had questions.

"So why wolves?" I asked. "If you weren't intentionally going for the whole werewolf thing, why not, I dunno. Bears. Or lions. Birds or dolphins or . . . anything, really."

Pushing his now-empty plate forward, Mr. McKinney stood and smiled down at me. "How about we ask the woman who was in charge of the project?"

"Who's that?" Tracie asked.

Finally meeting my father's sad, pleading eyes, I answered. "My mother."

10

I FIGURED IT OUT

Now two people short, Mr. McKinney led our party out of the cafeteria, into the elevators, and up to the second floor where all the offices were.

I already knew the layout of the building from the last time I was there. But this time I made a point of scanning the corners to see where the guards were stationed, to look in the cubicles to see what presumably innocent sales team member or customer service rep was still working that Saturday afternoon.

Mr. McKinney took us through the doors that led to the glass walkway connecting the two buildings. The window I shattered was fixed—no one would have known a werewolf had broken it a week before.

And then, we were in the labs. At least, the labs they wanted us to see. Something told me our tour wouldn't be taking us past the security door where we'd seen the vats of failed genetic experiments.

Holding a keycard over a pad on the wall, Mr. McKinney waited for the light on it to go from red to green, then slid open the glass door that led into a spacious computer lab. Unlike some of the other labs we'd passed, which were filled with plants and Pyrex containers and other equipment, this room was nothing but computer bays and giant, heat-emitting servers on three sides of the room.

Directly across from the door, a flat-screen monitor the size of a giant TV was mounted on the wall. Walking purposefully toward it, Mr. McKinney leaned over and pressed a button on a black box. Speaking into it, he said, "Jones, fire up the rings and the camera."

"Got it," a voice responded.

Turning back toward us, Mr. McKinney clasped his hands behind his back. "I understand that you three have been here before," he said. "And judging by the destruction of some of our equipment in the facility below us, you saw the ringed apparatus, yes?"

I nodded. "That has something to do with the other dimension, right?"

"Yes. You'll forgive me if I don't take you down there.

The shareholders would have my head." He waved a hand at the monitor. "But we've put together this setup so you can still speak to someone on the other side."

He pressed the corner of the monitor and it buzzed on. Like with the video he'd shown me on the tablet two nights before, the image was of static and liquidy bands of color fading into and colliding with one another. Like bad radio reception, whines and crackles came from the speakers.

Ever so distant, I could barely make out a female voice say, "Hello?"

My dad, who seemed to be doing his best to hide in the corner farthest from me, visibly stiffened. Pulling his hat onto his head, he shuffled closer to the rest of the group.

Just like in the video, a vague, human shape appeared in the midst of the staticky murk. As though someone was sketching her into existence, dark lines appeared showing my mother's features. Next to her, a darker gray shape also shaded in—a man around thirty, wearing glasses.

Someone grabbed my hand. I looked down at it to see Tracie's fingers threaded through my own. I could feel her trembling as she watched, wide-eyed, as her father appeared on-screen.

"Are we on?" my mother asked, her voice clear now. A muffled voice that sounded like Jones-from-the-speaker gave her the affirmative, and she smiled at the camera.

Behind her and Tracie's dad, I could make out the outlines of tall, spindly towers and giant machines hovering in the air. But they were just ideas of a world, barely there.

"Caroline," my dad said softly, so softly there was no way she could hear.

Near him, Mrs. Townsend turned away from the screen, her arm over her face.

"We're here," Mr. McKinney said, his voice much too loud. "Caroline, Thomas, can you see us?"

Mr. Townsend frowned. "No, sir, we cannot. But we can hear you fine."

Part of me was disappointed. Part of me wanted her to be able to see me standing there, even as hazy and indistinct as she was to me, just so she could see the girl she decided wouldn't be good enough without her meddling with my entire *self* first.

But another part of me was glad that she wouldn't be able to see the hurt and anger and longing on my face.

"Are they there?" my mother asked.

Gently letting go of Tracie's hand, I stepped close to the screen so that the gray-shaded images of my mom and Tracie's dad were all that I could see.

"I'm here," I said. "This is Emily."

"Is Tracie there with you?" Mr. Townsend asked.

I looked back at her. She shook her head, then looked down at the floor.

Turning back to the screen, I said, "She doesn't want to talk, Mr. Townsend. Sorry."

He didn't respond. His features went still, cold.

"Emily, oh, it's me, it's your mom," my mother started. "I don't even know where to begin. I've been waiting to talk to you for so long, I—"

"That's great," I snapped. "Wonderful. I'm glad you *wanted* to talk to me instead of abandoning me to go off to some crazy dimension and do experiments. But wanting to is not the same as doing. As far as I'm concerned, the only mother I have is Katherine. You, Caroline, are just some woman who messed with my body and mind without me having any say."

Everyone in the room fell completely silent. My mother—Caroline—on the screen sat there, mouth agape, speechless.

"I have questions," I said.

"Emily," Caroline pleaded. "I don't know what anyone has been saying, but—"

"Question one: Why wolves? It's not a huge deal." I shrugged, even though she couldn't see me. "But, y'know, just curious."

The shadowy form of Mr. Townsend stepped in front of Caroline.

"There are certain species that can perceive those on the other dimensional planes," he answered. "You ever notice a house pet stare at a corner or get spooked, as if something is there that no one can see? As we discovered, there *is*. Dogs are inbred, stupid creatures, so we went to their cousins instead—wolves."

I shook my head. "Why was it so necessary for us to be able to perceive the dimensional things—the shadowmen, I take it? I thought this whole HAVOC project was just about making us super strong or whatever."

No one immediately answered. I looked between the Holts and Mr. McKinney and the monitor. Just as I heard my mother start to stammer and give an excuse, Mr. McKinney interrupted.

"The ability to breach dimensions is the one thing the Akhakhu can't do, Emily," he said. "One of our directives back when we had yet to separate from our parent company was that we must find a way to interact with these beings, so as to help our trading of technology."

It sounded reasonable. But it was still a half answer, just like everything I'd been getting in this place.

Letting my brain and Nighttime's merge, I thought back to everything I'd seen and been told, both the truth and lies.

Dr. Gunther Elliott, BioZenith employee, discovered our existence and decided we needed to die before we could find "them," as he'd said just before we killed him.

The cheerleaders were sent by their parents—surely scientists who worked for some other branch of the company BioZenith was once part of, based on the technology—to keep us safe and to keep us from doing . . . something.

Mr. McKinney had told me the other dimension was some sort of scientific utopia where the kindhearted Akhakhu wanted to enhance our species. Since we're so deserving, I guess?

Evan described the devotion to the Akhakhu as almost religious—which fit with the way Mr. McKinney described their kindness and opulence. But when Evan slipped into the other dimension, he saw boil-covered humanoids in wastelands, not the magical mystery wonderland just on the other side of a rift in space and time.

The shadowmen I'd seen and interacted with ranged from observers to those actively out to get us—one even tried to get inside Megan's body.

So which version of the shadowmen/Akhakhu was real?

How about both?

I mean, our world isn't exactly homogenous. There's the superrich in their metaphorical palaces. And there's the poor, desperate destitute who would do anything to get out of their situation.

What better way for the upper class to abandon their

dying world first than to make friends with a new species and then pressure them to find some way to make the portals between worlds go both ways?

It was then, standing there in the middle of that lab room, everyone watching me silently and no noise save for the hum of the computer towers and the crackling from the monitor, that the puzzle of BioZenith and the Akhakhu clicked into place.

Snapping back to attention, I looked at Mr. McKinney and smiled. "I figured it out."

"What?" he asked.

"I know why you made us," I said. Pacing back and forth, I let it fall free as it all came together. "You needed some way to interact with these Akhakhu on this side. Humans can't perceive them, obviously, and I'm guessing the technology that lets you interact is inconsistent at best. You found out some animals can naturally see them, though, and so you decided to make the best of both worlds—humans with animal abilities." I stopped and looked at my two pack members, Spencer and Tracie, who watched me earnestly. "You made us so you could help them. Only it turned out they aren't exactly what you thought they were."

From the screen, Caroline spoke, desperate. "Emily, you're right. I'm so sorry." She took in a shaky breath and her words spilled out, an almost unintelligible torrent as she tried to speak as quickly as possible. "Thomas and I are stuck here, and the only way they keep us safe is if we do what they say. But I'm not going to stand here anymore and let them force us to treat you like this. You are more important, Emily. Don't let them destroy you!"

Muffling and shouts as someone dove toward the camera. As the image tilted I heard Caroline cry out one more time, "And don't let them hurt your father! He didn't know! He didn't—"

Mr. McKinney slammed his palm against the corner of the monitor, and the screen went black. Half of the parents jumped at the noise.

I rounded on him, shaking my head slowly. "Those rifts I see as a wolf, those are what the Akhakhu are after. They need them in order to completely slip from their world into ours. Only they can't come through whole. They need a body—like the body of my friend, who I saw one try to possess.

"And Dalton," I said, pacing once more. "I think I get why they took him: Those Akhakhu decided they were tired of waiting for you to help them cross over, so they found a way to drag Dalton into their dimension to put pressure on you to finally live up to your deal. I'm guessing they could take him because we're the only ones who can see and interact with them. Probably not something you expected, huh?

And that's probably the real reason you decided to stop 'observing' and step in."

Mr. McKinney glared, but he didn't speak, letting me go on.

I stopped pacing. "And that brings it back to Dr. Elliott, doesn't it?" I asked softly. "He found out about us and the real reason we were created: To help the Akhakhu take over people. And he figured the only way to stop it was to destroy us—the keys to the whole invasion."

Eyes darkening, Mr. McKinney's face lost any semblance of its cool. I met his glare with one of my own. "Yeah, that's it, isn't it?" I asked. "Maybe at one point you guys really were concerned with just making humans the best they can be. But going to other worlds, meeting incredible beings, that had to change some of you. Evan said his mom is a fanatic devotee of the Akhakhu. I'm betting some of you are, too. We may have been deactivated as babies to keep the bad members of the Akhakhu away. But I'm going to bet that the ones you worship are hardly any better."

Mr. Holt sputtered. "Evan? You know about Evan?"

I smirked at him. "Oh, there's a lot more I know, Mr. Holt. Thing about changing into a werewolf out of nowhere—it kind of makes a girl want to seek out some answers, you know?"

"You're smart."

Mr. McKinney's tone blistered with anger. I turned my attention back to him as he sidled up to the desk beneath the monitor. Before I could do anything, he pressed another button on his desk.

"I admire that about you, Emily, I do," he said. Nodding at my dad, he added, "Good job on this one." Back to me. "My own son is an incredible athlete but I always did wish he was brighter. It's almost as if we were prescient when we hard-coded you to be attracted to Spencer—the two brains of the pack *should* be together."

Spencer's brow furrowed and he stepped next to me. "What?" he asked. "What are you talking about?"

Mr. McKinney flicked his hand. "It doesn't matter anymore. I was hoping you would cooperate with me without raising even more of a fuss than you already have. But it turns out we'll have to take a harder tack."

From the hallways, we could hear hissing as doors whooshed open, then rhythmic, steady boot steps as men ran down the hall. I turned and through the glass door and windows on either side I could see armed men storming down the halls to block any escape. Hovering above them were the same floating robots that we had faced when we busted into the lower lab.

"No," my dad said. Louder, "No!" Grabbing Mr.

McKinney's arm, he shouted, "I didn't agree to this! Not any of this!"

Mr. McKinney flexed his bicep and whipped back his arm. I couldn't help but scream as my dad wheeled backward and slammed against a computer, shattering the glass of the monitor. Mrs. Townsend gasped and covered her mouth, while Spencer's parents clung to each other.

I wasn't sure yet if I forgave my dad for keeping secrets from me. But I knew in that moment that no matter what, no matter his faults or mistakes, he was still my dad. I still loved him.

And no one messes with me, my pack, or my family.

Clenching my fists, I stepped to stand face-to-face with Mr. McKinney.

"You," I said, "just made a big mistake."

11

JUST TWO LITTLE GIRLS
AND A SHORT KID

I shifted into Nighttime so fast that Mr. McKinney never had a chance.

All over my body, my muscles tightened and stiffened with strength. My shoulders rolled back, my thighs tingled with power. I stood taller, straighter, seeming to grow as the adults in the room watched.

And for good measure, I unclenched my fists and let my fingernails grow into claws, like little daggers jutting from my cuticles.

Mr. McKinney held up his hands and took a step back. "Calm down, Emily," he said. "We know your tricks. There is no way you're getting out of here. Why make it worse for yourself and your father?"

I don't like hurting people. Before, when I was full Nighttime or the werewolf, I could let myself get carried away with bloodlust. Now, I'd learned to weave my personalities together, to temper the worst urges and strengthen the best.

But that was before I'd seen my dad lay clutching his bleeding forehead.

My left hand whipped out. I grasped Mr. McKinney by both of his wrists and yanked his arms down. Then, lashing out with my other hand, I slashed four lines down his cheek with my claws.

He screamed. Pulling free from my grip, his hands shot to his face. Blood dripped between his fingers.

"You little bitch!" he roared.

Raising up my right leg, I shot out with my foot. It smacked against his chest and he wheeled back against the desk behind him, gasping for air.

Before he could move, I darted forward so that we were eye to eye, so close that our noses almost touched. I grabbed his face by his chin, my claws digging ever so lightly into his skin.

"Don't you call me that," I hissed. "And don't you dare lay a hand on anyone else again. That includes your wife."

He scowled, but didn't say anything.

I plucked his keycard off his pants pocket where he had

clipped it. Then, shoving his head backward, I let go of Mr. McKinney and spun to face my pack. Spencer and Tracie stood opposite each other, stoic. They both had the confident, tense posture of someone full hybrid.

"Let's do this," I said.

Tracie nodded, then turned to her mother. "Get out of here when you can, Mom," she said. "Help Emily's dad out."

"All right," she said, nodding vigorously. "I swear I didn't know he was going to call the army, baby girl."

"We didn't either," Mr. Holt said.

Spencer didn't look at them. "Ready, Emily?"

I glanced down at my dad, who was now being tended to by Mrs. Townsend. She pulled a bright orange handkerchief from her bag and pressed it against his forehead.

"Ready."

I strode purposefully to the glass door, Tracie and Spencer just behind me on either side. I waved the stolen keycard in front of the keypad, and the door hissed open.

On the other side, three dozen uniformed men raised their guns and pointed them at me. Above their heads, six hovering, mechanical orbs opened slots and pointed gun nozzles at us.

I couldn't believe BioZenith would go to all the trouble to observe us and then lure us here just to shoot us dead if we acted out. So of course they wouldn't—the guns definitely wouldn't contain bullets. A quick glance at the spare magazines on some of the soldiers confirmed my suspicions were correct. Their ammo was tranquilizer darts.

I could work with that.

Shoving the keycard into my pocket, I stepped forward and then raised my hands, as though surrendering. A quick glance over my shoulder and I saw that Spencer and Tracie did the same. The glass door whooshed shut once we were all the way through, leaving our concerned parents and one very pissed-off Mr. McKinney behind to watch us.

"We're here in peace," I called out. "We don't want to hurt anyone."

A couple of the guards snickered. The guard directly in front of me—a woman with her helmet pulled low on her forehead—shushed them.

"Quiet," she commanded, not taking her eyes off of me. "Remember the brief. These three are dangerous."

"You can't be serious," a man over her shoulder said. "It's just two little girls and a short kid." He started to lower his gun. "This seems a bit overboard, ma'am."

The lead guard's stern expression faltered. Her eyes darted, taking me in from head to toe. I let my claws shrink while she wasn't looking, and then offered her a confused smile and a shrug when she looked back up at my face.

"Yeah, this is all some crazy mistake," Tracie said next to me. "I mean, I'm class president! I'm not some sort of criminal."

More and more of the guards lowered their weapons, and I could hear some of them talking in low voices to their neighbors.

The lead guard darted her head back and forth. Seeing her team lose focus, she raised her hand to get their attention. "Hold position!" she shouted. "I'll call this in."

She reached for a radio clipped to the side of her waist. Nighttime and Wolftime twitched inside me, desperate for a fight. But if we could slip out just by convincing these guards we were helpless children . . .

A loud thud behind me. Hands still raised, I looked back over my shoulder to see Mr. McKinney pressed up against the glass door. The entire side of his face was covered in red, and his eyes were enraged.

Pounding his fists on the window, he shouted, his voice muffled by the glass. "What are you idiots doing? I pressed the alarm! It's them! Get them!"

So much for trickery.

The guard next to the lead guard raised his weapon, aimed it at me, and squeezed his finger.

I was too fast for him.

I was next to him in a flash. I gripped the barrel of the

rifle in both hands. Just as he pulled the trigger, I yanked the gun to the side.

A loud pop. The lead guard's hand leaped to her throat. For a moment the rest of the guards watched in shock as the woman's fingers grasped at the red-feathered vial that had plunged into her neck.

"Get . . . them . . ." she gasped.

Veins and capillaries turned into glowing green spiderwebs on her face, her neck, spreading quickly from the tranquilizer dart's point of entry. Then the lead guard's eyes rolled back into her head and she collapsed.

I took the opportunity to yank the rifle completely out of my guard's hands, wield it like a club, and slam the butt against his helmet-covered head. He too fell to the floor, unconscious.

"I told you I came in peace," I said. "But if you want to do this the hard way, let's go!"

Sixteen guns aimed at me, making a light show of red dots on my chest. A chorus of deafening pops echoed through the halls of the laboratory.

Ducking, I flung myself to the side, just as Spencer and Tracie did the same. The darts impaled and exploded against the wall behind where I'd just stood, some splattering into the windows and door and cracking the glass. Our parents, trapped on the other side, shouted out in horror.

And the fight was on.

Spencer bunched his legs and sprung up, like an enraged ape going in for attack. He slammed against the chest of the nearest guard, wrapping his legs and arms around the man's arms and neck. Using his momentum, he twisted the guard to the side and brought him down hard against the tiled floor.

Two other guards ran to capture him, but Spencer placed his hands on the ground on either side of the fallen guard's head, then kicked up and out with his legs. His sneakered feet hit one of the guards full bore in the gut.

Reeling backward, the guard slammed into the guard behind him. Both flew into the full-length window on the wall opposite the computer bay. The window shattered, raining down glass shards. The two guards, covered in scratches, collapsed into a pile atop an unfortunate potted plant.

Tracie, meanwhile, ran forward, used the closest guard like a springboard, and leaped high into the air. She grabbed the nearest hovering robot orb in both of her hands, then shoved it under her arm like a basketball right before she landed.

This got the other robots' attention. Their aiming lights focused on her. As if able to sense the lights, Tracie darted past and around as many guards as possible, weaving and ducking to avoid wild swings of guns or grasping arms.

The hovering robots fired indiscriminately, each one hitting a guard Tracie had just passed. She was forcing them to risk friendly fire to catch her. But there would be no catching her—the girl was a blur.

My turn.

I swirled the gun above my head, then swung it down toward any of the guards that tried to aim their rifles at me. I brought the butt down behind one man's knee, forcing him to the floor, then swung it up to connect with his lower jaw. He went slack, a marionette with his strings cut.

Another swing, another man down. And another. I was a hurricane of force, ripping a path through the men and women hired to shoot me and lock me up. Inside, I cringed with each slam of the gun against someone's body, knowing they were just doing their job, hating the pain I was causing them.

But at least I knew they were alive.

In less than a minute, I had no one else to hit. All the human guards either lay unconscious, held their hands up in surrender as they crouched down, or had run off.

All that remained were Tracie's robots.

Seeing she had no more targets, Tracie skidded to a stop in the hallway, spun, and lobbed the robot she'd captured at the nearest orb. They collided like two mini Death Stars and exploded into shrapnel.

Spencer picked up a fallen rifle and held it like a tennis racket. He easily whacked the two orbs nearest him out of the air. They slammed against the wall, leaving scorch marks as they fell to the floor.

I was farther away from the two remaining orbs than either Spencer or Tracie, but that wasn't going to stop me. I flung my stolen rifle through the air and it collided with one, bringing it down to crash on the hard floor.

The final orb darted its laser-sighting light onto me. Before I could duck or leap out of the way, a gunshot sounded, so close and so loud that my ears rang. The last robot went dark and dropped like a stone.

I looked down to find that one of the guards who'd sat there, surrendering, had pulled a handgun and shot the robot down. Seeing me focusing on him, he dropped the weapon and raised both his hands.

"I don't know what you are," he stammered. "But I know I don't want to be the guy who let you get shot. This is just a day job, I don't need to get hurt for it."

Smirking, I patted him on his helmet. "Good boy."

A muffled roar came from the computer lab. I looked back to see Mr. McKinney still slamming his fists against the glass door, shouting in rage. Raising my hand, I wiggled my fingers in a wave.

Stepping over unconscious guards, I walked over to Spencer and Tracie. They were both gasping for air with big smiles on their faces.

A distant alarm wailed.

A second later, the thud of more feet echoed from down the corridors.

More guards.

"As fun as that was," Tracie said while smoothing out her shirt and pants, "I vote we get out of here while we have a chance."

"I second the motion," Spencer said.

"Motion passed." I scowled in the direction of the computer lab. "We'll take care of this place later."

We ran down the hallway, back toward the covered walkway that led to the main building and our exit. I whipped the keycard in front of the pad and the lock opened with a *chunk*. Twisting the handle, I yanked the door open and ran through.

The door shut behind us just as we reached the center of the walkway. As we did, the door leading into the main building opened and a swarm of guards burst through.

The four in the lead crouched down, with the four behind them standing tall. All eight had their rifles trained on us, and there were undoubtedly more guards behind them.

BioZenith really had hired an army to try and control us.

Before we could even turn to run back into the labs, those doors opened as well and even more guards came through—including some of the ones that had previously run away.

Through the glass windows on either side of us I could see even more guards, dozens and dozens of them, standing beneath the walkway. These also had vicious Dobermans on leashes, their teeth bared and saliva dripping from their gums.

We were completely surrounded.

12

BACKUP

"Don't shoot!" I shouted, throwing my hands into the air. "We'll come without a fight!" Forcing my voice to go higher in pitch and tinging it with little-girl desperation, I cried, "I don't want to get shot. Please don't hurt me!"

Just like with the first round of guards, those aiming their rifles waffled at seeing us, their expressions wavering. I mean, I was just a helpless girl, right? What possible reason could a big corporation have for tranqing me?

Spencer, Tracie, and I stood back-to-back, our arms raised high. None of the guards spoke.

"Should we go full werewolf?" Tracie asked in a whisper, uncertainty in her voice.

"No," I whispered back. "We don't want to risk killing anyone."

"Then what's the plan?" Spencer asked.

A commotion came from the doorway that led into the labs. Guards were shoved aside as a bloody, disheveled Mr. McKinney, pressing a stained towel against his face, burst onto the walkway.

Shaking with rage, he spun around in a circle, glaring at the guards. "We aren't paying you to stare at them!" he roared. "Shoot them! *Shoot them now!*"

Tiny red dots circled our chests, our stomachs.

"Get ready to duck," I hissed.

And with the exception of the one that the three of us stood beside, all the windows facing the parking lot exploded inward.

The noise was deafening, like twin bombs gone off at once. Slivers of glass sliced through the air, smashing and tinkling against the windows on the opposite side of the hallway. The guards screamed and shouted in surprise, dropping their guns and covering their faces. Mr. McKinney barely missed being sliced by a million little glass pieces as he threw himself onto the pile of men desperately trying to get out of the hallway and back into the buildings.

Instinctively I'd covered my head too. Gaping at the destruction, I looked out the sole unshattered window facing the street and saw Nikki, Amy, Brittany, and Casey hovering in the air.

Our backup had arrived.

Each cheerleader floated in front of where two glass planes had once been, equidistant from one another. They held one hand down with the palm facing toward the crowd of startled guards beneath them, and the other with the palm facing toward the walkway.

Seeing us finally notice them, Amy raised her eyebrows and smirked at me. "So are you guys going to just stand there or what?"

"Hurry, jump out," Nikki called. "We'll get you down safely."

Nodding at Spencer and Tracie, we stood to our full heights and then ran toward the open windows. I went right, back toward the second building, while Spencer and Tracie went left.

Bunching my legs, I leaped off the windowsill and flew between Nikki and Amy. They aimed their hands at me and, as I started to arc toward the ground, it was though I hit some invisible trampoline. I bounced high into the air, jumping far past the crowd of guards toward the middle of the now-empty parking lot.

As I neared the ground, I pulled myself into a ball and did a flip in midair. I landed in a practiced, easy crouch, then jumped to my feet. Spencer and Tracie landed easily behind me, followed by the cheerleaders.

"Perfect timing," Spencer said, grinning broadly at them.

Nikki waved the phone at him. "We listened to

everything. As soon as we heard fighting go down, we made a plan."

Behind us, the guards started shouting. Dogs barked and howled and feet thudded against the asphalt.

You'd think seeing flying teenagers make a walkway explode would be enough to make you rethink your career choice. Maybe these guys were being paid *really* well.

"Thanks!" I said to Nikki. Turning on my heel, I began to run toward the entrance of the other building where the minivan was still parked. "But I think it's time to get out of here!"

No one argued. The seven us ran faster than humanly possible—which was surprising to see from the cheerleaders, but telekinetic speed boosts certainly didn't seem out of the question if they could make themselves, y'know, fly.

Dozens of pops sounded as rifles went off. I looked back over my shoulder to see Brittany and Casey raising their hands behind them just in time. The tranquilizer darts exploded in midair, as though hitting some invisible wall.

Veering left, we leaped onto the concrete walkway in front of the main building and hugged the wall. More guns were fired, but the cheerleaders deflected them easily.

And we were at the minivan.

The doors were unlocked. I leaped into the front passenger seat just as Spencer got in front of the wheel. Tracie ducked into the backseat. The four cheerleaders waited for us, their hands raised to block any bullets or darts that might be aimed for the tires. As soon as the car engine whirred to life, they leaped in.

"Open the windows!" Nikki shouted. "Brit, Casey, make sure they don't take out the tires. Amy and I are going to handle the gate."

"Got it!" the triplets responded in unison.

It was incredible to see the four cheerleaders work together as a team. Though they bickered and were in general their own people, focused like this they were like four parts of the same machine. Brittany and Casey shoved open the windows on either side of the car, then leaned halfway out simultaneously and looked back. Brittany didn't even complain about the wind messing up her hair, just aiming her hands at the pursuing guards to raise the invisible wall that would keep us driving.

As soon as space was available, Nikki and Amy shoved their upper bodies through the other half of each window, only they faced front. Their expressions were stone as Spencer whipped across the asphalt, tires screeching as he veered around a roundabout in the center of the parking lot and then went full speed toward the gate.

Facing forward, I gripped the sides of my seat and clenched my teeth, wide-eyed and pulse racing as the closed gate barreled toward us. Behind me, I could hear Tracie saying, "Oh God, oh my dear God," under her breath.

Right before we hit it, the gates exploded open. The force of Amy and Nikki's psychic blast was so intense that one of the doors snapped free of its hinges and clanged into the street.

With a squeal of rubber on road, Spencer yanked the van to the left and onto the main road. The cheerleaders pulled themselves back inside the car, gasping for air.

Remembering what Tracie showed me behind the bleachers at the football game, I took in one long deep breath, then exhaled for just as long, over and over again until I could feel my pulse begin to slow, my muscles lose their tension. Everyone was silent, and all we could hear was the grumble of the car as Spencer slowed it down to normal speeds and wound through as many roads as we could.

It didn't appear that any car was chasing us. Yet.

"Okay, wow," Brittany said from the back at last. "So that was actually kind of fun. I feel like Zoë Saldana." Gasping, her hands shot up to her head. "Oh my God, my hair is a tangled mess. I must look like I got put away wet."

Next to her, Casey sighed. "You look fine, Brit." Smiling at me, she said, "We listened to everything that went down in there. You were really impressive. I never liked Mr. McKinney."

"Yeah," Brittany said. "Who knew *you* were such a badass? Like, were you going for a whole Clark Kent thing?"

My cheeks warmed. "Uh, well, it's a recent change," I said.

"Good for Emily," Amy said. "She punched a couple of guys in the face while we deflected bullets. But whatever, all in a day's work."

Slowing to a stop at a stop sign, Spencer looked over at me. "So . . . where do we go now? What are we going to do?"

"I don't know," I said. "Let's just keep driving as far from there as possible. We probably shouldn't go home yet. Since they got all our parents involved, there may be people waiting for us."

"Maybe not at our houses," Nikki piped up. "They wouldn't have known we were coming."

Crossing her arms and scowling, Amy slouched down in her seat. "Didn't you hear what Dalton's dad was going on about?" she asked. "One of them specifically said that the science that made us came from these Ack-things."

"Akhakhu," I corrected.

She waved a hand. "Whatever. But that means that our parents were part of whatever bigger company this BioZenith place was a part of. Maybe they were in on this the whole time, too."

Casey clasped her hands on her lap. "Our parents would never," she whispered.

"Hate to break it to you," Tracie said from her cramped position in the middle of the cheerleaders, "but I never imagined I'd be seeing my mother here today. And yet there she was, eating like it was nothing that she let me go through hell for a month. And my dad was . . ."

A tear fell from her eye and she let it fall. I could tell she was trying to regain her composure—who wouldn't when surrounded by the popular girls—but her lower lip trembled anyway.

Reaching back, I took her hand. She squeezed it.

"I should have let you talk to your dad," I said softly. "I'm sorry."

She shook her head. "No. I didn't want to. I don't know how you were able to talk to your mom knowing what she did to us."

"I don't know either."

Spencer was being strangely quiet. Letting go of Tracie's hand, I looked over at him in the driver's seat. There was no excitement on his face from our near escape, none of his usual good nature in the face of dire events. In fact, he looked incredibly pissed.

"Are you okay?" I asked him, placing a hand gently on his thigh.

He shrugged, his eyes focused on the road. We were deep in a neighborhood I wasn't familiar with, but from the size of the houses I could tell we were in the affluent part of Skopamish.

"Spencer?" I asked again.

"I'm fine," he said. Meeting my eyes, he softened. "Just, I'm freaking out a little bit. We can't go home, can we? Can we ever? I don't think we have any money, and we've got a corporation that went and hired a bunch of mercenaries or something to come after us. Not to mention the Akhakhu and whatever they want."

I leaned back into my seat. He was right. In all my righteous fury at Mr. McKinney, Caroline, and BioZenith, I hadn't really thought beyond that afternoon.

"Oh," Tracie moaned in the backseat.

I turned around to see her clutch her head and close her eyes. Brittany grabbed her arm as the girl slipped down in her seat.

"Tracie!" I cried. "Tracie, what is it?"

Blinking her eyes open, she looked up at me. "It was *her*," she spat as she climbed back up into her seat. "She kept screaming in my head while you two were talking."

"Who's 'her'?" Amy asked.

"Nighttime," I answered for Tracie. "It's a sort of . . . alternate personality we have at night. Or at least we did until we learned how to get it under control."

"Oh." Amy smirked. "So that's your excuse for slutting it up lately."

I ignored her and turned my attention back to Tracie. "What did, um, *she* say?" I asked.

"Mostly nonsense," Tracie said. "As usual. But the general gist of it is that the one place the BioZenith people won't expect us to go back to is the place we just escaped: BioZenith."

I raised an eyebrow. "Actually, that's a really good point."

And I realized what had to be done.

Sitting back in my seat to look forward, I took in a deep breath to calm myself. My pulse had quickened as soon as the idea hit me, because the prospect of it was huge. Unimaginable.

I'd been delaying the end of life as I knew it for weeks now. The time was coming when I needed to face the only conclusion to this problem. And nothing would be the same after. Not after what we knew. Not after what we were going to have to do.

"All right," I announced before I could talk myself out of it. "Here's the plan. We're going back to BioZenith tonight, and we're destroying the place, starting with that portal to another world. All their records on us, all their new experiments, all their connections to the Akhakhu will be gone. It's the only way we can keep them from hounding us until the day we die."

"That sounds dangerous," Brittany said.

"Incredibly dangerous," Tracie agreed.

Spencer looked at them in the rearview mirror. "Really? After all the ass we kicked today?"

Brittany shrugged. "That was us taking them off guard. Who knows what will happen if they're prepared?"

Amy snorted. "Oh please, don't be such wusses." Meeting my eyes, she said, "I am one hundred percent down with blowing stuff up."

"Me too," Casey said softly.

I looked around at everyone in the car. Spencer, Amy, and Casey were clearly ready to go. Brittany's and Tracie's expressions seemed more or less resigned. Which just left . . .

"I can help," Nikki said. "We've come this far, and the fact is we got more answers about our own powers teaming with you for an afternoon than we have listening to our parents our entire lives." Leaning forward on her knees, she tilted her head. "I just have one question."

"What's that?" I asked.

"How are we supposed to save Dalton if we destroy that portal?"

Everyone in the car fell silent. It was true, I'd vowed to

save him after seeing him get taken. It was what I'd promised the cheerleaders to gain their trust, even. But I had no idea if I was able to get into the other dimension, let alone if I'd be able to find Dalton and get back out again before we'd need to blow the thing up tonight.

A buzzing sounded from the cup holders between the two front seats. My phone.

Swallowing down the anxiety in my throat, for I was certain it was my dad or Mr. McKinney or someone else involved with BioZenith, I grabbed my phone and flicked it open to see a text message.

And smiled in surprised relief.

"What is it?" Spencer asked, glancing at me as he stopped at another sign.

"I know how we're going to save Dalton," I said. "All it will take is a quick trip to, uh, Oregon."

"I don't care where we have to go," Nikki said eagerly. "How are we going to do it?"

I held the phone up so she could read the text:

2:53 PM PST: Emily, it's Evan. Things went down bad with my mom overnight. I know it's kind of far, but can you come get me?

Grinning, I said, "How about a little help from a guy who can jump between worlds?"

DID THEY FIND US?

Five minutes later, we were on I-5 South, heading full speed toward Portland, Oregon.

Last time I was in Portland, I was eleven, and my dad and I drove down for one of the special early showings of *Serenity*. We'd missed out on tickets to the Seattle show, but he managed to score these last minute. Just two—one for him and one for his little Leelee.

It was a six-hour round trip, and even though none of the cast or crew showed up like other screenings, and even though the movie randomly played out of order and had to be respooled halfway through, it was never boring.

Back then, life was much simpler.

I'd only summoned up the memory so that I could figure

out about how long it would be before we reached Portland, but the memories of singing songs with über-Whedon nerds and gasping at shocking deaths and sharing Junior Mints with my dad rushed over me.

The girls in the backseat all talked among themselves—curiously, Amy and Tracie seemed deep in conversation. Next to me, Spencer stared at the long stretch of freeway ahead of us, as lost in his thoughts as I was. The radio was on, but I could barely hear it over the hum of the engine.

Closing my eyes, I shook my head, and silently told myself to focus. When I opened my eyes again, I saw Spencer still staring glassy-eyed at the line of cars in front of us in the car-pool lane.

"Hey," I said, placing a hand on his leg. "Are you okay?"

He shook his head. "It's stupid."

Leaning in, I shook his leg playfully and grinned. "Try me," I said.

Meeting my eyes briefly, he sighed. "I know with all we just found out, I shouldn't be thinking about this. But when Dalton's dad said they made it so . . . well, they made it so that you're *supposed* to like me and want to be around me. Like you've only been spending so much time with me because your werewolf brain tells you to."

He was right, of course. My werewolf brain *did* tell me to be with him. His bioengineered scents were designed to draw me to him, vaporous magnets that tugged and pulled at my body and brain, leading me to him.

But I'd figured out long ago that wasn't why I wanted to be around him all the time.

"Look at my face," I said. "This is my super, one-hundred-percent-honest face. Okay?"

Unable to contain a small smile, he nodded.

Neither could I. My insides fluttered and my cheeks warmed, and my voice trembled slightly as I went on.

"And one-hundred-percent-honest me is telling you this: No matter what those people programmed me to do, I am always going to do what I want to do. And I want to be around you because . . ." I swallowed. Calling on Nighttime, I finished. "Spencer, you're an awesome guy, and I like you a whole hell of a lot."

His grin was at full adorableness now. "I like you too, Em Dub."

Behind him, someone snickered. Only then did I realize that Tracie and the cheerleaders had gone quiet and were listening to us.

I glanced back just in time to see Amy smirk. "How sweet."

Smirking right back, I leaned over and kissed Spencer on the cheek.

Eyes still on the road, his hand shot to his face where

my lips had pressed against his skin, and I could see a blush reddening his face.

Clearing my throat, I leaned back into my seat. Loudly I said, "Okay, we can stop listening to my conversations, thanks. Let's just keep making plans."

"Whatever you say, boss," Amy said, and I heard her and Brittany laugh.

I was the one blushing now. Scrunching down in my seat, I tried to hide from their view as much as possible.

Even when busy planning a rescue and a battle, the alpha could still get all embarrassed about crushing on a boy.

Glad to know that not all of me was lost to being a vesper.

For the next hour we discussed what we would do when breaking back into BioZenith, with the occasional detour into conversations about school and weekend plans.

I guess right then it still didn't feel entirely real. Even after our grand escape, the idea that our lives would never go back to normal didn't seem possible. That's a pretty big change, you know? How could I *not* be thinking about going back to school on Monday or sleeping in my bed that night?

We passed the water park and were then in the midst of downtown Tacoma when our phones started to ring and buzz, one after the other. Calls from blocked numbers, and from Dalton's dad, and from my, Tracie's, and Spencer's parents' phones.

So they hadn't forgotten about us. Damn.

We all clicked ignore and silenced our phones. The vibe in the car was much less chatty after that.

We were nearing the Tacoma mall when a car to my right matched our speed and began to honk.

"Whoa!" Spencer said, startled. For a moment he lost control of the minivan and it swirled out of the carpool lane, veering directly toward the honking car.

"Spencer!" Tracie screamed.

I gaped as I looked out the passenger window. We were inches from sideswiping the other vehicle when whoever was driving let go of the horn and veered to the right. Spencer got control at the same time and pulled us back into our lane.

"What the hell!" Amy shouted.

Spencer's knuckles were white as he gripped the steering wheel with both hands. My heart was pounding and I clenched the seat.

The other car pulled back toward us. Again the driver leaned on his horn. Peering through the window, I saw the figure on the other side of the tinted glass alternating between honking and gesturing wildly behind him.

"What's going on?" Nikki asked, leaning between the

two front seats. "Is it BioZenith? Did they find us?"

"I have no idea," I said. "He keeps gesturing behind us."

In the backseat, Tracie, Amy, and Casey all turned around to look out the back window. I looked in the mirror outside the passenger window and saw another car tailgating us.

"Oh," Tracie said. "It's Mrs. Cooke!"

"Evan's mom?" I asked, confused.

"Emily Cooke's mom," Tracie corrected. "She's trying to get us to take the next exit."

The car next to us mercifully stopped honking, though my ears still rang from the blast of noise. Instead he started to change lanes.

"Should I follow them?" Spencer asked me.

"No," Amy said from the backseat. "Absolutely not. We don't trust any of the parents, remember? That's what you said."

I thought back to the lunch at BioZenith three hours before. The Cookes had been massively upset. They claimed they were no longer a part of "this." And Evan's mom, who was apparently some crazed devotee of the Akhakhu, considered them enemies.

It was possible that Mr. McKinney had planned this in case we escaped—to have the Cookes pretend to be allies to try and trick us later. But he'd seemed so sure we'd never escape. And why would the Cookes go along with him after their daughter was murdered?

"Spencer," I said. "Take the exit. Follow their cars."

"Um, are you sure that's a good idea?" Brittany asked behind me.

I nodded. "They seemed to be on our side. And if they're so frantic about speaking to us now, maybe we should listen." Turning around, I met Amy's eye. "Besides, if they try to cause trouble, you guys can just blast them with your mind powers."

Grinning at me, Amy raised a hand and flexed her fingers. "You're not wrong."

Everyone seemed to calm down at that, at least for the moment. Spencer did as I asked and started changing lanes in time for the mall exit. The girls confirmed Mrs. Cooke was doing the same.

Curiously, throughout the entire exchange, Casey sat quietly scrunched up against the window behind Spencer. Out of all of us, she was the only one who offered no anxiety or enthusiasm about anything that was happening.

Instead, she just stared out the window, a sad look on her face.

It was midafternoon on a weekend, so the mall was packed. Families and teenagers and friends were out in force to chill at the food court or spend their cash at the department stores. An endless stream of people swarmed from the parking lot into the mall and back out again.

We slowly followed behind the two cars as they led us through the parking lot, looking for open spaces. Finally we pulled into the lot for Sears and found three empty spots toward the back, far away from the store entrance. The girls in the backseat opened the door and were jumping out before we were even to a full stop.

Taking a deep breath and hoping I was right about the Cookes, I unbuckled my seat belt and opened the passenger door.

In the two spots next to us were parked a pair of Lexuses, twins in every way save one was a sleek black and the other a glimmering silver. Apparently everyone who worked at BioZenith was a fan of the luxury vehicle.

Out of the black car stepped Mrs. Cooke. She looked a lot like her daughter, though the slight wrinkles at the corners of her eyes and the wisps of white hair mixed in with the blond gave away her age. The bags under her eyes were new.

She smiled at me. Behind her, her tall, attractive husband slammed shut the door of his car, then came to stand by her side. For a moment we all stood there in the narrow space between Spencer's minivan and the black Lexus—the

Cookes facing off with a line of superpowered teens.

I cleared my throat. "I'm trusting you two aren't with Mr. McKinney. But that only gives you five minutes. Which is more than you deserve for freaking us out and nearly driving us off the road."

Mrs. Cooke frowned and shot a glare at her husband. "You'll have to excuse him. It's his first car chase."

"I needed to get their attention," Mr. Cooke grumbled.

I sighed. "Make that four minutes."

Nodding, Mrs. Cooke said, "Of course, of course. It's just, you can't be in this car. It's been reported stolen, and all of you reported missing."

"What?" Tracie asked. With a moan, she put her head in her hands. "Oh now I'm going to have car theft on my record too. This is just great."

Nikki nudged her. "We'll be fine."

"How do you know the car was reported stolen?" I asked. "You left BioZenith before we did."

"Harrison—Mr. McKinney—called us," Mr. Cooke added, nervously stumbling over his words. "We don't know what happened after we left BioZenith, but we knew if you fled, then it was nothing good on their part."

"Thanks for the warning," Spencer said. "But we're not going back and we're not turning ourselves in. So unless you're offering new cars . . ."

"We are!" Mrs. Cooke said. She reached out and clutched his arm, smiling at him. "We've been waiting for a day like this ever since they . . . ever since what happened to our Emily. We want to help you. We want to keep you safe and tell you everything you need to know."

I scanned their eyes, looking for some flicker of deceit. I didn't find any.

But I hadn't found any in my dad's eyes, either.

"How did you even find us?" Amy asked, crossing her arms and glaring at them dubiously. "You just happened to be driving to Tacoma after leaving BioZenith in a huff?"

Good point. I crossed my arms and raised my eyebrows, waiting for an answer.

"Oh no, of course not," Mr. Cooke stammered. "It's nothing like that."

"Then what is it?" I asked.

Mrs. Cooke met my gaze. "We were already headed down I-5 when we got the call, because we got an urgent text message that said it was sent to you, too. We're on our way to save my nephew, Evan, from my crazy former sister-in-law."

14

WE JUST WANT TO HELP

Mrs. Cooke showed me her phone to prove it.

The text was there. Minutes before the one I'd received. From Evan's phone, begging for help.

I handed the phone back to Mrs. Cooke, who smiled at me, expectant.

"Evan said he hadn't seen or spoken to any of you in years," I said. "His mother wouldn't let him. How did he even know your number?"

Clutching her sweater at her neck, Mrs. Cooke shrugged. "I don't know. But if he contacted both of us, he must be in trouble. We want to help."

Putting his arm over his wife's shoulder, Mr. Cooke pulled her in close. "We just want to help," he echoed.

I looked between the both of them. They certainly seemed earnest. And like Evan, something about them made me feel like I could trust them.

"One sec." I held up a finger, then gestured at the others with my chin. We filed around to the back of the minivan in a line, leaving the adults behind, then formed a tight circle.

"What do you guys think?" I asked.

"I say we ditch the van and take the cars," Amy said.

Tracie nodded vigorously. "Definitely. I am *not* getting arrested for car theft. There is no way in hell."

I looked between Spencer, Nikki, Brittany, and Casey. "You guys agree?"

They glanced at one another, then shrugged their consent.

Straightening up, I prepared to head back to the Cookes and let them know we were down with their plan. As I did, Casey's hand shot out to grab my arm.

"Wait," she whispered. "There's nine of us, and each of those cars will probably fit around five people."

"Excellent," Brittany said with a grin. "More space at last."

Casey shook her head. "No, what I'm saying is, maybe now would be a good time to split up."

"What?" Nikki asked. "Why would you say that, Casey?"

Sheepishly, the girl looked down at her feet, letting her shoulder-length hair fall in front of her face.

"It's just, if we're going to attack BioZenith tonight, maybe some of us should head back to Skopamish to prepare, while some of us go for Evan."

Spencer nodded. "That's not a bad idea. It also means if some of us get caught, there will be others of us free to rescue the rest. Speaking of getting caught . . ." He reached inside his pocket and pulled out his phone.

Then Spencer promptly threw it on the ground and stomped on it.

Tracie leaped back to avoid cell phone shrapnel. "What on earth?"

"Everyone do it," Spencer commanded. "We don't know what kind of tracking tech they have, but if I know my movies, they can probably track cell phones."

Brittany pulled a purple phone encrusted with fake jewels out of her jacket, then held it close to her chest. "But I love my phone," she whined. "Do you know how long it took to get these crystals affixed? A long time, Spencer!"

Amy yanked the phone out of her sister's hand and threw it down. "I'll help you bedazzle a new one. Stop complaining."

One by one, the rest of us stomped on our phones or

smashed them against the bumper on the back of the van. People walking to their cars gave us strange looks, and a woman loading a baby into a car seat shook her head at us, but we didn't care.

Crouching down, Spencer swept up the broken cell phone pieces to throw them away. As he did, the Cookes appeared around the edge of the minivan, concerned.

"Is everything all right?" Mr. Cooke asked.

Looking as though she was on the verge of tears, Brittany watched the sparkly remnants of her phone disappear in the shadows beneath the van. "No," she said.

"We're fine," I said. "But with all that BioZenith has been able to do to keep track of us, we decided to smash our phones. Just in case."

Wide-eyed, Mr. Cooke began to stammer. "I-I don't think that's necessary. They won't be tracking us, and my phone was—"

Without a word, Mrs. Cooke reached into his jacket pocket, pulled out his phone, and threw it with all her force onto the asphalt. Her phone was next.

I met the woman's eyes and offered her a smile. "Welcome to the team."

She smiled back. "Thank you."

Nikki met my eye. "So what do we do now?" she asked. "Who goes where?"

"Let me think," I said, pacing.

The important thing, even beyond rescuing Evan, was to keep everyone out of sight until nightfall. Just long enough for them to think we were on the run before we doubled back under the cover of darkness. And then . . . boom. We blow up the portal device.

I didn't know what, exactly, that would accomplish. But I did know it was a giant flashing beacon the shadowmen could follow to look into our world. And I wanted it gone.

Only I wasn't entirely sure how we were going to do that. It's not like we had a bunch of C-4 lying around. Even if we did, it's not like I knew how it was constructed.

Though I might be able to access files that did have that information.

I stopped, stood as tall and confident as I could, and looked back over my group.

"Okay, here's the plan," I said, turning to my fellow teens. "All of you are going to take one of the cars and go back to Skopamish. I'm guessing the Cookes here have a tablet or laptop or something, anything that can read a thumb drive, right?"

Mrs. Cooke nodded. "We do. You're welcome to it."

"Thanks," I said. Facing my group, I continued. "Once you have that, lay low at their place or, if that doesn't seem safe, find somewhere else."

"Our parents can always help us too," Casey said softly. I barely heard her.

"You want all of us to go back?" Spencer asked, crossing his arms. "You're going to go get Evan alone now?"

I shrugged. "I'm the one he's been talking to and it just seems safer to keep everyone else here together. Bigger numbers in case they try to capture you. I doubt anyone will be able to find me in Oregon."

"But Em Dub," Spencer said, coming in close and taking my hand. "You can't go off alone. What if you *do* get found . . ."

I smiled at him. "I'll be fine. You know I know how to take care of myself."

He smiled back. "I do know. That's why I love yo—um." He swallowed the last word and his face went red.

I had to bite my lip to contain my smile. Behind Spencer, the cheerleaders did not look amused.

"Hate to interrupt," Tracie said, raising her hand. "But where are we meeting up? And when?"

"Let's say . . . after dark, in the woods behind the buildings across the street from BioZenith," I said. "If I'm not there by ten tonight, something probably happened and you'll need to storm the place without me."

Brittany raised a hand. I nodded at her and, tucking her wavy hair behind her ears, she asked, "So, how are we even supposed to know what time it is? You made us smash our phones."

"Maybe a watch?" I asked with a shrug.

"Ew," Brittany said.

"We'll have a laptop with a clock on it," Spencer piped up. "We'll be good."

"Sound like a plan?" I asked everyone.

Everyone nodded—except Amy. She crossed her arms.

"Did you forget each car only fits five comfortably? I'm not cramming myself into another backseat."

I tilted my head. "Is that your way of asking to go with me?"

"You could say that," she said. She jerked her thumb over her shoulder at the Cookes, still huddled next to the black Lexus. "Besides, I have some questions for these two."

I looked around at everyone. "Is that cool with you guys?"

They all nodded, except for Spencer. He raised his eyebrows at me, his mouth a line. I was guessing he thought if anyone should be going with me, it should be him.

"Listen to Spencer here on which tablet or laptop to take," I said, gently patting his shoulder. "He's the tech expert. That's the only reason you get to steal him away."

He grinned at me. "Uh-huh. But I'll choose to believe that."

As one, our entire group turned to face the Cookes once more. Brittany stepped forward and held out a hand. "Keys, please. The silver car."

"You're going to be driving my car?" he stammered.

"Marshall," Mrs. Cooke scolded gently. Again she reached into his pocket. Producing his keys, she plopped them into Brittany's waiting hand. The cheerleader smiled, her teeth as sparkly as her deceased phone.

"Thanks! I've always wanted to drive one of these." She bounced off around the black car to the silver one, and everyone except the Cookes, Amy, and Nikki followed.

Nikki grabbed Amy's hand and squeezed it. "Be careful, okay?"

Amy rolled her eyes, but it was clear the wild-haired triplet didn't mean it. "Yeah, yeah."

With a cordial nod at the Cookes, Nikki ran off to jump into the backseat of the silver Lexus, next to Tracie and Spencer.

Emily Cooke's mom smiled at me again as the car containing my friends came to life and Brittany backed out of the space. Wind rose up and caught Mrs. Cooke's white-and-blond hair, and for a second I saw the other Emily, my lost pack member, staring back at me.

"You handled that well," she said softly. "We made a good choice making you the alpha."

Amy's eyes went wide. "Her? The alpha? Isn't that usually a man?"

Mrs. Cooke shrugged. "Caroline—Emily's mother—and I felt differently. We thought . . ." She shook her head, then cleared her throat. "We should go."

"Yeah," I said, trying not to think about what grand plans my mother may have had for me when this all began. "Let's go."

15

THE MANIC GLEE

For the next two hours, we drove and we talked.

The car was definitely an upgrade from Spencer's mom's minivan. There was much more space, for one, and the backseat at least was supercomfortable. The air that whooshed from the vents was a comfortable seventy degrees rather than the temperature of the sun's surface, which was all you got out of the minivan. And the windows were tinted, which I found weirdly comforting. No one could look in and see me and call up BioZenith to give away my location.

As Mrs. Cooke drove, she and her husband took turns answering the lingering questions I had about this insanity.

It all began twenty years ago with a team of scientists who worked for a company called Vesper Industries.

This team specialized in quantum and multiverse theory—you know, the stuff of Michael Crichton novels. Purely by chance, this team discovered a hot spot, as the Cookes called it, while one of the scientists was working on an archaeological dig in Egypt. He'd been messing around with some equipment he brought with him—and the next thing he knew, he temporarily opened a rift to another world.

No one knew how he found the rift, especially since he was unable to perceive it, just like all humans. It was an accident, maybe. Right place, right time. All that mattered was that the rift opened into a proper portal through which he could see the other dimension. He described this other world as beautiful—an endless technological city that was at once familiarly ancient Egyptian and eerily alien. For a very brief moment, he stood face-to-face with a being from that world.

And then the portal was gone.

That man's name was Michael Handler and, obsessed, he returned to the offices in Washington State to try and find some way back through—some more *permanent* way.

As I stared out the window and watched the evergreen trees rush by, the Cookes told us how Handler and his team found another breach near their facilities in Volmond, a city north of where I lived. After years of development, they managed to send a team through and make contact with the Akhakhu.

And that was when the obsession with the beings turned into something else.

"It wasn't everyone," Mrs. Cooke said, her eyes focused on the long, empty stretch of highway before her. We were past Olympia by then. "But you could see it in the eyes of some of the ones who spent a lot of time on the other side. Manic glee is the only way I can describe it."

"It was religion," Mr. Cooke added, glancing back at me and Amy. "The more of their seemingly magic technology they shared with us, the more enamored many of those involved with the project became. I'd hear names of our Akhakhu contacts whispered in hushed tones, as though speaking the name of gods." He shook his head. "But we were discovering so much that we didn't want to question it."

Amy leaned forward between the seats. "So these Akhakhu people, they're like some advanced species? And they're the ones who made it so I have my powers?"

Mrs. Cooke nodded. "Basically. Mr. Handler grew through the ranks rather quickly after his discovery, and he was the one who started the various vesper projects. Marshall and I were part of Branch B, which you now know as BioZenith. We were a team of animal behavioral experts, geneticists, bioengineers, and early development specialists.

Caroline Webb"—she nodded at me in the rearview mirror—"Emily's mother—was the lead on HAVOC."

"Yeah, I heard that when we were listening in on Mr. McKinney earlier," Amy said, leaning back into her seat. "Something about how wolves can somehow see and interact with the Akhakhu things, so you mixed wolves with babies or something. We got the gist."

Mr. Cooke chuckled to himself. "What can I say, we were doing as ordered. But the basic idea, which came down from Handler and likely came from his conversations with the Akhakhu, was that working with the Akhakhu in our world was a matter of *perception*. We were aware that the Akhakhu were all able to peer into our world—they appear as shadows to those who have seen them, and those shadows only last briefly. Due to some sort of worldwide atmospheric radiation that altered their genetic makeup, even with our portals open they could not simply come through and visit our world as we did theirs.

"But they insisted that our wolf-hybrid children could assist them. That their ability to perceive the shadow forms of the Akhakhu would let them interact and aid them in some way. And from what Harrison told us about what happened to Dalton, it seems they were correct."

I looked away from the rushing trees and closed my eyes. Flashes of Dalton, terrified and naked and being dragged away by several shadowmen, rushed through my mind.

"So they can only touch us because we can see them," I whispered.

"Weird," Amy said beside me.

In the front seat, Mrs. Cooke clicked on her blinker and merged over into the next lane to get around a slow-moving pickup truck. She pressed on the gas and we zoomed past.

"So what about me and my sisters?" Amy asked. "How do we fit into all of this?"

"I wish we knew," Mrs. Cooke said. "Your parents were part of Branch A, which was handed Project COVEN. All we know is that they were experimenting with various psychic abilities, telekinesis and the like. When Project HAVOC was put on hold and we sealed our records away from Vesper Company and Mr. Handler, we splintered off and lost track of the other branches."

"But we were told we were made to watch and protect people like Emily and Dalton," Amy protested. "Are you saying my parents lied to me?"

Mrs. Cooke shook her head. "No, I'm not saying that. I just don't know. I'm sure Mr. Handler had some reason for having you created, just as he did the hybrid wolves. But we were never told the reason."

"You keep mentioning Mr. Handler a lot," I said. "How come he's not in the picture if he was the one who had us made?"

"We're not sure," Mrs. Cooke said. "We told him the

project failed and presented the mutated fetuses as evidence. Once we broke off into our own company, he left us alone."

"So he just let you guys make some new company, no questions?" I asked. "That seems really strange."

"There were . . . meetings," Mr. Cooke said. "We did everything we could to convince Handler and his people that our projects had failed, and that we were uneasy about the Akhakhu in general. He didn't want dissenters in his ranks, and since we brought in new backers to buy our facilities and equipment from him, he ultimately let us go without too much fuss. Of course, only our unease about the Akhakhu was true. And as you've found out, not all of us were entirely against joining their cult."

I sighed and leaned down in my seat. So much information to parse. At least the history behind all this was finally taking shape.

"So do you know what these Akhakhu *want*?" I asked. "We were made to perceive them, I guess, and let them interact with portals, and I saw one try to climb into a friend of mine. Am I right that they want to come into our world by jumping into human bodies?"

The Cookes glanced at each other, and for a moment they said nothing.

Amy's eyes went wide. "Uh, okay, don't stop being all forthcoming now. What are we dealing with?"

Mr. Cooke cleared his throat. "There were rumors," he said. "About Handler. That he'd . . . merged . . . with one of the Akhakhu. He supposedly claimed he and the Akhakhu coexist peacefully. Many others have visited him and have returned with that look."

"The manic glee," Mrs. Cooke said.

The man pointed at his wife. "That. Whatever he promised would come with helping the Akhakhu, they were buying it. A lot like Maureen."

"Who?" Amy and I asked in unison.

Mrs. Cooke met my eyes through the rearview mirror. "Evan's mom. She married Marshall's brother after they met while working on HAVOC, and it wasn't long after Evan was born that she started to be drawn more and more to the idea of the Akhakhu as gods."

"What about my—" My voice cracked. I coughed, then started again. "What about my mother and Tracie's dad? Are they like Maureen?"

Mr. Cooke shook his head. "No. They were made our liaisons to the Akhakhu once we found our own hot spot and made a portal at the BioZenith facility."

The portal contained within the giant ringed apparatus I'd seen in the basement.

"We splintered with Vesper Company, and our own portal malfunctioned while Thomas—Mr. Townsend—was on the other side. Vesper Company refused us access to their portal and, by the time we got ours working again, Terrance couldn't come back through due to his prolonged exposure to the irradiated atmosphere compounded with exposure from all his other trips. Caroline went after him through the repaired portal, but she became trapped as well."

"So they're stuck there with those things," I said flatly.

"Yes," Mrs. Cooke said. "They have been for a long, long time. But they are treated well, and they've made a life there. Together."

Together. No wonder my dad had moved on with my stepmom.

"Wow," I said softly.

"Is there anything else you want to know?" Mr. Cooke asked Amy and me. "There's just so much to say I don't even know where to go next."

"No," I said before Amy could say anything. "I think . . . I think I'm good for now. Can we just drive in quiet for a little while? Today has been a big day and I'd just like to . . . stop thinking about this for a minute."

"Of course," Mrs. Cooke said.

Everyone fell silent, and we drove in relative silence, the only sounds the whooshing of the wind past the car windows and the comforting hiss of the heaters filling the car with warmth. Eventually Mr. Cooke reached forward and switched on the radio. He flipped through the satellite channels and settled on smooth, lilting jazz.

I closed my eyes and leaned my head back, letting the music flow in to drown out the sound of my brain trying to process everything that had happened in the past and was going to happen in the future.

"Hey."

A nudge on my arm.

I opened my left eye and looked over at Amy.

"Yeah?" I asked her.

"Sorry about your mom," she said. "That sucks what happened to her."

I shrugged. "It's all right. Before last week I thought she was dead, and between then and today I thought she was an evil, mad scientist. I'm not really attached."

"That's a horrible thing to say about your mother," she said.

Mrs. Cooke glanced back at us through the mirror. "Everything all right?" she asked us over the music.

"Yes, Mrs. Cooke," Amy and I said in unison, like good little girls. Instinctively we met each other's eyes and then, despite ourselves, laughed.

"Thanks for saying that, though," I said as our laughter died down. "I appreciate it."

Amy shrugged. "Whatever." She looked out her window,

then quickly asked, "You think they're okay?"

"The others?"

She nodded.

"You guys flew and exploded a glass bridge today," I said. "You were like X-Men, the new class. I'm sure they'll be fine until tonight."

"Yeah," Amy said. "Of course they'll be. I just worry. You know."

"Yeah," I said, "I do know."

For just a moment, she glanced over and met my eye. I could swear, for a tiny instance, there was a flicker of friendliness. The she looked away once more.

"That's right," she said. "I forgot you're the alpha queen head bitch in charge. Don't mind me."

I grinned and looked out my own window. "Don't worry," I said. "I've learned not to."

16

IT'S A BIG DAY FOR US

It wasn't long before we were driving over the bridge spanning the Columbia River and were in Oregon. The sky was gray and a light sprinkle of rain clouded the windows. Using the GPS, Mrs. Cooke navigated the streets of Portland until we ended up in a residential neighborhood filled with nice, two-story brick homes.

At the end of a dead-end street was where we found Evan's house.

The place was sort of half-assedly gothic, with a wrought-iron fence surrounding the front yard, which had a weed-strewn stone path alongside which grew tall, spindly trees. Behind the house were towering evergreens, reminding me of home.

Mrs. Cooke pulled the car into a stop at the curb. The Cookes were going to wait for us to get inside, then follow, since Maureen would recognize them, so only Amy and I stepped out into the misty, cool air. I zipped up my jacket and shoved my hands in my pockets.

There was a a basic four-door car in the driveway, and though the curtains were all closed I could see a light on in the window next to the front door. Someone was home.

"After you," Amy said, gesturing me forward.

"Of course," I said.

I shoved the iron gate, which opened with squeaking hinges. Sneakers squelching in wet grass, I walked half on and half off the stone pathway to the front door, Amy behind me. Once we were all gathered on the porch, I took a breath and rang the doorbell.

We stood there, shivering in the wet and cold for what felt like a full minute.

No one answered.

I raised a finger and rang again.

A twitch of fabric out of the corner of my eye. I glanced over just in time to see someone peeking through the curtains. I leaned back so whoever it was could see me, and raised a hand in greeting.

The curtain snapped shut. A second later, I heard the deadbolt on the door turn, and then the door opened.

The person who answered was a short, slender woman

with frizzy gold-red hair. She peered out the half-open doorway.

There was something strange about her eyes. Something manic.

"Yeah?" she asked.

Her voice was deeper, gruffer than I'd expected.

"Hi!" I said, doing my best to sound chipper. "I'm a friend of Evan's. From school. I was wondering, is he home?"

The woman didn't say anything for a moment. She just looked me up and down.

"A girl," she said. "You have nice hair and teeth."

"Uh, thanks."

The woman gestured at Amy with her chin. "And her?"

"Just another friend," Amy drawled. "And my teeth better be fine. I had to wear braces."

The woman barked a laugh. There was something off about her for sure. Almost as if she was on some drug or drunk on all the boxed wine the corner store had on sale.

"So . . . Evan?" I asked.

The woman shook her head. "He's busy today. It's a big day for us."

I tilted my head and blinked my eyes, trying to look innocent. "Are you sure? Maybe—"

"Oh. My. God." Amy tilted her head back and sighed loudly. "I'm done."

Before I could make a move, she flicked her hand and

the door flew open. Startled, the woman wheeled backward into her living room. Without wasting a second, Amy shoved past me into the living room, and I followed. Behind me, I heard the car doors open and shut as the Cookes rushed out.

"Holy crap," Amy said, stopping a few feet into the living room.

I couldn't help but agree with the sentiment.

The living room would have felt homey, cozy, with plush carpet and new furniture. That is, if every flat surface wasn't covered with flickering candles. And if there wasn't a horrific painting of a naked, very hairy man with a wolf head set atop an easel.

Oh and mustn't forget the pile of tiny, bleached white bones beneath the painting.

"Get out!" the woman screamed, clenching her hands like claws. Only now that I got a full look at her could I tell she was wearing a homemade black robe trimmed in gold.

"The ritual must be performed!" she shouted, stepping menacingly forward. "It must happen today!"

A gasp behind us. Amy and I both turned to find the Cookes standing in the doorway, Mrs. Cooke with her hand over her mouth.

"Maureen," Mr. Cooke said, taking in the room, bewildered. "What are you *doing*?"

Eyes wide, Maureen's whole body began to tremble. She

pointed a finger at Mr. Cooke and said, "*You*. Why have you come? It's too late to be blessed by the Akhakhu now, Marshall! You turned your back on them after you convinced my husband to leave me! Only the faithful will be saved today!"

Lowering her hand from her mouth, Mrs. Cooke shook her head slowly. "Maureen, you're ill. You need help."

"Lies!" Maureen screamed.

Mr. Cooke raised his hands and stepped carefully toward the raging woman as though she were a feral dog. "It will be okay, Maureen. We're just here for Evan. He asked us for help. That's why his friends are here, too."

The woman's eyes darted to me and Amy. "My boy would *never*," she said, aghast. "He knows how important this is. How special he is. We made him in the Akhakhu's image to lead our people into the new future." She pointed at Mrs. Cooke now. "Don't you call me crazy again, Julie! You were both there! You all saw what I saw and know what I know! This is not irrational. This is the only thing that *is* rational!"

"Maureen," Mr. Cooke said.

"Don't you take another step," the woman said, reaching behind her.

"Where's Evan?" Mr. Cooke said as he stepped forward.

It happened so fast that neither Amy nor I could react.

Maureen's hand, the one she'd put behind her, shot up high in the air. Clenched in her fist was a hunting knife.

Screaming, she lunged forward.

And plunged the blade into Mr. Cooke's shoulder.

Startled, he couldn't even say anything. He tripped over a coffee table and fell backward, scattering candles. With a wail, Mrs. Cooke dove to his side, even as the couch behind the coffee table caught on fire.

Amy and I moved.

I slipped effortlessly into Nighttime. A blur, I darted forward, grabbed Maureen by both of her wrists, then yanked her arms behind her. She cried out and arched her back, but she couldn't escape my grip.

Amy meanwhile spun, flicked a hand at the door to slam it shut, then waved another hand. The air in the room swirled, a sudden gust of wind, and all of the candles extinguished. Another flick of Amy's hands and the lights came on.

"Vespers," Maureen gasped. "Oh, more vespers, here! Glorious day!"

"Shut up," I spat, still standing behind her and holding her wrists. "Mr. Cooke, are you okay?"

Mrs. Cooke crouched next to him, examining the wound and brushing his hair. Her husband clenched his jaw, struggling to hold back whimpers.

"It's okay," Mrs. Cooke pronounced. "It's just a flesh wound, all right, honey? Just a flesh wound."

"We have to call an ambulance," Amy said, spinning around to look for a phone.

"No!" Mr. Cooke shouted, then winced. "Not yet. They can't get here before you find Evan and leave."

Her eyes frantic, Mrs. Cooke looked up at me. "Hurry."

Amy ran to a hall closet, then returned a second later with a length of extension cord. The two of us tied Maureen to a chair in her dining room as quickly as we could.

"Where's Evan?" Amy demanded as she bound the woman's feet to the chair legs.

"So many vespers," the woman said wistfully. "They'll be so pleased."

"Hey!" I said, then shook the chair. "Evan. We need him. We vespers, uh, we need to be close to him for the ritual."

"Oh!" Maureen exclaimed. "Of course you do." She jerked her head behind her. "He's in the basement."

I turned around to look where she'd pointed. The dining room was at the base of a set of stairs leading up to the second story, and across from the foot of those stairs was a doorway.

"Come on," I said to Amy as soon as I was sure Maureen wasn't going anywhere.

The two of us dashed around the table. I reached the door first and yanked it open. Deep in the bowels of the basement, orange light flickered.

We rushed down the wooden steps, me in the lead and Amy behind. Seconds later we were standing on the concrete floor, gaping.

In the center of the room was a man-size wooden slab. Surrounding the base of it were more candles like upstairs, arranged in strange swirling patterns that reminded me of fractals I'd seen in math books.

And held to the front of the slab by leather straps beneath his shoulders and at his wrists and ankles, was a pale, naked boy wearing an elaborate golden mask in the shape of a wolf.

"Evan," I said. Then, running toward him, I shouted louder, "Evan!"

The boy stirred as I reached the slab and began fumbling with the straps on his wrists. Amy went to the other side of him and did the same, unsnapping his wrists before leaning down to free his ankle.

As soon as both his hands were free, the boy reached up and shoved off the mask. It clattered against the concrete floor. Gasping for air and looking wildly between us with wide, bright blue eyes was Evan Cooke.

The last member of my pack.

"Oh, thank God!" he gasped as he wriggled free of the straps that went under his armpits. "Emily, I'm so, so glad you're here. I can't believe you came all this way! I don't know what my mother did to me, but she was screaming all sorts of crazy stuff about it being time, and then she started chasing me with a needle and . . ." He glanced down. "Oh my God, I'm naked."

"Here," Amy said, tossing him a pile of wrinkled clothes she'd found next to the slab. "I'm guessing these are yours." She smirked. "And don't worry, you've got nothing to be ashamed of, trust me."

The boy's cheeks went red. "Oh God." He scurried around the other side of the slab and proceeded to dress.

"Your mother's gone wacko," Amy said, pacing impatiently as we waited. "She stabbed your uncle, so we need to hurry."

Buttoning his jeans, Evan popped out from behind the slab, gaping. "She did *what*? Is he okay?"

"Yeah," I said. "But we need to get out before the ambulance comes, okay?"

He stood there, stricken and tiny looking. He was shorter than I expected. Not Spencer short, but with his slender frame and tousled hair, he seemed young, innocent. My wolf side ached to protect him.

"Where will I go?" he asked softly.

"That's the question of the day," Amy asked. Looking pointedly at me, she said, "Come on."

I hated not giving the kid a moment to catch his bearings. But Amy was right. There wasn't any time to waste.

The three of us bounded up the basement steps to find the dining room and living room as we'd left it. As soon as we rounded the table and rushed past Maureen, who rocked in her chair silently glaring, Mrs. Cooke jumped to her feet.

"Oh my," she said. Her lip trembled and her eyes glistened. "Evan. You're so big."

"Auntie Julie," he said. He ran forward and grabbed the woman into a hug. The two of them stood there, holding each other and rocking back and forth.

"My own son," Maureen said. "Betraying me."

Evan let go of his aunt and turned to glare back at his mother. "You knock me out, strip me naked, and tie me to a big piece of wood and I'm the one betraying you?" He shook his head, anger in his eyes. "Just . . . shut up, Mom."

"Here," Mrs. Cooke said, coming forward and putting her car keys into Amy's hands. "You three need to get out of here. Go find your friends and try to bring these bastards down."

"Oh, we will," Amy said, holding the keys up and jingling them.

I nodded at Mrs. Cooke. "Thanks," I said. "For all the help."

"It's the least I could do after all we did." She went back to her husband, still lying on the coffee table. His eyes were closed and he grimaced. Sweat beaded on his forehead.

"Get him help," I said, grabbing her arm reassuringly. "He'll be okay. We'll all be okay."

While Evan put on his shoes, he directed Mrs. Cooke to the landline. Amy and I waited by the door, ready to run to the car as soon as Evan was done.

Before we could leave that house of crazy for good, Maureen stopped struggling in her chair and looked directly into my eyes.

"Thank you for all you've done, Emily," she said, her tone flat, cold. "Those who have devoted themselves to the Akhakhu will ascend because of your actions, you'll see. You are a true prophet."

More mutterings from the mind of a woman who'd apparently been pulled into some freaky, alien-obsessed cult.

But that didn't stop the chill that gripped my spine.

17

IT'S TIME TO MOVE ON

Not even a three-hour car ride feels like a breather after the dose of insanity we'd gotten at Evan's house.

I couldn't believe that it was the same day we'd stormed out of BioZenith in a blaze of glory. It felt like ages ago. And I could barely believe that the day wasn't done.

Of course, we still had a company to destroy.

After the cursory reintroductions—Amy and Evan remembered each other better from elementary school than either did me, what with my lifelong invisibility and all—I took a deep breath and told our story. I laid out everything that happened since last we talked, ending with the big escape we'd pulled off—and our plans to go back.

"Do you think you're up for it?" I asked him when I

finished. "I mean, I know you just went through a lot."

"He has to be up for it," Amy said, steering the car expertly north on the freeway. "You can . . . slip between the dimensions or whatever, right? You're the only one who can go through and get Dalton and come back. So you have to go."

Mouth agape, Evan looked between me sitting next to him in the backseat and Amy up front.

"I don't want to force you into anything," I quickly added. "But these people are just like your mom. They want to help the Akhakhu come and possess us all."

Evan sat there, quiet, thinking. He was exactly as he looked on cam: angled features, blond hair, slender build. The biggest differences were his exhausted eyes and that the hair on the back of his head stuck up, disheveled. His blue windbreaker, zipped up to his throat, was also a wrinkled mess.

But even though he was probably only a few months younger than me, I couldn't erase the feeling I'd also gotten in the basement. Motherly. Protective.

"So how about it?" Amy asked after Evan didn't answer. "What do you say, big guy?"

"Uh, yeah," he said. He swallowed and ran a hand through his hair. "If it'll stop those things on the other side, then yeah. I'll help."

Amy glanced back and winked. "I always knew you would."

It was fully dark by the time the freeway arced toward Skopamish. The lights of the small city glittered through the ever-present trees.

We drove to the Cookes' house first, but the silver Lexus wasn't there. Worry nibbled at the back of my head, but I refused to let it take over. The cheerleaders had said they'd go their parents' house if need be.

The car wasn't at Nikki's house either. I held my breath when we turned down the street on which the Delgados lived.

And let out a sigh of relief when I saw Casey in the driveway, leaning against Mr. Cooke's car, as though waiting for us.

Amy pulled partway into the driveway, then rolled down the window. Casey ran over and leaned in.

"Is everything cool?" Amy asked, her voice hushed.

Casey grinned, nodding at Evan and me in the backseat. "Yeah, we're doing great. We were hoping you'd meet up with us before we went to BioZenith." She waved at the backseat. "Hi, Evan! You look really good."

Blushing, he ducked his head. "Thanks . . . uh, Brittany?"

Casey shook her head. "The third one."

"Yeah, of course," he said. "Casey. You're more outspoken than I remembered."

Hell, she was more outspoken than I remembered from only half a day earlier.

Amy turned off the engine, then looked back at me. "So what now, Alpha? Should we head to the rendezvous and get ready for our big attack?"

I shook my head. "Not yet. I had you guys come back to scout out a tablet for a reason. I need to sneak back into my room and grab those files we stole. We're going to need them with us to figure out how to actually take apart that portal thing."

"All right," Amy said, already opening her door. "So you want the car?"

I climbed out and slammed the door shut behind me. I heard Evan do the same on the other side.

"I'd love to," I said. "But I, uh, can't drive. Besides, we can't risk someone seeing me pull up. They may be scoping out the place waiting for me to arrive."

"So we're sticking to the same timetable then," Amy said. "We meet up at ten. If you're not there, go in without you."

"Exactly."

Casey tugged her sister's arm, trying to drag her away from the car and into the house. "Come on, Amy. We need to talk to Mom and Daddy before this all happens."

Amy yanked her arm free. "Yeah, Casey, fine," she said, scowling. "Why are you acting so weird?" Her expression softening, she nodded at Evan. "You coming?"

Head ducked, Evan came to stand next to me.

"Maybe I can go with you?" he asked me. Before I could answer, more words rushed out. "It's just I think I'll feel safer with you for some reason. I can't explain it."

Amy raised her eyebrows at me.

I nodded to her and Casey. "You two go," I said. "Make sure everyone stays on track, okay, Amy?"

She shrugged. "Yeah, okay. Whatever."

"All right, Evan," I said as the two cheerleaders walked up the driveway toward the front door. "Looks like it's you and me."

"Sorry," he said again. "I know I must seem like a giant wimp. It's just, you and Amy are the only ones I've talked to so far, and Amy seems kind of . . . intense."

I laughed. "That's one word for her." We watched as the two sisters disappeared inside the house.

Turning to meet Evan's big eyes, I asked him, "Ready to go all stealthy and break into my house?"

"I have no idea," he said with a shrug. "But hey, first time for everything!"

* * *

Living in the Pacific Northwest can come in handy when you need to sneak through a city without being seen.

The whole place was once a giant rain forest, and luckily the people who built cities here more or less respected that and kept a lot of the forests intact. Especially in Skopamish.

My trip home was a matter of darting between trees and bushes in the woods behind the Delgado house, and then making our way through some backyards to the next wooded area, all the while keeping one-hundred-percent alert for any sign of, well, *anybody*.

Evan, for his part, zoned into his powered state with no issue. One moment he was the vulnerable young guy freaking out over fleeing his mother, the next he was a hyperfocused, superstealth badass, moving slick through the woods like he'd walked these overgrown paths hundreds of times.

His movements were smooth and sharp at the same time, each twitch of his head or flick of his eyes or step of his foot a deliberate, practiced motion.

"You sell yourself short," I whispered to him as we darted through the woods that would lead me to my house. "You're definitely ready for this."

"I am always prepared," he said. His voice was flat, monotone. Robotic. There was more inflection in the computer voice on board the *Enterprise*.

I was so surprised I almost ran face-first into a

low-hanging branch. Instead, my hand shot out just in time to keep it from slamming into my face.

"Evan?" I asked as he whooshed past me. "You okay?"

He stopped, freezing in place. Then, his body slacking slightly, he turned to look at me. He offered a sheepish smile.

"Uh, sorry," he said. "Sometimes I get like that."

"It's all right," I said, ducking beneath the branch and coming to stand next to him. "Just, maybe let a little bit of normal Evan slip into Robot Evan. I'm afraid you might go all Terminator on us."

He laughed. "I promise I won't. But I'll try to be less . . . *that*."

Both of us more at ease, we continued on. Veering to the right, I led Evan to the edge of the tree line, where we crouched down. In front of us was a quiet, suburban street.

And beyond that was my house.

Everything *looked* quiet. The windows were all dark. There were no cars in the driveway. There was no one on the dark street at all.

But I had to be careful.

"Look everywhere," I whispered to Evan. "If you see anyone at all, let me know."

"Okay."

We sat there for what must have been ten minutes, scanning the street in its entirety. I focused on windows in neighboring houses, thinking maybe someone could be watching there. Or in the trees, camouflaged.

Nothing.

Tepidly, I stood. They had sent the police after Spencer's minivan. They had to be after us still. Could they have already come by the house and decided I wasn't dumb enough to go there? Could I have gotten that lucky?

Only one way to find out.

Waving Evan forward, the two of us went full hybrid and ran across the street so fast that we would have been a blur to anyone watching. Just a flash of color that would mean nothing if they weren't looking for it.

Around the back of the house and I crouched down again, my eyes on the shed, the trees bordering the fence. Still no one that I could see.

Crouch-walking, I went to the back door. I pulled my keys out of my pocket, unlocked it, and slowly pushed the door open.

The room contained our washer and dryer, and beyond that was a hallway that ran by the kitchen, to the stairs. I stood slowly to my full height, then took one step into the house, then another. Floorboards creaked beneath my feet despite my hybrid prowess, and I gritted my teeth in frustration.

Still nothing.

Again waving for Evan to follow, I walked slowly down the hallway, stopping every few feet to look left and right and even above me, certain that there would be hired guards hiding in the shadows with more guns.

The attack never came. Evan and I made our way through the hallway, up the stairs, and into my room. No one popped out at me. I even checked the other rooms on the second floor while Evan sat on my bed waiting for me.

No one was home.

Finally relaxing, I went back to my room and plopped myself down into my desk chair.

"Looks like we're safe for now," I said to Evan as I dug through my desk drawer to find the thumb drive.

"Awesome," he said, then flung himself backward to lie on my bed. "Man, you've got a comfy bed. I wish I could just *sleep*."

Finding the drive, I pulled it out of the drawer and then stood from my desk chair. I opened my mouth to respond.

Then, from outside my window, I heard the sound of a car pulling into my driveway.

I ran to the window and pressed my face against the glass to try and get a look, but the vehicle was just out of view. Car doors slammed shut.

I had no idea who it was. It could just be my stepmother back from visiting friends.

Or it could be Mr. McKinney with a tranq gun.

"Okay," I said, stepping back and running my hand through my hair. "We can get out of this. You ever jump out of a two-story window?"

Evan didn't respond.

"Evan?" I asked as I spun to face my bed.

He sat there, staring at the corner by my closed bedroom door, mouth agape. I followed his gaze and stiffened in surprise.

Megan was standing there, glaring at us.

"Megan!"

I blinked and shook my head. Was I really seeing her? How had I missed her after searching the whole house? There's no way she could have been standing there the whole time without me seeing. No way she could have slipped through my door without me hearing.

"Megan," I said again, running to her side. "What are you *doing* here? Why are you in my room? Now is not a good time!"

"Emily," Evan whispered.

Megan didn't say anything. Like at school against the tree, her pale flesh was waxy, her body completely still. Only her gray eyes moved, slowly turning to look at me.

Deep inside, a primal fear began to rise up through my legs, into my bowels, forcing its way into my throat to choke me. Even though I was mostly hybrid—supposedly my fearless, confident self—I began to shake in fear.

"Megan?" I asked.

"Emily," Evan said louder. Bedsprings creaked as he jumped to his feet. "She just appeared there. She's not human. She's—"

"Oh, shut up," Megan said, her face coming alive and her lip curling into a snarl. Before I could react, her right hand shot up, her fingers pointed at Evan.

I spun around to see Evan leap to the side as the air where he'd just stood shimmered like water in daylight. In a flash, the water burst into a boil. Icy heat emanated from the spot, making my skin tingle. In a moment, the weird distortion disappeared—leaving part of my carpet and bed-spread in tatters.

"What?" I managed to stammer out. Rounding to face Megan, I said again, "What?!"

"Emily, you have to get out of here," Evan said behind me. "You can't hurt her."

I turned just in time to see Evan's big eyes glow white. Next to him, a rip tore through the air, just like the portal I'd seen the shadowmen come through when they came to take Dalton. Only this portal had never existed in my room before. He'd somehow summoned it with his mind.

"I can't control this!" he shouted, his voice a distant echo. "I'll come back to help you!"

And though Evan seemed to be struggling to pull himself away from the rip in the air, the force of its pull was too much. Slipping sideways, he was sucked through.

The distortion disappeared.

I was alone with Megan. Or whatever it was that was pretending to be her.

Spinning and leaping back at the same time, I pointed my finger at Megan. "What are you?" I demanded. "What did you do to my friend?"

Megan stepped forward, hands at her side. "It's me, Emily," she said. "Megan. Same friend you abandoned for"—she waved her hand at where Evan had just stood—"whoever the hell that was."

The back of knees met my mattress and I stopped walking backward.

"You can't be Megan," I said. "Megan can't teleport or make the air boil."

Megan shrugged. "To be clear, I'm not actually here. I'm in a car a street away and I'm sort of . . . projecting myself here? Something like that."

"That's great," I said. "But still: not a thing Megan can do."

"Let's just say this is Megan . . ." She waved her hands, presenting herself. *"Enhanced."*

The image of Megan in front of me doubled and tripled

up, going out of focus. She disappeared.

And reappeared next to me, sitting on the edge of my bed, her legs in front of the tatters her power blast had made. She patted the bed next to her.

"Sit," she said.

Not taking my eyes off of her, I slowly lowered myself to sit down. I still couldn't shake the unearthly fear, the primal terror of the wrongness of it all. I knew it was coming from the wolf side of me. But the wolf side of me was only afraid of the shadowmen.

Of course.

"I didn't save you, did I?" I whispered. "I thought I pulled you free of that shadowman, but he got inside you."

"She, actually," Megan said. "But you did stop her. All that's left of her in me is a shadow of herself. I mean, I can still hear her thoughts, and she can hear mine. And I can do things like . . ." She waved her hand. "You saw. But she didn't come through completely like she had been waiting to do her entire life."

I reached forward to grab her hands, but my own hands went right through her. I yanked my arms back.

"I told you," Megan scolded. "I'm not really here."

"Megan, I can fix this," I said. "I don't know how, but I can fix this."

She gaped at me. "You think I want you to *fix* me? Look, Emily, I get it now. Why you left me. Once you . . .

change . . . once you grow up . . . sometimes old friends aren't good enough anymore. You need to branch out." A smile spread across her face. An honest-to-God, genuine *smile*. "I'll always remember our lives together, Em. I would never, ever forget all we've been through. I know you won't, either. But it's time to move on."

Was this why she was here? For some big breakup speech?

I didn't have time for this.

Jumping to my feet, I walked away from her. "Megan, I'm sorry about everything. I've said it hundreds of times now, and I'm glad you finally get it. But I can't stay here. I need to go. I have to—"

A shimmer of air, and Megan was standing directly in front of me.

"You have to go to BioZenith and destroy their labs," she finished for me. "I know."

"You know?" I asked.

Another smile. "I know. I'm sorry I messed with you, but you were right—I have been watching you. *She* told me it would be a good idea, and she was right."

My body tensed. She wasn't just hearing the shadowman's—woman's—thoughts. Megan had been actively talking to her somehow.

"And what does . . . she . . . want from me?" I asked.

Megan shrugged. "Oh, she doesn't care about that

portal. That's for the *bad* ones." She took a step forward. "The only problem is, no one knows what will happen if you close it. Only you and those like you are able to activate and interact with the portals, so I need you to take me to the rift behind Dalton's house before you attack. She'll be waiting for me there."

Closing my eyes, I shook my head. This was too much, all at once—this wasn't in the plan. This wasn't how the night was supposed to go.

"Megan," I said softly as I slowly opened my eyes. "I can't do that."

Her smile fell and her lip trembled. "But you have to, Em. Only people like you can interact with the rifts. If you're not there, she can't come through. I can't become whole!"

"Whole?" I spat. "Megan, that thing wants to *possess* you!"

"She wants to make me better!" she shouted, stomping her incorporeal foot on my floor. "I'll finally not be such a screwup. I'll finally be good enough. Why won't you help me?"

Raising my hands, I stepped back, away from where Megan's projection clenched her fist and glared at me with rage-filled eyes.

"You're not you right now," I said. "Once I stop BioZenith, maybe you'll lose whatever connection you have to the other side, maybe—"

"No!" Megan roared.

She leaped forward, momentarily forgetting she wasn't solid. She ran through me and stopped, confused.

At that moment, my bedroom door burst open. Dawn rushed in, Deputy Jared in full uniform behind her.

Dawn smiled at me, relieved. "There you are," she said. "Em! We've been out looking for you. We were told you were missing."

Jared shook his head. "Emily, this has got to stop." Looking at Megan breathing heavily behind me, he asked, "What's going on in here?"

The car downstairs had been them. I'd completely forgotten about it in my fear and surprise at seeing Megan.

Before I could do or say anything, Megan turned to face the two intruders, anger distorting her features. She raised a hand, her fingers aimed at Dawn and Jared.

18

WHAT DID YOU DO?

It all happened so quickly.

One moment, Dawn was herself, staring at me with concern, oblivious to the insanity that had been happening in my room moments earlier.

The next, her mouth opened into a horrified O as the air around her shimmered.

And she screamed as the world boiled around her.

Jared reached for her with both hands, instinctively trying to grab Dawn and pull her free from the distortion. But as soon as his hands went into the boiling mass, he wailed in agony.

All I could do was shout at Megan. "Stop! Stop it!"

Then it was over.

The air returned to normal. Dawn collapsed to the burned and melted carpet beneath her. Jared stared at his hands, which flopped from his wrists unnaturally. They were pale, dead things.

Dead.

I dropped to my knees at the same time Jared did. Ignoring his own injured hands, he shook Dawn with the back of his wrists. I could only stare, numb.

I wasn't the wolf, or Nighttime Emily, or Daytime Emily, or the hybrid of all three. I was a shell with eyes that could not look away from my beautiful, kind stepsister lying motionless in front of me.

Jared was shouting, but it was like hearing someone try to yell at me while I swam deep in a dark ocean. Just mumbles and vibrations, hints of sounds but nothing I could make out clearly.

Swallowing down the bile that had risen in my throat, I looked up at Megan, or her apparition. Whatever the hell she was. She stood there still, her hand raised. Her jaw was slack, her eyes wide, disbelieving.

I finally found words.

"Megan," I whispered over Jared's desperate shouts of Dawn's name. "Megan, what did you do?"

Slowly, she lowered her arm. "I didn't mean to," she said, sounding young, afraid. "I didn't want to hurt anyone."

Forcing myself to my feet, I stepped in front of her. "What was that, Megan?" I asked, my voice trembling, shrill. "What did you do to her? Is she alive?"

Her lips parted, her eyes darted between me and Dawn's still form. Then, her mouth closed into a tight line and her eyes narrowed. She was back to wearing the waxy Megan mask.

"Show me the rift, Emily," she said, her voice flat, emotionless. "Take me there right now or else Jared will be next. And if even that doesn't convince you, well, I guess I'll need to go put a stop to your friends at BioZenith before they can ruin everything."

"Emily, what is she talking about?" Jared said, looking up at us from where he crouched on the floor next to Dawn.

I sobbed and turned to face my window.

"Wait, Emily," Jared gasped. "She just breathed. It was shallow, but she breathed!"

Gasping in relief, I spun around to see him getting to his feet.

"We need to call an ambulance," he said. "I'll—"

"No!" Megan shouted. I looked just in time to see her raise his hands at Jared. "If you try to call anyone, then you're next. Got it?"

"Megan, what is wrong with you!" Jared bellowed, angry for the first time that I'd ever seen. He stomped forward and reached out to grab Megan's wrist—but his useless, floppy hand passed through Megan's incorporeal arm.

Jared almost didn't seem to notice. Again he raised his hands to his face, his expression twisting in terror.

I leaped forward and grabbed Jared by the shoulders. "Jared, Jared, listen to me. Listen, okay? Things are happening you won't understand. So just do what I say for now." Looking back over my shoulder at Megan, I said to Jared, "Megan can hurt us. So for now we're going to do what she says." Facing him once more, I pleaded at him with my eyes, silently begging him to go along. "Will you listen?"

"Yeah," Jared said quietly. "I'll listen."

Behind me, Megan spoke. "Downstairs. Now. There will be a car parked at the curb out front. Get in it. And don't try anything."

Glaring defiantly at Megan, I picked up Dawn's limp form. Carrying her in both arms and with Jared following me, I walked purposefully and quickly down the stairs, through the living room, and into the foyer.

The beats of my stepsister's heart echoing through my palms were so slow, so distant, that I expected them to stop at any moment. Images of Dawn kept creeping into my thoughts the entire way, but I couldn't think about her now, couldn't think about how happy she'd been the last time I'd seen her, how she'd done her best to help mold me into a confident young woman, how—

I couldn't think about it.

I opened the front door and, just as Megan had said, there was a gray four-door car waiting at the curb. Megan was in the passenger seat, staring straight ahead, eyes blank. In the driver's seat was a visibly anxious Patrick.

Jared and I walked side by side over the lawn. I opened the door and let him slide in, then awkwardly set Dawn's torso on his lap. Squeezing beneath her legs, I got in as well.

Dawn let out a soft whimper, then went still, silent.

Still breathing, though. That was good.

As soon as I slammed the door shut, a click echoed through the car as each door locked.

"Who are they?" Patrick asked. "Is that girl all right?"

"I don't know what Megan did to her, Patrick," I said. "I don't know what all she can do. You're the one who's been hanging around Megan lately, not me. How are you involved in all this? Why are you helping her?"

"W-we're mates," he stammered. "And she told me all about you and showed me things she could do. She said I could learn how to pop around like she does. I—"

Megan stirred in the passenger seat, then snapped awake. Patrick clammed up and turned his attention to the road. Putting the car in drive, he pulled away from the curb and started heading down the road.

Megan—the real, solid Megan this time—leaned over the seat to face me and Jared. Grim-faced, Jared stared back at her. He cradled his dead hands in his lap, beneath Dawn's head.

"Sorry, Jared," Megan said. "I didn't want to involve any of you normal people in this." She shrugged. "Wrong place, wrong time."

"That's all you have to say, Megan?" I said, seething. "You hurt Jared and Dawn, and it's just, 'Whoops'?"

She glared at me, not saying anything for a long moment. Then, finally, "Yeah. Whoops. Guess I'm just as evil as all the idiots at school say I am." Sighing, she turned away to sit back in her chair. "Can we not talk anymore? I don't want to talk."

We rode in silence, my mind racing. This wasn't supposed to be happening. I was supposed to be on my way to stopping BioZenith and the Akhakhu, not being kidnapped to *help* one of the creepy shadowmen come across.

For a moment I thought about trying to surreptitiously text Spencer and the others. Until I remembered our phones were now a bunch of plastic and glass shards scattered across a mall parking lot.

Feeling my pocket, I did find the hard nub of the thumb drive, at least. Despite the commotion, I'd managed to not leave it behind. Not that it would do me much good if I couldn't get to the meeting place in time.

I briefly considered going hybrid or even full wolf and busting myself out of the car. But that would just lead to an accident, or let Megan go free to cause even more trouble. No, I decided in that moment that I'd just have to sit it out and try and figure something out on the fly.

It didn't take us long to get to the McKinney house. Patrick pressed on the brake hard as he pulled into the driveway, and we all jerked forward. As he and Megan opened their doors and came to open mine and Jared's from the outside, I peered over the car seats at the front door of the mansion, hoping that Mr. McKinney would be there with his team of guards.

I couldn't believe I actually *wanted* to see that man.

But I didn't have that much luck.

"Emily, what's happening?" Jared whispered in the few moments we had before our doors opened. "What I saw Megan do . . . That was impossible."

"I'll explain later," I whispered. "Just make a break for it when I say. Okay?"

"But what about Dawn and—"

"Just do it," I interrupted. "You've helped me a lot. Now let me help you."

He didn't get a chance to answer. Both of our doors

opened at the same time. Megan's hand gripped me around the bicep and she yanked me out. Dawn's feet plopped heavy on the backseat.

"You know the way," Megan said, shoving me off the driveway and onto the mansion's front lawn. "And don't try anything, Emily. Even if you take me down, I can pop somewhere else and . . ." She raised her hand and wiggled her fingers. "Got it?"

"Yeah, Reedy," I said, using my old nickname for her. "I got it."

She snorted. "Reedy. Whatever. Go."

I did as she asked. Leaving Dawn unconscious in the backseat of the car, I led confused Jared, jittery Patrick, and determined Megan around the side of the house and toward the woods at the back of the property. We passed the pool, covered for the cold months, and a fenced-in area where Dalton's dog was usually kept.

My mind kept searching for some solution. I didn't want Jared to get hurt. Not Patrick, either, even if I didn't know how he fit in with all this. My only plan was to tackle and knock out Megan, but she was right that she could pop out—astral project or whatever it was that she did. I actually had no idea what the extent of her abilities were now that she was connected to an Akhakhu.

So I made a choice I hoped I wouldn't regret.

I decided to do exactly as she asked and hope that she would let me go.

We reached the tree line where a week before I'd chased wolf-Dalton as he'd dragged a screaming Megan into the brush. The bushes were still trampled, branches still broken and scattered. I followed the makeshift path, the others behind me in a line, until we were there.

The clearing.

The last place I'd seen Megan as herself.

It was just how I remembered. A small, treeless space covered with fallen leaves in red and orange and brown. It would have been a lovely place for a picnic or something when it was warmer out.

That is, if it weren't for the rippling, oval distortion that I knew was hovering in the air to my left. The one I'd seen a shadowman crawl through toward Megan while others dragged Dalton away. It was awfully convenient that there was a portal right behind Mr. McKinney's house, but I got the feeling there were probably rifts everywhere—it's just no one could see them.

Focusing, I let my eyes shift from Nighttime's strong human vision to the gray-tinted vision of the wolf.

And the rift came into view.

The distortion was larger than I remembered, having grown from the size of a window to that of a door. I could see through it, too, those same spindly dark cities I was familiar with by now.

A shadowy figure stepped into view just on the other side of the portal. I knew right away that it was Megan's Akhakhu. She'd been waiting.

The shadowwoman tilted her head at me, watching me.

Megan came to my side, spinning to take in the clearing. Her hands were shaking, and a crazed grin spread across her face. "Where is it?" she asked me. "I can feel her, she's so close!" Grabbing my shoulders and staring into my eyes, she shook me. "Where?"

Last chance. I could point her in the wrong direction and, when she was distracted, try to take her down and risk ending up like Dawn.

Or I could point her toward the awaiting Akhakhu and hope that the thing would let me finish my plans for BioZenith. Which could mean losing Megan forever.

I raised my left hand. And I pointed at the distortion.

Crossing her arms, Megan turned from me and walked slowly across the clearing. As she did, the portal expanded and contracted, like a pupil with a light flashing on and off in front of it. The shadow figure on the other side trembled with excitement.

Megan stopped a foot away from the portal. Strands of her long blond hair wisped away from her face in the breeze. Closing her eyes, she raised her hands like a woman at church.

"I can hear you," she said. Then, louder, "I hear you! Come into me! Take me! Please!"

With Megan focused on her possession, I turned to Patrick and Jared. "Run," I hissed.

Still cradling his dead hands, Jared looked at Megan, then back to me. "What about you? I can't just leave you with her."

I grinned wryly at him. "Yes you can, Boy Scout. Go get medical help. Save Dawn and get your hands fixed so I can hear you play drums again. And get the police to find my stepmom and my dad." I swallowed, realizing I didn't know if my dad ever made it out of BioZenith.

The wind had picked up more now and Megan's hair was a streamer of white behind her. Face so full of joy that she looked like another girl altogether, Megan raised her head toward the sky.

"H-hey," Patrick said, stepping toward me and Jared. "I'm with Megan. I'm not supposed to . . ."

"Then stay," I snapped at him. "But you don't need a hostage anymore. Megan got what she wanted. You won't get in trouble." I raised my right hand and tensed my fingers. Dark claws shot from my nail beds. "At least not with *her*."

"Emily," Jared said, wide-eyed.

"Go!" I said.

He didn't need to be told again. He disappeared through the underbrush.

Patrick took a few steps away from me, but he didn't leave.

Megan moaned, half pleasure, half pain, and I turned to see what was happening.

The Akhakhu was halfway through the portal. Her dark, wispy hands connected with Megan's own, and Megan shivered.

The shadowwoman stepped one foot out of the portal and onto Megan's, then another. As I watched, horrified, the creature slowly pulled its inky blackness into Megan's chest, her hips, her legs, and finally, her head.

Megan convulsed and dropped to the ground. With my wolf vision I could see a wispy, smoky aura surrounding her. Tendrils of darkness wrapped around her limbs like creeping vines. As the girl gasped for air, the shadows disappeared into her nose and mouth.

Finally Megan lay still.

"Is it done?" Patrick asked me.

I didn't answer. I didn't know.

Snapping back to Nighttime vision, I crept forward, slowly, not sure what to expect. Hunching down, Patrick followed me.

When I was not two feet from Megan, her eyes snapped open. I stiffened, seeing them. The iris was gone altogether. All that remained were engorged black pupils.

Megan—ShadowMegan, at least—smiled.

Flexing her fingers, ShadowMegan raised her hands to look at them. She twisted her hands this way and that, studying her palms, her knuckles, her nails. Then, pressing her hands into the dirt, she pushed herself to stand up.

"Megan?" I whispered.

ShadowMegan looked at me as though seeing me for the first time. Then, tilting her head and biting her lip, she glanced away.

"Hmm," she said, her voice deeper than normal. "Megan. Yes, I will be called this."

So, not Megan.

"Is she still in there?" I asked.

ShadowMegan laughed, then patted me on the cheek like I was an adorable child asking silly questions. I jerked away.

"She must be here somewhere, I suppose," Shadow-Megan said. "I'm not sure. This is all *quite* new to me."

"Why are you here?" I asked. "What do you want?"

Sighing, ShadowMegan stepped past me, stretching her legs with each step. "So many questions. Everyone has so many questions." Looking at me, she smiled, her lips spreading farther and farther until Megan's face no longer looked human.

"I am here to stake my claim first, child," she said. "You know not what we fight on the other side. But I made it here *first*. I shall be the one who is bowed down to." She tapped her index finger against her cheek. "But first, of course, I need an army."

And then she was gone.

I blinked and took a step back.

There was no poof. No wisp of smoke or other wild particle effect. Just there one moment, gone the next.

Rounding on Patrick, I shoved him in the chest. Even though I was much shorter than the boy, he cowered as though I towered above him.

"Tell me where she's going," I demanded.

"I don't know," he stammered. "This isn't what she said it would be like. She said we'd have superpowers like you, not get taken over by some spirit and hurt people! We were supposed to—"

Letting out an exasperated sigh, I shoved past him and started to race through the broken brush toward the McKinneys' backyard. "Come on!" I called over my shoulder. "You get to be my chauffeur."

"Where are we going?" Patrick huffed as he raced to keep pace with me.

There was only one place ShadowMegan would be going if her goal was to raise an army. The same place where Mr. McKinney and Evan's mom and all the other scientists-turned-fanatics would go to bring the Akhakhu over if they could.

"We're going to BioZenith."

19

YOU WANT ME TO DRIVE
TOWARD THE GUNSHOTS?

When Patrick and I reached the car, we found Jared struggling to open the back door with his limp hands. I could see his fingers moving—life was coming back into them—but they were slow, uncontrolled. Just as I ran across the lawn to meet him, he kicked the car door in frustration.

"Hey," I said softly. I placed a hand on his shoulder, but he jerked away, angry.

"I don't understand," he said. "All of this is crazy. And my hands." Meeting my eyes, I could see the fear distorting his face. "My hands!"

Brushing past him gently, I opened the backseat door. Dawn still lay there, but she was squirming now, moaning louder and louder. I let out a deep, relieved breath.

"I think you guys are going to be okay," I said as I looped my arms under Dawn's shoulders and dragged her out of the backseat. "She's coming to, and your hands are starting to work again. Whatever Megan did to you, she wasn't strong enough to be fatal."

Jared blinked, gaping at me. "Megan did this. She waved her hands . . . and she teleported. . . . I swear, she teleported. I'm going crazy."

I laid Dawn out on the cool, manicured lawn. As I did, Patrick ran up, gasping for air.

"You can sure run fast," he said, leaning on his knees.

"Yeah," I said. "Get in the driver's seat. Don't forget." I showed him my nails. They were still normal—but he remembered.

A second later, he was in the front seat, slamming the door shut behind him.

Jared crouched down next to Dawn, caressing her hair as best he could. "You promise to explain all this to me one day?" he asked quietly.

"I promise. But I need to go. Ask the woman who lives here to call an ambulance. She'll help you."

He looked up at me. "Whatever you're doing, Emily, be careful."

I shook my head. "Always so worried about me. I'm just some teen girl you barely know."

He shrugged. "You're certainly not like any girl I've ever met."

I offered him a grin. "Thanks. But when Dawn wakes up? Make sure you tell *her* that."

Rounding the car, I opened the passenger door. Jared stood to go call the police and try to get ahold of my dad and stepmom.

"Good luck!" he called to me as I climbed inside the car.

Luck. I could certainly use it.

I only just had an evil corporation to bring down and a possessed best friend to stop, after all.

Patrick rambled next to me in his lilting English accent, one hand waving to express himself while he spoke, the other on the wheel as he followed my directions and drove me toward the industrial district.

"See, and she showed me the things she could do, and I thought it was neat, yeah? But I didn't know she would hurt anybody, or that—"

I gathered he only got involved in this through Megan. That his showing up when I was searching for another werewolf was literally just a confirmation-biased coincidence—I had been paying extra-special attention to him since I thought he was cute, and therefore I saw him everywhere. Not the most astounding answer to that little mystery, but I guess not all of them can be.

I didn't care.

I sat in the passenger seat of Patrick's car, knees to chest, my brain ping-ponging back and forth.

Ping. Need to get to BioZenith. Need to meet up with my pack and the cheerleaders. Need to storm into the facility, stop ShadowMegan from bringing over an Akhakhu army, and destroy the portal.

Pong. Dawn and Jared had been hurt. And it was all my fault because I was at the center of this madness, I was the one who let Megan get possessed by some otherworldly being, I was the one who had disappeared and she decided to look for.

Ping. I needed to stop the scientists and shadowmen who were trying to control me.

Pong. If half-possessed Megan could almost kill people with a flick of her hand, what was full ShadowMegan capable of? How many more of my friends would be hurt before the night was done?

Ping.

It was dark by the time Patrick turned onto the street where we would find BioZenith. I glanced at the dashboard clock. It was almost ten p.m. The day was gone. The time for me to put my plan into action was here.

I was supposed to be the alpha, the leader. But I didn't

know if I was ready. Seeing Dawn on the verge of death . . . it had suddenly made things much more real.

Patrick had stopped talking by then. I guess he figured out I wasn't listening to his life story.

Putting my feet back down on the ground, I leaned over the dash and pointed at the building opposite BioZenith.

"There," I said. "And turn your headlights off."

He nodded and did as he was told.

Quietly he veered the car into the parking lot of the other office building. Following my directions, he drove down the side of the building, past big air-conditioning vents and closed Dumpsters. He parked at the edge of the lot, just in front of the woods.

"Come on," I said, opening the passenger door and leaping out.

Leaning from his side of the car over the passenger seat, Patrick looked out the open door and asked, "Why do I have to go? I don't want any more part of this. I just want to go home."

"You should have thought about that before you teamed up with Megan," I spat. "Out of the car. Now."

Turning off the ignition and pocketing the key, Patrick did as he was told. Slouching, he came to my side and then followed a half step behind me as I took him into the woods.

I darted through the grass and bushes to where Spencer

and I had had our little practice fight a few nights before. I expected him to have taken the others there.

But no one was around.

Letting myself shift slightly into the wolf, I scrunched my nose and sniffed the air. Spencer's scent was all over the place, but it was an old, stale scent. I couldn't smell any of the others. If they had met in the woods, it would have to have been farther away, but that didn't make any sense.

Unless something was wrong.

Something was always going wrong.

Grabbing Patrick by his arm, I wordlessly led him back through the woods and to his car.

"Get in," I commanded him as I gently shoved him toward the driver's seat.

"Ow," he said, rubbing his arm and glaring at me. "You don't have to be so rough."

I didn't answer. I rounded the front of the car and was about to slip back into the passenger seat when I heard a gunshot.

Then another. And another, and another, until they became a staccato, deadly rhythm.

I spun and looked across the street to BioZenith. Floodlights had burst on outside the building, illuminating the parking lot. I could see shadows in the lot huddled behind dark cars, some with rifles aimed at a lone figure who walked slowly, casually toward the main entrance. The figure waved a hand and the gunshots stopped.

The attack had already begun.

I jumped into the car and slammed the door shut. "Get in, get in!" I shouted at Patrick.

"I'm in, I'm in!" he shouted back as he slammed the door shut.

"Drive us across the street and up to the guard box."

He gaped at me, his hand hovering over the keys in the ignition. "You want me to drive *toward* the gunshots?"

I craned my neck to look back. I could see more figures running to hide behind vehicles, though some tepidly approached the person who'd made the gunfire cease.

"Yeah, I do," I said. "You don't want me to hurt you, do you?"

"No, I don't," he said.

The car cranked alive and the next thing I knew we were reversing fast down the side alley. When we reached the parking lot, Patrick slammed on the brakes, put the car in drive, and spun us around to face the main street, then pressed on the gas.

"Whoa, Speed Racer," I said.

Glowering over the wheel, Patrick mumbled, "I bloody wish."

Not bothering to look either way, Patrick barreled into

the street, then aimed toward the open gate and drove us through. Tires screeching, we skidded to a stop just past the guard box.

"I thought Brits were good drivers?" I gasped.

"I'm on visa," he said. "I might as well be pure-blood American now."

Before he could stop me, I reached over and yanked the keys from the ignition. As I leaped out the car door once more, he shouted, "Hey!"

Crouching down so I could look through the open door, I met his eye. "You're the only one who's been with Megan and I may need you. You don't have any super-powers, right?"

"No," he said, furiously shaking his head.

"All right, then wait here. I'll be back."

Shoving the keys into my pocket, I opened the car door and slipped out into the cool night, trying to absorb the scene in front of me. As far as I could tell, everyone was so distracted by what was happening in the center of the parking lot that they hadn't heard me arrive.

Standing halfway between the front gate and the building entrance, and glowing as though in a spotlight, was Megan.

She glided over the asphalt as though hovering. Arms outstretched, she turned in slow circles as she walked, the wind catching her long white-blond hair and swirling it around her. At her feet, a pile of brass bullets lay scattered.

Near the glass doors that led into the lobbies of BioZenith, guards crouched down behind planters and black trucks, their guns still aimed at Megan but no longer firing. Several scientists in lab coats huddled behind the guards, including the scratched and disheveled Mr. McKinney.

I was confused. Why were they attacking Megan if they all worshipped the Akhakhu?

I didn't have time to try and figure it out. Mr. McKinney wasn't looking at Megan like everyone else. Next to him, almost hidden in the shadows, were two of triplets. From their hair I could tell it was Brittany and Casey. And standing behind them, holding handguns aimed at Mr. McKinney, were a Hispanic man and woman, and a white man with gray hair.

The triplets' parents? And maybe Nikki's dad? But what were they doing here?

Mr. McKinney and the cheerleaders' parents spat words at one another that I couldn't hear. The two girls slouched, wide-eyed, as they looked between their squabbling parents and the strange girl twirling in the parking lot in a beatific haze.

I needed to get closer. Crouching down, I ran alongside

the barbed fence, and then into the parking lot to hide behind an old white car. I was closer to the group at the entrance now and, slipping into hybrid, I could finally hear them.

"What do we do about the girl, sir?" one of the guards asked, not taking his eyes off of giggling, gleeful Shadow-Megan.

But Mr. McKinney ignored him. He was too focused on the cheerleaders' parents.

"Tell them to stand down, McKinney!" the Hispanic man bellowed. He stood in front of Brittany and Casey, one hand aiming a gun at Mr. McKinney, the other held back to keep the girls from jumping in front of him.

Mr. McKinney shouted back. "We didn't involve your daughters! They aren't a part of this! If you just *leave*, no one has to get hurt!"

"Oh no," the triplets' mother said, switching her gun from one hand to the other. "We've been waiting two decades for this. We were cut off. Aim your guns away from the Rebel or we go for your precious wolves."

"Why are you working with Rebel?" Mr. McKinney asked. "You know what she is, who her people are. She is a peasant upstart, not one of the glorious leaders!"

"And that's why she is in the right! That is why her people's *ka* are pure!"

Whispers tickled my ears to my right. I looked over in the shadows to see Spencer, Tracie, Nikki, and Amy huddled together behind a concrete divider. I sighed in relief—they were safe.

Crouch-walking, I made my way as quickly as possible to the huddled group. I pressed my hand against Spencer's shoulder. He jumped, startled, then grinned wide when he saw it was me.

"What happened?" I hissed.

Eyes ablaze with fury and her wild hair more a mess than usual, Amy answered. "My idiot sisters are what happened," she said through gritted teeth. "Casey was working with our parents the whole time. That's the real reason she went with you. Apparently they're all caught up in this shadowmen crap too."

"Nikki, yours too?" I asked.

The red-haired girl nodded. Shiny streaks ran down her cheeks and I could tell she'd been crying.

"They tricked us," Nikki said softly. "They said they wanted to help us, just like Mr. and Mrs. Cooke."

"And now we're here," Tracie finished for her. Craning her neck, she looked past me. "Where's Evan?" she asked. "Is he in the car you drove up in?"

"No, that's Patrick," I said as I dug through my pants pocket. "Evan slipped through to the other side, however it is he does that. I don't know when or how he'll get back. But something happened I didn't expect."

Tracie rolled her eyes. "I'm going to take an educated guess and assume that your friend Megan acting like she's on crack has something to do with it?"

Before I could answer, ShadowMegan's voice boomed across the BioZenith grounds.

"I tire of your arguments!" she said. "I demand silence!"

Her words echoed endlessly between the buildings, like a priest's commandment in a chapel. The bickering parents fell silent.

"What is Megan *doing*?" Spencer asked, eyes wide with bewilderment.

Swallowing back my fear and sadness, I shook my head. "That's not Megan. Not anymore."

Together, the five of us rose to peer over the top of the concrete divider.

In the center of the parking lot, beneath the glimmering stars and the yellow moon, Megan stood with her hands raised. A swirling, mystical aura the colors of deepest night and impossibly bright daylight surrounded her, becoming a pulsating ball of energy.

As we watched, she rose into the air like some divine being sent down from above.

"Whoa," Spencer said beside me.

"She has powers too?" Amy asked. "When did *this* happen?"

I couldn't answer her. The wolf side of me was terrified and from the way Spencer and Tracie trembled beside me I could tell they felt it too. We were seeing something old and dangerous, hidden within something designed to be beautiful.

But every instinct told us the truth.

The ball of energy spun slowly so that ShadowMegan could take in the people surrounding her. All of the adults, and Brittany and Casey, watched her with awe. The rifles the guards were carrying slipped from their fingers and clattered to the metal floor. The cheerleaders' parents dropped their weapons as well.

"I am what you have been waiting for," ShadowMegan declared as she smiled down at the scientists. A few on Mr. McKinney's side that I didn't recognize fell to their knees.

"All your years of work have brought us to this point," she went on. "You created the vespers who would lead you to your salvation. How long we have all waited for our worlds to unite." Smiling her inhumanly broad smile, she exhaled rapturously, closed her eyes, and aimed her face toward the dark sky above. "That time has come now!"

Movement caught my eye by the glass doors. Mr. McKinney stepped past his awestruck guards to walk toward

ShadowMegan. His cheek was covered with a large bandage that was stained in the center with blood. His hands were clenched into fists, and he trembled with anger.

"The Rebel," he spat at her. "You're the one who's been holding our people—my *son*—hostage."

ShadowMegan nodded, not looking at him. "Yes," she said distantly. "That was me. I thank you for keeping your promise to manipulate Emily."

"This isn't right," he shouted, pointing an accusing finger up at ShadowMegan. "We only agreed to help you come over, not the rest of your *filth*. You're here for the portal to bring them over, aren't you? Well, it's not going to happen! Give me back my son, you unclean—"

With an absentminded flick of ShadowMegan's wrist, Mr. McKinney's voice caught in his throat. Choking and gurgling, he took a wild step back.

And then, one by one, each of his limbs twisted and snapped. The sound was sick, horrifying, but I couldn't cover my ears, couldn't do anything but watch. His gurgles struggled to become screams.

His neck snapped last. Mr. McKinney collapsed to floor. Dead.

"Oh God," Nikki said, her hands covering her face.

No one else made a move as ShadowMegan spun within her energy bubble.

"What are we supposed to do now?" Tracie whispered to me, frantic. "Getting inside BioZenith and blowing up the portal was going to be hard enough. But how are we supposed to fight that?"

"I don't know," I said. My mind raced, trying to find some answer, but the wolf side of me kept howling and thrashing inside of me, and I couldn't think. "Just . . . I don't know yet."

"I know I have acolytes among you," ShadowMegan called down. "Step forward. You will find salvation with me."

"Here!" Mr. Delgado bellowed. "We're here!"

He and his wife shoved Brittany and Casey forward, forcing them to leave the safety of the shadows and the protection of the awestruck guards. Along with Mr. Tate, they pushed past the cowering scientists and wound past the cars to stand in front of Megan.

The three parents bowed their head. Brittany reached out and grasped Casey's hand, but the quiet triplet smiled up at Megan, tears in her eyes.

"We did as you asked and told the other acolytes of your arrival," Mrs. Delgado said, her words halting, jerky, as though she had a sob in her throat. "Our daughters helped. We ask that you bless them, too."

ShadowMegan tilted her head, her lips parting into a

radiant smile. "Of course, my children. Your vespers are precious things. They shall ascend higher than us all."

"Thank you," Casey said, her voice almost a whisper.

Next to me, Amy trembled, her features contorted in rage.

"Traitors," she spat. "I can't believe this. I can't . . ." She shook her head.

As the ball of black-and-white light that surrounded ShadowMegan swirled like oily streaks on a soap bubble, she hovered forward toward the entrance to BioZenith. The Delgados, clinging to their daughters, followed, with a quiet and stoic Mr. Tate at their heels.

ShadowMegan casually flicked her hand and one of the cars the guards huddled behind crumpled like aluminum foil. Glass crunched and shattered as ShadowMegan closed her hand into a fist, and then the totaled vehicle spun away as she flicked her hand once more.

The dumbstruck guards backed away until they hit the wall next to the entrance. Then they parted to let Shadow-Megan pass.

She was going for the portal. And no matter how upsetting it was to see my friend like this, no matter how terrifying she was to the feral third of my brain, I knew one thing for certain.

I caused this mess. And I had to stop it.

I looked over at Spencer, Tracie, Nikki, and Amy. "All right, no more sitting around. We need to follow them in and stop whatever it is she's planning."

"How are we supposed to do that?" Nikki asked.

I shrugged. "Seems like the whole blowing-up-the-portal plan should still work. You ready?"

Tracie sighed. "No."

At the same time, Amy grinned deviously. "Definitely."

"All right," I said. "Let's—"

I never got a chance to finish. Headlights flashed behind us, and the buzzing of engines thundered down the darkened street. We turned just in time to see four black vans come roaring down the road, tires screeching as they veered through the gate, past the car in which Patrick still hid, and pulled to sudden stops in the middle of the parking lot.

Caught by surprise, ShadowMegan twisted in the sky and looked down at the sudden intruders. The guards, the scientists, the cheerleaders' parents, and all of us vespers watched, stunned, as the backs of the vans burst open and dozens of men dressed in black military gear poured out.

ShadowMegan grinned. She raised her hand to crush these newcomers and resume her plans—and then stopped when a man in a crisp suit climbed out of the back of one of the vans.

The man brushed smooth his jacket sleeves, then held his hands behind his back, his white beard–covered chin held high. In his tailored gray suit and red silk tie, he looked imposingly rich and important. He actually looked a little bit like Anderson Cooper with a goatee. An evil-twin Anderson Cooper.

And seeing him, ShadowMegan's face twisted into revulsion.

"You!" she spat.

The man nodded. "Hello, Rebel."

ShadowMegan raised both of her hands, the swirling energy whipping into a tornado. But before she could break the man apart like she had Mr. McKinney, who still lay dead atop the asphalt, the man's eyes glowed and he waved his own hand.

The energy exploded into smoke and drifted away. ShadowMegan hung in the sky, her pale skin tinged blue, frozen in place. Even the wild, flowing strands of her hair hung mid-whip, as though we were now looking at a photograph of the possessed girl.

Like a block of ice, ShadowMegan dropped to the asphalt, landing on her side with a heavy, echoing thunk.

"What the hell," Amy whispered.

"Emily, do you know who that is?" Spencer asked me.

Again I didn't get a chance to answer. Footsteps

crunched behind us. Tracie, Spencer, and I heard them first, and we spun around to see four of the black-clad military men trying to sneak up on us, rifles raised.

"Hey!" I shouted.

But it was too late. With a series of pops, four darts flitted from the end of the rifles and into the necks of everyone except Nikki. My hand shot instinctively up to my throat and I yanked out the needle, then tossed the vial of green liquid onto the ground.

Spencer, Tracie, and Amy collapsed to the ground. Startled, Nikki noticed the guards just in time to try and stop their shots with her own powers, but a dart pierced her chest. Eyes rolling back in her head, she crumpled.

The Nighttime part of me seethed with rage. I let her take over. Adrenaline flooding my veins, I clenched my fists and ran over the asphalt to attack the shooters. Behind me I heard voices rising and someone screaming as more pops sounded. A car door slammed and glass shattered.

The four shooters pulled their triggers. *Pop-pop. Pop-pop.* As each dart pierced my skin, I roared and tore the needle free. My skin tingled and my vision went hazy, blurry, but I refused to stop until these men lay unconscious. Even when my own feet threatened to give out beneath me, I kept running—at least, I thought I was running. Distantly, I felt myself fall onto my hands and knees, the rough street scraping my palms.

The man in the suit stepped between me and the guards. Heaving in anger and frustration, I looked up at him.

His pale eyes glowed. He waved his hand.

And then everything went black.

FIGHT THIS, EMILY

I was ice.

I couldn't see, or taste, or hear, and I constantly faded in and out of consciousness, but when I became briefly, hazily aware of myself, I could feel.

My skin was frozen to the point of burning, hard and smooth. Blood rushed through my veins slowly, sluggishly, a slush slurry. Cold air swirled around me, somehow seeping through the icy carapace of my flesh and chilling my insides until I trembled.

It was unlike anything I've ever felt before, and when my dreams faded and the blackness gave way to dim light seeping through my sealed eyelids, I forgot all about who and what I was and everything that had happened to me.

My world was nothing but endless cold and I lost all

sense of time. Sometimes I sensed lights brightening beyond my closed eyes, and then turning off and coming back on. Days passing, or maybe only someone coming in and out of a room at minute-long intervals.

The only respite was my shocked body alerting my brain to sleep, black out, go unconscious, and let me drift off into dreams of loping wolves and flying cheerleaders and shadows that hovered in the sky.

Then, one day, my eyes snapped open.

All I saw were plumes of white fog curling in front of me, at first, anyway. My vision was blurred—normal Daytime Emily vision, I realized in the back of my brain. It didn't help that my lids hung heavy, my crystal-laced lashes hanging in front of my pupils like icy bars. Vaguely I could see a solid, curved metal wall to my left and right, with plastic strips spaced at intervals.

My mind came back to me then in a way it hadn't before and I tried to move, but couldn't. Panicking, I jerked my shoulders side to side, but if I moved it was only a fraction of a fraction, nothing I could feel.

My breath was ragged, quick. The chill fog swirled up through my nostrils, frozen fingers that clawed at my brain and sent sharp lances of pain through my head. My lips parted, the skin sticking together and tearing until my mouth finally opened. Blood only marginally hotter than my skin seeped from my mouth and made tracks down my chin, but all the scant warmth did was remind me again that the rest of my body felt as if I'd walked naked into the Antarctic. Only without the numbness that soothed the freezing as they accepted death.

I tried to scream, but my voice came out ragged and hoarse.

Pull it together! I instead screamed in my mind. *Go Nighttime! Go feral! Use your strength!*

I closed my eyes and willed my breathing to slow. My muscles twitched, vibrating beneath the shell of my skin. I wiggled my frozen fingers and slowly, slowly, they responded. A crunching, snapping noise met my ears, though the sound was dulled, distant. I hoped it was just ice breaking off of me and not my bones breaking apart.

You can do it, I commanded myself. *Fight this, Emily. Fight it!*

With a flex of my biceps, my forearms snapped up. I opened my heavy lids to find my hands intact, though they shimmered blue in the dim light that surrounded me. I raised back my fists then punched forward.

Knuckles met glass, and the force of my motion sent fog swirling away to reveal a curved, opaque window in front of me. Light seeped through, and I could see shadows beyond the ice crystals that formed curling fractal leaves atop the glass.

I was in some sort of upright tube or capsule or something. A Mr. Freeze chamber meant to keep in me in stasis.

All I could think was *I failed. Those BioZenith bastards got me.*

I didn't know where I was or how I got there, but I guessed a sterile lab. I pictured scientists, possessed by shadowmen and driven mad in their messianic lust, hovering over my frozen body with scalpels and whirring saws.

Not going to happen.

I screamed again, and this time air scraped up my throat, past my vocal cords, and a tinny, enraged shout echoed through my chamber.

My fists pounded against the glass again, and a dozen jagged cracks snaked away from where they landed. I slammed my fists again and the glass splintered, fragmented. The icy patterns split into a thousand pieces.

I screamed.

This time, when I hit the curved glass door, it shattered into a million tiny pebbles. They rained down, clattering and scattering atop white linoleum like hail.

Bright, blue-white fluorescents hummed and flickered on behind the plastic strips in the back of my chamber. The freezing white fog whooshed out, and hot air took its place, melting my skin with its touch.

But that just made it worse. I had been numbed, after all, and now every inch of me felt as if millions of tiny needles were piercing my skin. I stumbled forward, tripped on the metal lip of the door, and fell into a gleaming room.

Lights seared my eyes, blazing as bright and hot as if I were looking right into the sun. Clutching my eyes closed, I collapsed on my hands and knees to the hard ground. Glass sliced into my palms, shredded the knees of the wispy white pajama pants someone had dressed me in.

Pain. It was all I felt. The screeching of voices slicing into my eardrums. The needles digging deeper into my skin, into my muscles. The light trying to melt my eyes through my closed lids.

Strong, rough hands grabbed me beneath my shoulders and hauled me up to my feet. The hands of those who had taken me captive, or those who worked for them. It didn't matter. My heart beat an angry rhythm as it sent molten blood surging through my veins.

I screamed again and shoved the grabbing people off of me. I heard a great, bright crash of noise as they landed against equipment, and one shouted while the other tried to speak to me in soothing tones, but I couldn't focus on their words.

Forcing my eyes open, I blinked and blinked until I could see again under the harsh white lights shining from above me. I was in some sort of white hospital room, complete with the countertops lined with gleaming silver medical equipment and vials of medicine behind glass cabinets.

My eyes darted back and forth. Two men dressed in scrubs lay on either side of me. One had crashed into a gurney with leather straps connected to its railings. He cursed as he climbed to his feet. The other one, the one with his hands raised and trying to calm me down, had knocked over an IV rack. A plastic bag filled with syrupy orange liquid lay on the floor next to it.

I stood equidistant between the two of them with my hands raised.

"Stay away from me," I said, my voice an undead rasp. "I will hurt you. You better stay away."

The calm orderly—or nurse, doctor, scientist, whatever he was—took a tepid step toward me. He was short and stocky, but had a kind face.

"It's all right, Emily," he cooed. "You woke up earlier than we expected. We know you must be hurting and wondering where you are. We can help you."

"Yeah," I spat. "Just like you helped me get freeze-dried in the first place."

I spun in a slow circle, meeting the two men's gaze with narrowed eyes. On the back wall I saw the chamber I'd busted out of. It looked like a clear-lidded metal casket set on its end, only with wires and tubes snaking out of it, and blinking lights and LED screens on its front.

Next to it sat another, unmolested chamber. Fog swirled

inside and I could make out a shadowy figure.

And for just a moment, the fog parted and through the frozen glass I could see Megan.

Her eyes were closed, her face slack and neutral. Her skin and hair were as blue as if she'd been dyed. She was frozen. My friend was frozen!

Only it wasn't her at all. It was ShadowMegan, wasn't it?

The last events I remembered before blacking out came back to me in a rush.

Rescuing Evan. Being forced to take Megan to the portal.

ShadowMegan killing Mr. McKinney while the cheerleaders' parents acted as if she was their born-again prophet.

The vans showing up with the men in assault gear. The tranq darts shot into the bodies of my friends.

And Anti-Anderson, the man in the suit with the glowing eyes who froze ShadowMegan and then froze me.

"Emily, if you'll just let us help you—" the short man said.

I snapped my head to look at the bigger guy. "What happened to my friends?" I asked. "Who was the man that froze me? Where am I?"

The big man sighed. "Look, vesper, I'm just here to make sure you don't die. Don't make me get rough with you."

"I could say the same thing," I snarled.

He smirked, regarding me with crossed arms. Then, with a shake of his head, he rushed at me, opening his arms wide to try and tackle me.

I dodged to the right, letting him barrel past like a bull seeing red. I spun around and shoved him in his back, and he tumbled into the smaller orderly. They fell in a heap next to the fallen IV rack.

I turned to the wall opposite the frozen chambers and saw the exit. Leaping forward, I grabbed the handle and swung the door open.

And almost ran right into a large woman in a lab coat. Without missing a beat, she jammed a needle into my neck and pressed her thumb on the plunger.

I tried to shove her away, but whatever was in the syringe acted quickly and my limbs slackened, went numb. I stumbled into her and the woman grabbed me around my middle, holding me up.

"Go to sleep," she whispered. "That's a good girl."

Another stab, this time in my side, just above my hip. I tried to speak, but my words came out slurred, unrecognizable.

And once more the world went black.

21

IT'S NOT THE FUTURE, IS IT?

The squeaking of wheels over linoleum met my ears. With a sharp intake of breath, I opened my eyes and found myself staring up at a white ceiling. Big glowing rectangles of light whooshed by above me.

I lay atop a mattress, so thin that I could feel the metal supports underneath it biting into my back. I was on a gurney, and it vibrated and thumped beneath me. Instinctively I tried to move my arms and legs, but thick leather bit into my wrists and ankles.

Before I could think to summon my genetically engineered strength, a face appeared above my own. The kind man from the room where I'd been held captive.

"You're going to be a good girl, right?" he asked me.

"You're kidding," I said.

He shook his head. "You wanted answers to your questions, and the boss wants to speak to you. But we can't put you in there unless you agree to behave. Will you behave?"

I thought about saying no. About telling the man to screw off and then ripping the binds off of me and making a run for it.

But I still didn't know where I was, or how I got there, or where any of my friends had been taken. So instead, I kept my mouth closed and nodded.

A door whooshed open just beyond my feet, and I tried to crane my head up to see, only to find that my neck was bound too. So instead I forced myself to relax as the short orderly leaned out of my line of sight, and the gurney moved forward once more.

The squeaking of the wheels faded as we left linoleum behind and instead rolled over what I guessed was carpet. The top of the door frame flashed by overhead, and suddenly the ceiling was much higher up, and tan, and painted with shimmering gold hieroglyphics.

The gurney jerked to a stop and rough hands fumbled with the straps that bound me to the mattress. That done, whoever had escorted me into this new room walked away, shadows out of the corners of my eye. The door whooshed closed behind me.

I sat up, rubbing my wrists, and took in my new surroundings. I was in a wide-open office that was three times the size of my living room back at home. Whoever it belonged to seemed to have a thing for Egyptian-themed decor. There were small, potted palm trees in the corners, and gold-gilded chairs with the heads of ancient gods on each side. On the dark brown carpet I could barely make out symbols in a slightly lighter shade of brown—hieroglyphics that mirrored the ones on the ceiling.

And opposite me, in the far back of the room, was a wide, gleaming black desk, a row of bookcases behind it. Sitting there with hands atop the lacquered surface was the man in the gray suit with the white hair and goatee.

"Hello, Emily," he said.

His voice was deep, authoritative, but not unfriendly. Keeping my eyes on him, I kicked my pajama-clad legs over the side of the gurney and hopped down. The carpet was plush beneath my bare feet, and only then did I realize that the pain that had overwhelmed my body after I'd escaped my chamber was completely gone.

"Ah, yes, hello," another voice said.

I darted my head to the right to find another man sitting in one of the ornate chairs. He was a slender, petite man wearing a too-large suit, with big glasses barely hanging onto his nose and his bald head gleaming beneath light cast from iron sconces on the wall.

I recognized him immediately: Mr. Savage. The supposed grief counselor who had tried to wheedle information out of me after Spencer and I killed Dr. Elliott.

"I suppose I should have guessed you'd be part of all this," I said.

Fumbling with manila folders in his lap, Mr. Savage got to his feet. He let out a nervous chuckle. "I suppose so."

"So what was your deal, then?" I asked. "Were you sent to spy on me? Is that why I saw you with Megan, too?"

Eyes darting between me and the man at the desk, Mr. Savage's head beaded with sweat. "Sort of. We caught wind of, erm, strange reports near BioZenith. I was sent to talk to any child around your age who had been seen acting strangely. But, ah, Vesper One—Emily—shall we? Mr. Handler is waiting. He'll answer your other questions."

He gestured for me to walk ahead, and so I did, rounding the front of the gurney and striding down the center of the vast room to the desk. The man in the suit—Mr. Handler—sat there, watching me with a strange smile playing at his lips.

"Mr. Handler," I said as I approached. "Michael Handler. You're the one who started all this."

He nodded at me. "It's nice to finally meet you."

Squirrelly Mr. Savage rounded the desk and set the

stack of folders to Mr. Handler's right. Mr. Handler's eyes darted to a flat-screen computer monitor to his left, then back to me.

"I've heard a lot about you," Mr. Handler said." He didn't move, didn't unfold his hands or lean back in his chair. He just watched me, his pale blue eyes filled with curiosity. "From many, many different sources, in fact. You have become more than I ever could have imagined."

Shrugging, I walked over to one of the nearby antique chairs and plopped down. I rested my hands on the gods' heads—cats, so, Bast, if I remembered my ancient history right—and crossed my legs. Mr. Savage fidgeted with his glasses and looked back and forth between me and Mr. Handler, but Mr. Handler didn't seem perturbed.

"I never knew so many people would be so interested in me," I said. "I mean, two months ago no one ever gave me the time of day. Now I have whole teams of people, like, obsessed with everything I do."

Mr. Handler smiled. "Becoming an important person changes things. And you are definitely an important person, Emily. You are one of my vespers. And that makes you precious."

Mr. Savage nodded. "Quite precious, quite."

Sighing, I glared at the squirrelly man, then back at Mr. Handler.

"If I'm so precious, then why did you have goons shoot my friends up with drugs?" I asked. "And why did you freeze me in a chamber? Are they all frozen like me and Meg—like that shadowwoman?"

"Akhakhu," Mr. Handler corrected me. "Rebel is what we call her. And no, they are not frozen. They are . . . here."

I leaned forward, resting my elbows on my knees. "So why freeze me?"

Smiling, Mr. Handler shook his head. He chuckled, and Mr. Savage tittered along with him—until Handler shot the small man a glare.

"You're the alpha, aren't you?" Mr. Handler said. "The strongest of the bunch? I needed to make sure the other vespers were acclimated before we worked on you. That took some time."

My forced calm facade fell. "Time? How much time?" My voice shaking, I asked, "How long was I frozen? It's not the future, is it?"

"Oh!" Mr. Savage said. "Nothing like that, Emily. You were out for, erm . . ." He produced a pocket watch from his breast pocket, flicked it open, and peered down his nose at its face. "Ah, yes. A little over two weeks."

I leaped up from the chair. "Two weeks?" I shouted.

Shrinking back, Mr. Savage mumbled, "And three days."

Running my hands through my hair, I paced back and

forth, the soft carpet squishing between my toes. I couldn't imagine all that could have happened in the time I was out— so much had gone down in such a short time even before that. They could have done all sorts of things to my friends, to my family, to bystanders like Dawn and Jared. . . .

Mr. Handler stood up and placed his palms flat against the smooth desk. "Your friends are safe," he said as though reading my mind. "And if you cooperate, you might be able to see them again sooner rather than later."

I stopped pacing and glared into his pale eyes. Eyes that could cast an unearthy glow.

"Cooperate, huh?" I asked. "If I don't you'll, what, wave your hand and break my body into pieces like Meg— like Rebel?"

He shook his head, then walked around Mr. Savage and leaned against the front of the desk nearest me. He crossed his arms.

"I'm not like Rebel," he said. "For one, I am still human."

"Oh, so you're still the same man, then," I said, forcing myself to remain cool. "I heard all about you. You're the pioneer who went to a new world and came back a cult leader."

He laughed. "A cult? No, cults are created by the charismatic mentally ill and are joined by the gullible and needy. The existence of the Akhakhu is not a guess. It is not faith.

It is fact. You have seen them and interacted with them yourself."

"Yeah," I spat. "They sure did a lot to mess up my friends and, y'know, destroy my . . ." My voice caught in my throat. The anger threatened to choke me.

"Oh, you have it all wrong," Mr. Handler said softly, his face falling. "You've been dealing with the insurgents, Emily. The seething, diseased masses that plague that world. They were led by the Rebel, the one that took over your friend." He shook his head. "Poor Megan Reed. She couldn't have known."

I uncrossed my legs and stomped my foot on the floor. "Don't say her name," I said between clenched teeth.

"She couldn't have known," he went on, ignoring my outburst. "None of the fools at BioZenith knew how to distinguish between our true lords and those who would deceive us. The Rebel twisted their devotion to the true Akhakhu gods to make them aid her, and then she took over your friend in whole. That is not the way of our lords."

"So what is the way of your lords?" I asked.

Spreading his arms wide, Mr. Handler stood up straight. "Me, Emily. Or I should say, Us. I am the only living human who has merged with our true lords. I am blessed to provide the host body for his soul, his *ka*. I am his receptacle, his escape from a world that is dying. In exchange, he provides me with power and knowledge that will help propel humanity forward. And at times of great emergency, he deigns to let me use some of his power."

"Praise them," Mr. Savage said, nodding slowly from where he stood behind the desk.

Mr. Handler went on. "People like us, Emily—hosts for the gods and our vesper creations—are the future. We are the brightest stars in a sea of miserable black holes, and we shall lead the way for any who care to follow."

I sat there for a moment. Silent. Considering what he'd said. I had to give it to the man—the words he spoke crackled with promise and salvation. No wonder a bunch of otherwise rational scientists fell prey to him and to the Akhakhu.

Too bad I wasn't about to buy any of his crap.

"So what you're saying," I said slowly, "is that your special Akhakhu—the good ones—just want to possess people too. Only it's a *good* possession, right?"

Mr. Handler lowered his hands. Annoyance flashed for just a moment on his features. "No, that's not—"

I started walking slowly toward him across the luxe carpet.

"I mean, it couldn't *possibly* be that your Akhakhu companion is only letting you have control now—or even pretending to be you—to whip people up into a frenzy

263

about the possibility of being more than human, so they'll be willingly taken over. Like my friend Evan's mom. You know her, right? She went nuts, made up rituals, stabbed a man?" I stood chest to chest with Handler, reaching my arms around his torso so I could slam my hands on his desk. I looked him directly in the eye. "Right?"

He glared at me. I glared back. His eyes flicked away, losing him the win of our staring competition.

The man's expression softened. "I'd like to show you something," he said.

I took my hands off the desk, stood up straight, and crossed my arms. "What's that?"

Mr. Handler snapped his fingers. Startled, Mr. Savage twisted his glasses, then sat down in the leather desk chair. He fumbled with the lid of an ornate gold box embedded into the polished wood, then got it open and pressed the button inside.

A whirring noise sounded behind him. He and Mr. Handler turned to watch as the bookcases that stood there slid to the side, revealing a series of monitors. They showed images from throughout the building—people working in offices, mostly. I thought I caught sight of someone who might be Tracie, but the image shifted, taking the girl or woman out of view.

Mr. Savage tapped at a keyboard in front of the computer

monitor. "Ah, yes, just one moment."

With a click of one last button, the images on the monitor changed. Instead of multiple camera views it was just one, blown up to fill all the screens.

At first I didn't know what I was looking at. It looked like an ancient stone archway with vines and tree trunks growing out of it. But the image gradually became clearer and I could see two rings within the arch, spinning slowly. And the branches and vines were neither—they were inky black, tendrilous wires swooping out and connecting to massive machinery inset on the walls.

"This is my portal," Mr. Handler said. "The one inside BioZenith is inadequate, a pale imitation of the one I discovered here in Volmond that started everything. With our machinery installed around the portal we can pass back and forth between the dimensions, though of course our gods are sadly incapable."

"Why are you showing me this?" I asked.

He turned away from the monitor and smiled down at me. "You'll know in good time, Emily. But first, you must do us a favor."

Backing away from him, I threw my arms into the air. "A favor! How about you show me my friends are actually safe first? How about you tell me why you kidnapped us all, and where my family is? Or better yet, let me go, then

I'll gladly do you a favor."

Mr. Handler shook his head. "I can't do that, Emily. As you've experienced, there are factions outside these walls that have their own agendas. I can't let you fall into their hands, not when you're so important. Now that we know you exist, we can't let you out of our sight. You will stay here."

"But—"

"You will stay here," Mr. Handler repeated, his voice growing loud, thunderous. "And you will give us a detailed account of everything that happened to you from the moment you discovered your enhanced abilities. I must know everything you've seen and experienced before we proceed with . . . well, we'll discuss that at a future time. Once your account is written, then I will give you more answers than I have already so graciously done."

I took in a long, shaky breath. Then exhaled. In and out, again and again, just like with Tracie behind the bleachers.

"No," I said.

"No?" Mr. Handler asked, raising his eyebrows.

"You heard me," I said. I crossed my arms. "And you're lucky I've seen what your possessor can do or I'd take you down right here."

He grinned. "Ah, yes, that's our alpha. The killer."

"I'm not a—" I started to protest.

Mr. Handler snapped his fingers. "Savage!"

The tiny man leaped out of the boss's chair and raced around the desk to Mr. Handler's side. "Yes, sir?"

"Get Limon. Have her assign Emily a new home. And I'm putting you in charge of making her . . . agreeable."

Mr. Savage glanced at me and then swallowed nervously. "Me?"

The white-haired man slapped his lackey on the back. "Of course! Who else here knows her as well as you do? And if you succeed, know that you will have my favor."

Nodding rapidly, Mr. Savage said, "Ah, yes. Thank you. Thank you very much."

The squirrelly faux counselor took me gently by the arm, and I let him. I turned purposefully away from Mr. Handler the cult leader and let myself be led back down the center of the room to the door where my gurney still sat.

"I'll be seeing you soon!" Mr. Handler called after us.

I didn't respond.

RECESS

They called my accommodations my new "room." But *my* room had a bed that wasn't a hard, twin-size mattress covered with gray sheets. My room had a desk with a computer connected to the internet, not a glorified word processer screwed into a tabletop that they hoped I'd use to tell them my life story. My room had DVDs and a TV and yellow curtains and a stuffed toy dog named Ein.

This room—this *cell*—had a fake window made up of a glowing panel that showed different outdoor scenes. It was the only thing I had to watch—while they watched me from the camera in the corner opposite my bed.

Yeah, no. Not *my* room at all.

I was led there by a woman in a suit-skirt combo, over

which she wore a lab coat. Her brown hair was in a bun, and she wore glasses. It was all very cliché of her. While two of the blank-faced guards pointed their guns at me, she undid my cuffs and ushered me into bed.

And that's where I spent the next few days.

I vaguely remembered different people coming to my door and trying to speak to me. But all I did was lie in bed and sleep. And when I couldn't sleep, I'd stare at the blank gray wall opposite me and try not to think about what they were doing to my captive friends or how much my dad and stepmom would be worried about me.

I refused to look at the fake scenery out of my stupid fake window.

I didn't eat at first, even though they provided some pretty decent meals. Even having been in stasis for a few weeks, I wasn't trusting the food Vesper Company would serve me. It wasn't until I found myself doubled over with ravenous hunger pangs that I stopped worrying about potential sedatives in the food and chowed down.

They also let me have a small, private bathroom with a shower and everything. When I got bored with all the wall staring and thinking, it was a nice respite to take off the thin button-up shirt and pajama pants they gave me to wear and climb into that shower, turn on the hot water, and let the jets scald my skin until a timer clicked and the shower turned itself off.

Still, each night when they asked if I'd written anything for Mr. Handler, reminding me that answers awaited only if I told him everything that happened to me, I refused.

Why? Partly because my first instinct was to resist being told what to do, especially by some guy who'd turned me into a Popsicle right when I was about to finally take down BioZenith. I had no idea why he wanted the information or what he planned to do with it, but it couldn't be anything good.

It was also in part because I wanted to frustrate them into giving me more and more leeway to try and woo me into cooperating. Which would give me better chances to escape.

It worked.

After three days of refusing to do Mr. Handler his favor, they let me have a couple books to read. No one ever dared step fully into my cell without a bunch of armed guards— and, I mean, who could blame them—but it's not like I wanted to hang out with them anyway.

They started feeding me five small meals a day, and better food, too—grilled chicken instead of boiled, roasted vegetables, garlic mashed potatoes. And that was just dinner.

Good books and good food. It was actually kind of nice after all the stress I'd gone through back at home. I found myself feeling actually comfortable, adapting to this new life—but all it took to keep me focused was remembering my friends were out there.

I needed out of that room.

The same woman who had put me in my cell the first day came to collect me at the end of my first week in captivity. She introduced herself again as Mrs. Lemon or Mrs. Limon or something like that.

"Enjoying the book?" she asked me from the doorway to my cell.

I stared at her and didn't answer.

Clearing her throat, the woman gestured behind her. A younger man, also in a lab coat, scurried past her, dropped a pair of rubber-soled slippers next to my bed, then scampered out of the room as quickly as he could. He was clearly afraid of me.

"What are those for?" I asked.

Mrs. Lemon or whatever her name was smiled at me. "You've been cooped up in here for days now. We thought you might like some exercise."

I could barely contain my grin.

I nodded in agreement. "I'd love to stretch my legs. Thanks."

I slipped on the funny slippers and brushed past Mrs. Citrus Fruit into the bright, blank hallway. Of course, there were guards with guns waiting to escort me. I'd have been insulted if they didn't think I was worth the trouble.

My entourage led me down several hallways to a pair of double doors, where the entire group stopped. Mrs. Limon and her skittish assistant opened the doors, and immediately cool, fresh air gusted through.

I stepped outside. I was in a big, square field surrounded on all sides by towering evergreens. It was a crisp, clear day, with cottony clouds swabbing clean a blue sky.

In the center of the clearing was what looked like an obstacle course. There were ropes and a rock wall to climb, tires to jump through, pipes to use as monkey bars.

The double doors slammed shut behind me and I heard a click as they locked. As they did, a hum sounded and all around the clearing a thin, almost transparent, mesh glowed with blue electricity for just a moment. The mesh was built inside glass walls that rose high up along the side of the five-story building I'd just exited.

I turned to study the wall of the Vesper Company facility, scanning everything to see if there was some path to freedom. There were lights inset in the wall, flush with the smooth bricks. I saw a few windows as well, but everything was designed so that the walls were a smooth surface— impossible to climb onto. At least for me. I wondered how they'd keep the telekinetic cheerleaders from hovering their way out.

"Hello, Emily."

I spun, startled. Sitting in an old-fashioned leather armchair next to the doors, clutching a yellow legal pad and a fountain pen, was Mr. Savage.

I couldn't help but clench my hands into fists. "What do you want?" I demanded.

He swallowed nervously, noticing my fists. "I, ah, uh, I'm just here to observe," he said. "Don't worry about me. Go ahead, run. Play."

I considered going full hybrid, brutalizing the man, and then stealing his keycard. In the back of my Daytime mind, my Nighttime self urged me to do so. The wolf howled in agreement.

But it occurred to me that if they'd gone to such trouble to keep this square of land werewolf-proof, they weren't going to give the man a key I could easily steal. Which explained the nervous sweat beading on his forehead—he was as trapped out here as I was.

Besides, this guy wasn't Mr. Handler. Maybe I could weasel some information out of him.

"Oh, goody," I said to Mr. Savage. "Recess! It was always my favorite subject."

He gave an obliged chuckle, then coughed into his fist. "Whenever you're ready."

I hadn't realized until that moment how stiff my body had felt since I was frozen, how atrophied and rickety.

I cracked my knuckles and then ran forward and leaped. My hands grasped the first of the monkey bars and my feet swung forward. I let go of the bars and let my forward momentum lead me to the next and the next. I was across in a flash.

I glanced over at Mr. Savage. He scribbled furiously on his legal pad, consumed with detailing my movements. I dropped to the grass.

"So how do I compare to the other vespers?" I called out. "I beat their time?"

"The dev—ah, vespers—all made similar time on the monkey bars. You slightly edged out Tracie and Spencer, but were beat by Dal—" Clamping his mouth shut, he looked up at me.

I gaped back at him. "Dalton? Were you going to say 'Dalton'?"

He shook his head. "No. Not at all. No." My mouth shut and my surprised eyes narrowed into a glare. "Erm, maybe. Perhaps. Yes."

Hands on my hip, I tilted my head. "How did he get back?"

The fidgety man crossed and uncrossed his legs, then crossed them again. He wiped his forehead with the back of his jacket sleeve.

"Vesper 0—ah, Evan Cooke—we managed to capture

him in your home," he finally said. "He came back from the other side in your room, where I gather you last saw him. Mr. Handler sent Evan through the portal to collect Dalton from the Rebel's people. They were told if they did not return the boy, Mr. Handler would kill Rebel. So they complied."

"Are they all right?" I asked.

Mr. Handler shrugged. "More or less."

I let out a sigh of relief. So Spencer, Tracie, Dalton, and Evan were all here too, at least. And apparently Handler had a vested interest in keeping us alive if he made the effort to get Dalton back.

I turned away from Mr. Savage in his armchair and then bounded through the tires, my knees rising up to my chest as I bounced back and forth.

"Thanks for telling me," I called. "You know, like I told Mr. Handler, you answer all my questions and maybe I'll cooperate."

"He felt that you might be more inclined to help us if you didn't know their fates," he called back. "That you, erm, might succumb to the worry."

I leaped up and twisted in the air. I landed with one foot on either side of a tire's rim, facing Mr. Savage.

"He doesn't know me at all," I said. "Maybe the old Emily might have writhed in worry. But after all that I've been through? I just get mad. You don't want me mad, do you?"

He shook his head.

"Cool, I didn't think so. So tell me, who else is here at Camp Vesper?"

Clearing his throat, he flipped through the pages of his legal pad. "All of the deviants have been taken—the vespers of branches A and B."

So the wolves and the cheerleaders.

"One non-vesper is also being held captive. A Patrick Kelly."

"Patrick?" I asked. "Why him?"

Mr. Savage looked back up at me and let his pages flop down. "Ah, well, he spent a lot of time with Rebel's host body, who we've surmised had some sort of cross-dimensional link to Rebel for a time. He may have information that can help us squash the rebellion."

Poor Patrick. To think he only ever got involved in all this because I thought he was hot and mistook him for a werewolf.

I dropped down from the tire and made my way to the base of the rock-climbing wall. Dusting off my hands, I jumped up and gripped two of the hard plastic nubs. My feet found purchase below, and I started to ascend.

"What about our parents?" I shouted as I stretched my

arm high to grab another fake rock.

"They were questioned and released," Mr. Savage said. "They were . . . convinced to let us hold you. But they're safe and at home."

"Convinced, huh?" I muttered under my breath.

I hated that the last I'd seen of my dad I'd been so angry, so unlike myself. And I hated that Mr. Handler and his cultists forced him to let them keep me here.

Once I got out of here, I was going to go home and give that man a big hug.

I surged up the wall, then thrust off with my legs. I flew through the air—and grabbed on to the climbing rope that dangled from a tall pole. Shimmying down, I tried to think what to do with what little information I'd gotten out of my observer.

I walked back to Mr. Savage and said, "I think I'm done for the day."

Standing up, he flung his pen and pad on the armchair behind him. "Good. I hope you enjoyed yourself." He wiped his sweating forehead once more. "You, ah, wouldn't happen to want to give us your account now? Now that I've told you the fate of your friends."

Crossing my arms, I smirked at the man. "Nah."

He blinked at me. "Why not?"

"Well, you see, I was all set to destroy BioZenith, and

277

you guys took that away from me. But I also never would have had to deal with that, would still be a normal girl and my friends would all be safe, if you people hadn't ordered BioZenith to create us in the first place." I reached out and patted his shoulder. "You have a lot more to do to make all this up to me."

"Would it help if I told you that after all the destruction you caused at BioZenith, we were easily able to claim it as a branch of Vesper Company once more?" he asked.

I shook my head. "Not really. But good start!"

He cleared his throat. "Thank you," he mumbled.

Someone must have been watching and listening in because there came a buzzing from the door, then a *thunk* as it unlocked. It opened to reveal armed guards waiting to escort me back to my cell.

I waved at Mr. Savage. "See you tomorrow."

They walked me down the stairs and long hallways and deposited me in my room. As soon as the door shut behind me, I went into my bathroom and peeled off my sweaty pajama clothes.

I twisted on the shower, nice and hot. Then I climbed in and tried to process all that I now knew—about my friends and about the defenses they had to make sure I didn't get out.

I was sitting on the floor of my shower, knees to my

chest, eyes closed as water pelted my face and dripped down my nose and chin. The hot water was timed to only last five minutes before shutting off, and I was determined to enjoy every last bit of warmth I could before I was forced to towel off, get dressed in a clean set of the thin clothes, and go back into my blank, boring cell.

That was when I heard someone's footsteps on the linoleum. Immediately my eyes darted open. Blinking away water, I saw a shadow through the plastic of the shower curtain.

So they couldn't even let me take a shower in peace, huh?

I didn't even think. I leaped to my feet and willed my fingernails to extend into long, shredding claws. Snarling, I tore the curtain open, prepared to attack.

And came face-to-face with Evan.

23

YOU IN?

Evan stood there in the foggy bathroom, appearing no worse for the wear, dressed in the same pale blue pajama clothes they forced me to put on. His blond hair was longer than I remembered, disheveled. Looking at me in all my naked glory, his eyes went wide.

"Oh God," I gasped. Not because I was nude. But because seeing him, knowing for certain that he was actually one-hundred-percent okay, made my heart swell and my inner wolf-pack leader howl with joy. Tears streaming down my face, I let my nails turn back to normal, then lunged forward and pulled him into a sopping-wet hug.

"You're okay," I said. "You're okay, you're okay, you're okay."

"Yeah, I am," he said, his voice muffled by the wads of my wet hair I'd shoved his face into. "But um, you're sort of not wearing any clothes."

Laughing, I pulled away. "What do you care? I thought you'd be immune to naked girls."

As soon as I let him go, he turned away from me, then fumbled for the towel on its plastic hanger. Shoving it back toward me, he said, "I'm sure tons of guys would love naked hugs from you, but it's sort of awkward, so please." He shook the towel. "Just so we can talk before your shower runs out."

I'd been so excited to see him that I didn't realize why he chose the bathroom, of all places, to pop in on me. It was the only room with privacy, and the water would drown out any recording devices. That is, until the timer shut it off automatically—and the people watching my room on camera would expect me to exit the bathroom.

"Are you decent?" he asked.

I wrapped the towel around me and held it closed. "As decent as I'm gonna be."

Grinning shyly, he peeked over his shoulder. Seeing that my lady bits had been put away, he turned all the way around.

"Man, it is so good to see you," he said, running a hand through his hair. "I've been popping between worlds for weeks now, trying to find your room. I mean, we only knew each other for like a day before getting kidnapped, but . . ." He shrugged and looked down at the floor.

"I know," I said. "Trust me, I know. Ever since this werewolf-hybrid-vesper thing started, meeting any of my pack members has felt like reconnecting with an old friend. And—hey, you've been popping between worlds? Like by accident or what?"

Shaking his head, he said, "No. Not by accident. Mr. Handler tried to tell me about how this worked, but it wasn't until he made me go get Dalton that I finally figured out how to control it. Apparently all of us were supposed to have this ability—I was just the only one who turned out like they wanted. No offense."

I shrugged. "None taken. I'm not sure I'd want to go over there anyway."

"So okay," he said. "Before the shower stops. First, they have no idea I can slip between worlds—I figured it out but I didn't tell them. Second, I only managed to find one other person here, and that's Amy."

"Amy?" I asked. "Is she okay?"

He shrugged. "She's . . . Amy. It's hard to tell what she feels with the way she acts. I think she's sad, though. About her sisters."

I looked down at the puddle forming around my bare

feet. "Yeah. I can't believe they turned on us like that."

He nodded. "But Emily, she and I have been talking every day. We're not going to let them hold us captive. And I'm guessing you don't want that, either. We're going to break out of here." He grinned, showing off his perfect teeth. "You in?"

I met his eyes, my gaze firm. "Oh hell yes, I am in. It's all I've been thinking about since they unfroze me. If we can escape your crazy mother and BioZenith, we can definitely get away from these people."

He laughed and raised a hand. "Awesome. High five!"

"Seriously?" I asked.

Blushing, he shrugged again. "Yeah. It's like . . . go team, go! High five?"

I raised my hand and slapped his. "Go team, go."

Just then, the showerhead squeaked and the water abruptly shut off. Raising a finger, Evan placed it in front of his mouth. We fell silent, the only sound in the bathroom the dripping of the faucet.

He mouthed, "Same time tomorrow?"

I nodded.

Evan's bright blue irises faded as his eyes began to glow white. The air beside him rippled, then tore, revealing black nothingness beyond. Every part of his body seemed to stretch, like strands of taffy pulled by unseen hands.

In a flash, he was sucked through the distortion, which zipped itself closed immediately following.

And I was alone once more.

I walked to the mirror above the sink, then wiped my hand across the glass to clear it of steam. I saw myself staring back, skin flushed, hair hanging limp and wet. Just a normal girl, fresh from the shower.

Only not a normal girl at all. A girl with a plan.

For the first time since I saw Dawn and Jared fall at Megan's hands and my old friend be possessed by a shadowman, I smiled at myself.

I still had a pack to lead and friends to save.

And the first step was to get back on Mr. Handler's good side.

The next week was somehow both the longest and shortest of my life.

I woke up each morning to a tray of steaming coffee and whatever they felt like serving for breakfast that morning— usually a veggie omelet or breakfast sandwich. I was never much of a coffee person, but I liked the heat of it in my gut, the way it made my hands jitter.

The first half of the day was spent writing furiously at the word processor, fingers a blur as I zoned out and let every last memory flow from my brain and onto the page.

I pretended I was a fancy writer in some wintry chalet, but mostly that was just so I wouldn't think too much about how real all the events were.

After lunch I was sometimes taken out to the obstacle course—a prize for cooperating—while skinny, balding Mr. Savage watched me and tried to engage in conversation. I did my best to play along like I enjoyed talking to him.

"So, ah, Emily," he asked me, legs crossed, a folded newspaper on his lap. "What all did you learn about the vespers while investigating BioZenith?"

I was hanging upside down from the monkey bars, my knees curled over the poles. With a quick glance at him, I swung myself forward, let my legs go, then grabbed the bar three rungs across with my hands.

"It's all gonna be in my pages," I told him. "Just like I promised."

He chuckled. "How about you give me a sneak peak?"

I dropped to the trampled grass and wiped my hands on my flimsy pants. My clothes did little to keep the fall chill away from my skin, but the exercise and my determination kept me plenty warm.

Turning back to Mr. Savage, I forced a grin. "There's us wolves and the telekinetic cheerleaders. But I know there are more."

He looked at me over the top of his glasses. "You, ah,

know that for a fact?"

Shrugging, I stepped forward to stretch my legs, one by one. "I don't know the specifics. But those shadowmen sure had some crazy technology, huh?"

"Hmm. Yes."

He jotted a note down in the margins of his legal pad. I went back to tackling the rock wall.

After daily exercise and forced bonding with Mr. Savage came my shower. While I washed my hair and let the warmth of the water envelop me, Evan stood on the other side of the curtain and we talked. Planned. They'd attached some device to Amy to keep her from using her tech powers, but they apparently figured out where the keys to remove it were being kept.

"She'll easily be able to blast the door open," he told me. "And then she'll pull you out, and the two of you can free whoever else we can find in here."

Running my fingers through my hair, I let soap bubbles rinse free and swirl down the drain.

"And what exactly will you be doing while us girls handle the rescue?" I asked.

"I'll be making sure the way is clear once you're done."

Afternoons and evenings were devoted to more writing. Sometimes I was so hyper-focused on telling my story that I wrote long after they shut my lights off. My eyes burned from the glow of the computer monitor; my body ached from sitting in one position for so long.

I didn't care. At some point during my writing spree, I decided that if they wanted to know everything that happened, they were going to know.

Vesper Company were the ones who started all of this. They were the ones who allied with the Akhakhu and ordered the creation of all us mutant kids, with the sole purpose of using our abilities to bring the Akhakhu into our world and then put them into power.

I figured, since they were the ones behind everything that had upheaved my life the past two months, it was time for them to stop thinking of me as a "subject" or a "vesper." If they wanted my account, they were going to get all of my thoughts and feelings about what they did to me, too.

I was a girl whose body they changed against her will, and whose life they tried to control.

But the truth was, despite everything, I was still me.

And they were about to get a big dose of what being Emily Webb was all about.

24

I'M TIRED OF BEING TRAPPED HERE

I'm typing this in the last few minutes I have stuck in this place.

Any second now, I'm going to be whisked out of my cell—and then it will begin.

I didn't expect, with what I had planned, that anyone at Vesper Company would actually get to the final pages of my account. Which is why I was so terribly forthcoming.

But just for fun, I'm going to pretend they might. Allow me to switch things up on you for just a page or two:

Hi, Mr. Savage. Just FYI: I'm tired of being trapped here. Hence all the fake cooperation while we hatched our plan.

Yeah, I said hence. What of it?

Just one thing I want to say to you before I finish these pages and send them off to you.

I offered you this: I'd write out a long, detailed report about the events as long as you promised to release all of us vespers, and Patrick, too. You couldn't answer yourself, but you got a call on your cell from whoever was listening in, and you more or less confirmed that you agreed to my incredibly simple terms.

Now *that* wasn't shady at all.

But, whatever. I did as you asked. And now we've reached the end of my story up until now. It's a *lot* of pages. But I think you'll find them enlightening.

And I have a feeling things are going to really get interesting around here at Vesper Company, very soon.

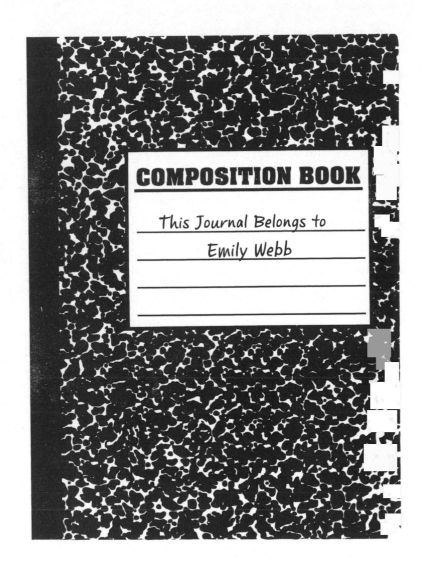

COMPOSITION BOOK

This Journal Belongs to

Emily Webb

25

MY NAME IS EMILY WEBB.
I AM SIXTEEN YEARS OLD.

Before the events of the past two months, I never considered myself much of a writer. Maybe I'm still not much of one. My abilities aside, as a fan of books, comics, TV, and movies, it made me itch all over to think of ending the story with that final chapter in my last account to Vesper Company. The dangling plot threads would drive me absolutely insane if I hadn't, y'know, lived this. I'd be super surly on the internet. *Super.*

So I'm gonna crack my knuckles and scrounge up some pens and complete this story, even though now no one is making me write it.

By the end of that week, I'd written 680 double-spaced pages, separated into three parts. As instructed by Mr. Savage, I found a menu option that said SUBMIT TEXT and clicked it. Off it went through digital space, presumably to the computers of Mr. Savage, Mr. Handler, and whoever else cared to read my words.

The morning I turned in my final pages was the day of our big escape.

I still didn't entirely know why I was being held captive anyway, or why they were so damned interested in me writing down everything that happened.

But it didn't matter to me right then. My story was all told. Now it was time to get the hell out of that place.

And maybe wreak a little havoc along the way.

I woke up that morning long before my lights turned on to signal it was a new day. Heart thudding and mind racing, I lay there in the dark, staring at the ceiling. In the corner the little red light on the surveillance camera blinked, over and over and over.

After what felt like hours, the fluorescents inset in the ceiling clicked on with a buzz and a hum. Tossing my gray sheets aside, I jumped onto the cold tile floor, then strode purposefully to the food slot on my door. Right on cue, a tray popped through with a Styrofoam cup of coffee and a paper plate of eggs Benedict.

I plopped the tray on my bed and sat at my desk. I opened up the file and added one last chapter—a message to Vesper Co. that I had no idea if they'd ever read, though I hoped they would—after I was free.

I sent off the file, then spun my desk chair around to face the door. Leg shaking restlessly, I ate, not taking my eyes off the door.

Then, finally, a shadow crossed in front of the food slot. Men spoke in hushed tones on the other side of the door. A beep as a keycard was accepted by a security reader, then a *thunk* as the heavy lock inside the door unlocked.

The door opened to reveal short, slender Mr. Savage standing there. His balding head was shiny with sweat, and he offered me a shaky smile. He carried a large black brief-case.

"Are you ready to discuss these pages?" he asked me.

I downed the last of my coffee, tossed the cup onto my empty tray, then jumped to my feet. The broad grin on my face was anything but forced.

"I am definitely ready, Mr. Savage."

My good mood lasted only so long.

I realized the day wasn't exactly going to be a breeze when, instead of leading me to Mr. Handler's office with the plush carpet and the wood-paneled walls and the antique leather couches, the gun-toting guards guided me into an interrogation room.

Concrete walls. Concrete floor. Another black camera in the corner with its intrusive, blinking red light. Steel door and table and chair—the first of which was fitted with three locks, the other two bolted to the floor.

And, oh yeah, the chains they attached to my hands and feet after two of the guards shoved me down onto the chair.

The guards left after that, the heavy door slamming shut with a resounding thud behind them. The fluorescents above flickered, and Mr. Savage cleared his throat as he plopped the briefcase on the table, took out the first part of my account, and then produced a recording device.

I raised my hands and shook my wrists. The chains clanged.

"Is this really necessary?" I asked.

"Hm?" Mr. Savage looked up from straightening the pages, then blinked at the sight of my bindings as though he'd never seen them before.

"Oh," he said. "I'm afraid yes. The people upstairs were a little, erm, perturbed by some of the things you wrote. I insisted the precaution wasn't necessary, but . . ." He shrugged, his shoulders minuscule in his oversize suit.

Leaning forward, I glanced over the first page of my report. I WAS HALFWAY OUT MY BEDROOM WINDOW WHEN MY CELL RANG. It felt like ages since I'd written those words. Even longer since it had happened.

"You guys read all of this already?" I asked.

"Just part one," he said, fussing with the recorder. "We separated it into chunks, and then we each wrote a report on our chunk, and then there was a meeting to give our individual feelings on each, ah, chunk."

"Say chunk again," I muttered.

"Hmm?"

"Nothing."

Mr. Savage cleared his throat. "All right. Yes. Today you and I are going to clarify the things in these pages that weren't entirely clear to us."

That was when my mood entirely deflated.

Not only was I not in Handler's office where Amy could quickly find me and bust me out, but I was actually going to be forced to spend my entire day in this tiny, cold room, chained to a table, talking about my life with a weaselly Vesper Company employee.

The only silver lining was knowing I could mess with him a little before my friends completely blindsided him.

Finally figuring out the recorder, Mr. Savage set it in the center of the table, then clicked it on. He shoved his seat back, sending it squeaking over the concrete floor, then sat down.

Coughing into his hand, he leaned forward, looking down his nose at the recording device as though it was some crazy new technology.

"Testing," he said. Waving his hand at me, he added, "Say hello."

I leaned forward and said, "Hi."

Nodding and smiling encouragingly, Mr. Savage waved

his hand again, as if I was supposed to know what he wanted. "Please state your name and age for the record."

I cleared my throat. "My name is Emily Webb. I am sixteen years old."

It was midafternoon when we first heard the commotion in the halls outside.

At first it was just distant rumbles. Thunder, maybe; a storm outside that was raging so hard that we could hear it even in our concrete room. As the day grew longer and we neared the end of part one of my report, though, there was no denying it—something was happening outside the interrogation room.

But even as the noises outside grew louder—the screams of startled guards, sickening thuds of bodies hitting walls and floors—Mr. Savage insisted on finishing the review of my account. Not even frantic texts on his phone could deter him from his task.

Can't say the guy wasn't dedicated to his job.

I barely paid attention as the man read about how Spencer and I killed Dr. Elliott and our first investigations into BioZenith. Leg tapping, I focused on the door, waiting. I couldn't even keep up the faux innocent personality, and every time I was forced to respond to one of Savage's queries, my words came out snarkier and snarkier.

Pages dwindled. Amy was getting closer. I could sense it, sense her power. It wouldn't be long before she found me.

Across from me, Mr. Savage read the final pages. Musky, salty sweat dripped down his head, soaked his collar. He didn't even bother to wipe it away now. The scent of it was strong with fear to the wolf side of me.

Good.

I watched him, stoic, silent, as he read aloud the last pages of the first account. It ended exactly where I wanted it to: the moment this man snuck into my life, pretending to be a school counselor as he investigated BioZenith and the potential that Project HAVOC was alive and well.

"Looks like we've come full circle, Mr. Savage," I said.

My eyes bored into his face as he held the final page in shaky hands, his look glossy, distant.

"Because that week ended the day I met you," I went on. "Or at least who you pretended to be."

Setting down the last page, Mr. Savage cleared a throat. He stuck a finger under his collar and ran it back and forth, trying to let air in. "I apologize for all the initial deception, Emily," he said. "But like I've said—"

I slammed my palms down against the table. My chains clanged.

"You did all this for my own good, yes," I snapped.

Outside, a woman's screams echoed down the corridor—

then fell abruptly silent. Footsteps thudded, then became echoes.

Finally meeting my eyes, Mr. Savage looked at me pleadingly. Begging. "It's the truth, Emily, I swear to you it's the truth."

Licking my lips, I looked the man up and down. "Are you sweating, Mr. Savage?" I asked sweetly. "I think you are. I can smell you. You're afraid, and the stench is totally nauseating."

Shrinking in his chair, Mr. Savage started to say, "I—"

"What did the text message say, Mr. Savage?" I interrupted. Loud. Forceful.

Alpha.

He raised his tiny hands, as though they could protect him. "Everything's under control, i-i-i-it's—"

"What were those noises in the hall?" Palms still on the table, I stood and leaned over, putting my face as close to his as my chains would allow. "Are things not going as you planned? Did it turn out that you and your freak bosses and their shadowmen underestimated us . . . ?" I smirked. Using the slang term he told me the scientists used to refer to us rebel vespers, I finished, "Deviants?"

In that moment, I slipped easily into Nighttime's strength and righteous anger. Clenching my fists, I raised my hands as high as the chain's slack let me. Teeth gritting, muscles straining, I willed every last ounce of strength

I could muster to my arms. Veins bulged on my forearms.

And the chains snapped. They clattered to the concrete floor, useless. Focusing on my legs, I kicked one, then the other, snapping the chains at my ankles as well.

Mr. Savage gaped at me, all the color flushed from his face. Still holding his hands high, he tried to scoot his chair backward.

"Emily, please," he begged. "Please, I—"

Jumping to my full height, I darted around the table so that I towered over the cowering, simpering man.

"You know, Mr. Savage, my friends and I thought about it and we guessed that you weren't actually going to let us go." I put my lips next his ear, speaking almost in a whisper. "Because we know what you and the Vesper Company have been up to all this time. We know all about BioZenith and how we were made and what we were made for. I know that all of the horrible, awful things that have happened have been because of you and the other deluded people like you. And so we're not going to sit here and take it. Not after you made me . . ."

Memories flashed into my head.

Dr. Elliott, his throat torn out.

Dawn on the verge of death, with Jared, crippled, looking on.

Megan smiling happily as a being from another dimension stole her body.

Trembling, I stared past Mr. Savage, my eyes blurring as I stared at the blank gray wall.

"You made me . . ." I whispered again, unable to finish the thought.

With a whimper, Mr. Savage twisted to the side and fell off his chair. Thrusting himself up with his hands, he made a mad dash for the door, his loafers squeaking on the concrete.

And that's when I sensed her on the other side. Listening. Waiting.

Shaking my head to catch my bearings, I called after my interrogator, "You can't really run anywhere, Mr. Savage."

A second later, the steel door buckled as easily as if someone had punched a sheet of aluminum foil. With one more thunderous boom, the door exploded inward and flew across the room, slamming into the opposite wall, almost swiping a terrified Mr. Savage.

Chalky dust from the broken concrete swirled around us in a cloud. Hacking, Mr. Savage backed away from the shadowy figure who stood in the doorway.

Hands on her hips, the figure stepped forward. With an eyebrow raised, she took in the pitiful Vesper Company employee who'd been tasked with gathering all my secrets.

"Going somewhere?" Amy asked.

I grinned. At long last, the cavalry had arrived.

26

LET'S MOVE

We let Savage go.

Not that I was really planning on, you know, killing him. I had never wanted to kill anyone—I still don't want to. I made the man feel like he only escaped by some merciful whim on my part, but I really let him go for the same reason I left behind the recorder and the pages with my account.

After all the work of writing down who I was and what I'd become, I wanted as many people at Vesper Company to know my story as possible.

"We're not going to kill you," I told him before he scurried off.

Amy shot me a look. "We're not?" she asked between clenched teeth.

I forced myself to keep my expression static, unreadable.

"No. Like I told him, I'm not a big fan of blood."

After my interrogator was gone, I took in Amy. I hadn't seen her for a month, not since the day her sisters and parents betrayed her. Physically, she looked the same—average height, tan skin, pretty face, wavy black hair.

But there was a look in her eye that unsettled me. She had always been sarcastic, flippant. In your face if she thought you were threatening her or her friends. Now, she seemed to be filled with an anger that threatened to boil over.

At that moment, I didn't have time to worry about it. I hated to admit it, but I needed her anger to fuel our escape.

Oh, the girl I'd become.

We stepped out of the jagged hole in the wall where the steel door had once been. The hall was littered with bodies— mostly guards, but also a few people in business wear. I took in a breath at the sight of them, thinking for a moment that Amy had killed them all.

A chest rose and fell. Another person stirred, moaning. I let out a shaky breath—they were just unconscious. Good.

Without a word, I stepped over the guard in front of me and headed down the hall. Like all the corridors in that place, it was blank white with glaring fluorescents above and tile below.

As we stalked through the halls, stepping over more unconscious guards and stomping on scattered paperwork,

Amy filled me in on what she and Evan had planned.

Whenever he was able, he'd been popping between the Akhakhu dimension and our own, figuring out the layout of the place. He described it to me during one of our shower sessions—the world over there was half overly elaborate city, half wasteland. When he was there, he could see our world sort of layered on top of theirs.

"Like ghosts or mirages or something," he'd said. "I'll be walking down a street there, but I can see the shadows of trees in the middle of the road. It took a while to get used to."

Though he'd only managed to find my cell and Amy's, by doing this he'd more or less mapped out the rest of the facility and its important landmarks.

Which is how Amy knew directly where to go next: the control room where they watched all of us.

The room was occupied day and night, which is why Evan couldn't look at the monitors himself. But no amount of staff was going to stop us now.

Following the placards next to the doors in the hall-ways, we followed Evan's instructions until we stood outside the control room doors. Distant footsteps echoed down the hallways, fading as people ran. I guessed the scientists in the place had figured out we'd escaped and were getting the hell out of there.

Smart people.

Amy raised her hands, and the steel door to the control room buckled, burst inward. It didn't fly off its hinges like the door to my interrogation room, but it did slam against the wall with a satisfying *clang*.

And we came face-to-face with a slew of guards. As one, they kneeled, aiming their guns at us.

"Don't move!" an older guard shouted. "We don't want to shoot you!"

I looked to Amy, and she looked to me.

"You ready to do this?" I asked.

She grinned. "Oh yeah."

Before any of the guards could react, Amy raised both hands again. An unseen wave of energy burst from her palms and all of the guards fell backward, their guns flinging from their hands. The bays of monitors and computers sparked with electricity, and the lights above us dimmed and blinked.

Gasping, Amy dropped to her hands and knees on the linoleum. I grabbed her shoulders.

"Are you all right?" I asked.

"I'm fine!" she shouted back. "Don't just stand there, get them!"

Groaning, the guards were starting to get back to their feet. Letting go of Amy, I stood up straight, rolled back my shoulders, and thought of Spencer and Tracie and everyone else, huddled in cells, alone and afraid.

And I shifted into Nighttime.

I was a tornado of kicks and fists. I punched one guard in the head, so hard that his helmet cracked. His eyes rolled back in his head and he collapsed.

I roundhoused and knocked another one's feet out from under him, then stepped gently on his neck until the lack of air sent him to sleep.

Two heads clanged together and two more guards dropped. A couple tried to flank me, but they flew backward, and I glanced back over my shoulder to see Amy back on her feet.

Darting behind one of the remaining officers, I kicked him in the back of his knee, sending him sprawling. His gun flew from his hands and I grabbed it by the barrel midair. I swung it, clubbing the man on the back of his head.

In seconds, all but one of the guards was knocked out, a heap of uniform-clad men on the floor. Only one remained.

He was a slender man, and what I could see of his face behind his mask was young. He clutched his gun and backed slowly away from us, eyes darting to look at the open doorway.

"You want to go?" I asked the guy as Amy came to stand next to me.

He nodded, jaw slack as he gaped at me.

I jerked my thumb for the door. "Then get out of here before I change my mind."

Hugging the wall, the young guard kept his eyes on us until he reached the exit. Then he turned and ran as fast as he could down the hall.

We scanned the monitors and used a fire exit map that was tacked on the wall to plot our route. Tracie was easy to find and close by. And I spotted Spencer who was in an adjoining building. Dalton's camera was black, but labeled by his vesper number, and he was apparently on a lower floor of the building we were in.

There was no sign of Nikki or Patrick.

Amy and I decided to start near and then work our way out. So our first stop: Tracie's cell.

Amy and I made our way there easily enough. But with each step closer I took, the more nervous I became. Tracie had only a day to learn to go hybrid before we were captured, and I couldn't help but worry about what being left alone would do to her.

Amy burst open her cell and the first thing I saw were the drawings. Dozens and dozens of crayon drawings taped to the wall opposite the door, making up a fake bedroom wall. Perfect brown rectangles represented shelves, atop which were books with brick red and goldenrod spines.

There was a window plastered over the fake, glowing window that was in all our cells, showing a scene in pine green and midnight blue.

Tracie sat with her back to us at a table in the center of a room. Crayons were arranged in a neat row next to her—sorted in rainbow order, of course—and she drew purposefully on a piece of plain printer paper.

"Tracie!" I said.

Setting down the crayon, she turned to us, blinking.

"Oh. It's you."

It didn't take much convincing to get her to join us. She seemed in a strange haze, but I couldn't worry about it.

We still had more people to find.

Now a trio, we stalked the halls to our next destination: Dalton.

We met some more resistance along the way—a few of the more audacious guards and some of Tracie's old friends, the hovering robots. But they were easily dispatched, especially since they seemed hesitant to shoot us.

Seemed even in escape, Mr. Handler wanted us alive.

Dalton's cell was far north of the hallways where Tracie and I'd been held, according to the map we yanked off the wall. We had to descend a flight a stairs and walk down a long stretch of concrete. The lights went from bright fluorescents to dim red, and steam burst from pipes that ran along the top of the wall. It felt like a set straight out of *A Nightmare on Elm Street.*

Finally, we were there. The cell was at the end of one last dingy hallway, its door old and rusted. It had a metal wheel on the front, almost as if it was some hatch on a submarine.

Arms trembling, Amy reached out and clutched her fists closed, grabbing an invisible steering wheel. Twisting her arms around, the wheel on front of the hatch screeched and turned. A bolt thunked free, and the door swung open.

The cell was padded on all sides—dingy beige walls and floors and ceiling that looked like some oversize quilt. The lights were pale and orange.

And sitting in the center of the floor, torso constrained by a straitjacket, was Dalton.

I ran forward and dropped to the soft floor next to him. I fumbled with the straps constraining him while Amy and Tracie hung back by the open door, watching.

Dalton looked over to me, his jaw slack, his eyes distant, glassy. His red hair had grown longer, shaggy, and sweat plastered it against his forehead. He smelled rank, as though he hadn't bathed in weeks.

He inhaled deeply, his body going calm, slack. He smiled at me.

"Emily," he whispered. "It's really you. I thought I smelled you coming, but I thought that before and it was . . ." His smile faltered. "It was never you. Maybe this isn't you now."

"What's wrong with him?" Amy asked, crossing her arms. "Did they drug him?"

Tracie gently slapped the girl's arm. "He was kidnapped by shadowmen, remember? Who knows what happened to him over there."

Dalton's head snapped to face them at the mention of the shadowmen. His lips moved, but nothing came out.

"Dalton, it's me," I said as I unbuckled one strap and moved on to the next. "It's Emily. We have to get out of here, okay? We need to run."

Clenching his eyes closed, he moaned, "It's too late."

I released the final strap, and his arms fell free. I grabbed the jacket by the shoulders and wriggled it to free him from its grasp.

"What is?" I asked him as one pale white arm and then another pulled out of the long, scratchy sleeves.

"It's too late, Emily," he said, opening his eyes to meet my own. Pleading with me. "They're already here. We've already lost."

Amy peered back down the hallway behind her. "Uh, no one's here. But that doesn't mean we shouldn't move."

Though I was curious about what Dalton had just said, it was more important for us to continue our escape.

I hauled Dalton to his feet, and he clung to my shoulders, even though he was a head taller than me. He stood on legs that trembled like a newborn fawn's.

Half carrying him, we exited the padded cell and went back into the dingy hallway. Amy took the lead, and Tracie took up the rear as the four of us backtracked down through the sublevel.

"They're here," Dalton said again. He leaned his head into the crevice between my shoulder and neck.

"Who's here?" I asked him. "You're going to have to be a little more specific."

He chuckled. "I missed you guys," he said with a sigh. "I was with the creatures for years and years, and they would never let me see the light, but I thought about all of you and about Nikki and I knew you'd save me."

"I didn't, though," I said as we reached a cross-hallway.

Amy looked both ways, then referred to our map. She gestured for us to go right, down a section we hadn't been through yet.

"You found Evan," Dalton said. "And Evan found me. He's a nice guy. I remembered him from third grade."

"You never said who's here," Tracie said from behind us.

Dalton peered back at her and smiled. "Hey, Tracie. You joined the pack. That's cool."

She shrugged. "I didn't have much of a choice. But it's

not all that bad being one of us once you get used to it."

Steam hissed and water dripped, the sound pinging and echoing down the long, empty hallway along with our footsteps. We hadn't seen any guards or robots in a long while. It was making me nervous.

Dalton let go of me, walking on his own now. "I never gave up," he said to me as his cheeks flushed red, his arms bulging with muscle. He was going Nighttime. "I thought about attacking those creatures, but I told myself, *Dalton, no. You are not a killer. Emily said that. So don't kill.*" He met my eyes. "We're still not killers, right? They wouldn't tell me, but . . . is Megan alive?"

The image of Megan's blue, frozen features inside the glass chamber entered my mind.

"You didn't kill her," I said. *I did,* I added silently.

Dalton exhaled. "Good. I'm glad." He reached out, grabbing my arm urgently. "But, Emily, they're already here. The shadowmen, those creatures. Their leader is Rebel. She's the only one who would ever talk to me up until she disappeared. And then the others told me she was here now, and they'd be coming soon."

Swallowing, he peered ahead into the gloom of the hallway. "They kept coming to me even after Evan helped me escape. They kept coming as shadows into my room and watching me, and touching me, and it made me scream and scream. But Mrs. Limon wouldn't believe me. They said I was just traumatized. That's why they gave me the padding."

A lump rose in my throat and my eyes burned. Poor Dalton. Lip trembling, I forced myself to keep from crying. But I did lean over and wrap my arms around him.

"I'm so sorry," I said as I leaned into his broad chest. "It was my fault you got taken. I should have tried harder to save you."

"You did try," Dalton said, hugging me back. "It wasn't your fault. It wasn't."

Ahead of us, Amy came to a stop at the base of a flight of grated steps. She regarded us with a raised eyebrow.

"Uh, yeah," she said. "Whenever we find Nikki, try not to get all up on her boyfriend like this."

Grinning, I let Dalton go. "Don't worry, I've only got eyes for one wolf. I'm not trying to be Dalton's girlfriend. Just his alpha."

Dalton smiled at me. "I knew there was a reason the wolf side of me always told me to listen to you, even when it really didn't want to."

Tracie patted Dalton on the back and offered him a warm smile, then walked past us to stand at Amy's side.

"I'm glad you're all right, Dalton," she said. "But we should probably be quiet from here on out."

I nodded. "Let's move."

We climbed up the steps, the grating cutting into the bottom of my bare feet. With another blast of Amy's telekinesis, the doors at the top of the stairs burst open.

And crisp night air whooshed over us.

I hadn't realized how stifled we'd been inside the building, how stale the air was in the hallway, until I stepped onto rough asphalt and inhaled fresh, cool air. We were in a parking lot behind one of the Vesper Company buildings. A few streetlamps attached to the wall and hanging from poles lit up small spotlights amidst the darkness.

Ahead was another building, several stories high and unremarkably white. That was where Spencer was being held. I strode forward, intending to take the lead.

That's when the alarms sounded. The noise was screeching, piercing, and I instinctively clutched my ears. Small lights attached to the buildings swirled red and white.

I saw shadows moving behind windows in the building across the way, and distantly heard the engines of large trucks rev to life.

Vesper Company was sending in reinforcements.

Amy dropped the map and darted forward, racing across the parking lot to the dark line of trees beyond. "Come on!" she shouted over her shoulder.

Tracie and Dalton started to follow, but I grabbed their

arms and held them back. "No! We're not all free yet. We need to get Spencer!"

Amy stopped and spun around, throwing her hands in the air in frustration. "We can come back for him. But this is our only chance to get out of here."

I knew she was right. The new guards would be equipped with tranq guns now that they'd rallied. If we got captured again, they'd step up the security even more, and then . . .

But luck was on my side that night. I didn't need to make a decision at all.

Tires squealing, a dingy, old gray car veered into the parking lot and raced toward us. I noticed Evan in the passenger seat right away, but it wasn't until the car squealed to a stop right in front of me that I saw past the glare in the windshield and realized who the driver was.

Spencer leaned out the window and grinned at me. "Hey, Em Dub," he said. "Need a ride?"

27

ALL GOOD SUPERHERO TEAMS
HAVE A NAME

Amy, Tracie, Dalton, and I dove for the car. We yanked
open its ancient, heavy doors and piled into the backseat.
It was cramped and we were basically sitting on top of one
another, but hey, you don't look a gift escape car in the radi-
ator. Or however the old saying goes.

"Spencer!" I cried as he pressed on the gas and spun us
in a tight U-turn. "We thought we'd have to come back for
you. Are you all right? Did they hurt you?" I ran my hands
through my hair, almost elbowing Tracie in the nose. "Oh
wow, I missed you guys. I so missed you guys."

He glanced at me through the rearview mirror as he
drove around the back of the building. His smile was lit up
by the blinking red alarm lights.

"I'm good," he said. "And I'm glad to see you, too. But I kind of need to focus on driving now."

Amy reached over and slapped my wrist. "Yeah, shut up. Let the man drive."

We reached a small access road that disappeared into the woods and veered onto it just as the big black trucks of the Vesper Company security personnel pulled into the parking lot behind us. It led to a big concrete bunker, beside which Spencer parked and turned off the engine and headlights.

"Why are we stopping?" Tracie asked.

Spencer and Evan both leaned past the front seats to look back at us.

"It's a dead end," Spencer said, his voice hushed. "We need to get back to the main road, but we can't with all those guards out there." He raised a hand in greeting. "And, hey! I'm glad everyone is in one piece. They wouldn't tell me who was here and who wasn't."

"Me neither," Tracie said. "They were pretty rude about everything, in fact. I still don't even know why they were holding us there all this time."

Evan shrugged. "I tried to listen in on conversations when I was leaping around. But I couldn't figure out much, just that Mr. Handler has a plan."

Tracie tilted her head. "Evan, right?" she asked. "We never actually officially met."

"Oh yeah," he said. He reached into the back, offering her a hand. Tracie shook it. "I'm Evan Cooke."

"Tracie Townsend," she said with a smile. "Nice to meet you."

"You too," he said, pulling his arm back.

"So you found Spencer?" I asked Evan. "What about Nikki or Patrick? We couldn't find them on the monitors."

Evan shook his head. "I don't think they're here. I know they were captured, but they're not in any of these buildings."

"Nikki?" Dalton asked. "They took her too?" His face fell. "They'd better not hurt her."

"Don't worry," Amy said next to him. "If they try, they'll have to deal with me."

"Hey, big man," Spencer said softly to Dalton. "You all right? Evan filled me in on how he got you back. Sounded rough."

Dalton shrugged and tried to look casual. "I'm good."

Not what he'd said when it was just him and us girls. But I let him have his posturing.

I reached forward and grasped Spencer's hand and he clutched it back. We smiled at each other.

"How did I know you'd end up saving the day?" he asked.

"It wasn't just me," I said. "It's a team effort."

"Oh, that's right," Amy said. "You know what they

called our two groups? 'Deviants.' All 'cause they didn't get to observe us from birth or whatever."

Tracie gaped. "I am in no way a deviant. How obscene."

Evan laughed. "I've heard worse insults lobbed at me. I say we claim it! All good superhero teams have a name. The Fantastic Four, the Avengers, the Scooby Gang . . ."

I grinned. "The Deviants."

We spent half the night sitting there in the dark car, catching up and sharing tales of our captivity. I told them about how I was frozen and my run-in with Mr. Handler, and how Megan—ShadowMegan, Rebel, whoever she was now—was similarly frozen.

They were all curious about the possessed girl in the frozen chamber. But again I pictured Megan's silent, peaceful face, knowing what it felt like to have your body turned to ice but unable to imagine what it would be like to have another soul controlling my limbs on top of that.

I changed the subject.

Flashlights pierced the darkness of the access road, but no one came down, and soon we figured that the guards must have given up and assumed we escaped into the woods. Slowly, carefully, we drove back into the parking lot with the headlights off—none of us wanted to go anywhere near the place again, but it was the only way out.

The alarms no longer screamed. There were no trucks in sight.

Spencer drove us slowly around the front of the building and then onto the main road. All of us but him ducked down, our heads in each other's lap. I saw him go tense when another pair of headlights drove by, but it was just someone else leaving the facility. To anyone who wasn't working frantically inside to try and figure out a way to track us down, and who instead was just going home after an insane night at work, we just looked like another employee getting the hell away from Vesper Company.

The Vesper Company facilities turned out to be a sprawling set of buildings on a large campus in a city called Volmond, which was across a bridge from and to the northeast of Seattle. Volmond is home of lots of rich tech companies and so the streets are pristine, clean, and the neighborhoods look like the suburban sets in old 1950s family sitcoms.

Not too far from where we'd been kept prisoner was a new, in-development community Evan had found while zipping between universes. The safe house he found for us? A model home. How very *Arrested Development*. It even had a conveniently unlocked garage in which we could store our stolen car.

Spencer, Amy, Tracie, Dalton, Evan, and I spent the

remainder of the first night together, huddled under blankets we'd stolen off the flimsy beds, trying to sleep. I'm not sure any of us got more than a few hours. The next morning we set about making the place more homey. We blacked out the windows with cardboard and tape we found downstairs so that no one would see us, then we claimed our rooms and did our best to make them warmer, adding towels and curtains to the blankets. Our breakfast was a box of gourmet cookies we found in a cupboard, apparently there to serve when showing off the home.

Thank our crazy parents for giving Evan the ability to cross dimensions, because if it wasn't for him we might have frozen or starved. He was the one who snuck into the corner stores, grabbed a basket of food, then hid in a corner and disappeared . . . only to show up back in our kitchen with goodies to share. He was the one who also jacked us some battery-operated space heaters from a nearby hardware store.

We didn't know when, or if, anyone would come to the house. As far as we could tell, construction was on hold due to the weather. I tried not to think about it, tried to pretend we were just a bunch of kids camping out.

It was just good to be free.

We spent the next days hiding out in the house, trying to lay low and not draw any attention to ourselves. It was getting colder by the day, and sheets of rain came down outside. The grounds around our squatting residence turned to ice and mud. We spent a lot of our time huddled underneath our blankets around heaters, trying to keep one another entertained.

This couldn't last forever.

Most of our time was spent talking. Planning. Avoiding speaking about how we were now a bunch of teen runaways.

For all my bravado and righteous anger inside Vesper Company, now that I was free I felt weirdly lost. Empty. I mean, it was nice to be surrounded by my new friends, and really nice to have Spencer back, to cuddle with him on the living room couch. But for all our talks of where to go and what to do next, and reminders from Amy and Dalton that we needed to find Nikki—and Patrick, when we remembered the poor guy—I could tell we all felt uneasy. Like there was some giant, Old Mother Hubbard shoe hovering above us just waiting to drop.

And it didn't help that I got the distinct impression from my fellow Deviants that they were all waiting on me to make the plan that would save us all.

Sometimes I needed to be away from the others. I snuck off to one of the dark, cold rooms and sat on the cheap particle board furniture and just stared at the walls, remembering the people who made up my whole world before that first night when I found myself climbing out of a window.

Dawn. My beautiful, peppy, social butterfly stepsister who saw a fellow monarch in me despite my old cocooned caterpillar ways. Last I'd seen her she was just stirring back to life in the back of Patrick's car. I hoped she was fine after her temporary coma, that she was as vivacious and full of life as ever. I hoped they fixed Jared's hands, and that he'll continue to be the best damned police deputy/drummer in all of Skopamish, Washington.

My dad. The last he'd seen me, I'd been so angry. I'd never been mad at my dad—well, at least not to the degree I'd been during those last few days before we were captured. I couldn't see a way that I could go back to him without drawing Vesper Company's attention. I didn't even know if he was as all right as Mr. Handler claimed he was.

My home, my life with him, was all warm, sappy memories, and I wanted so bad to go back to him and be his normal little Leelee. He was sort of involved in making me the deviant I am, but screw it, we all make mistakes. I'd have to find him one day. I vowed to.

And Megan. I didn't like to remember her in her in those final, desperate moments before she gave herself over to the Rebel. I hated the visions of her as a frozen corpse. With the exception of forcing myself to write about it in my account for Vesper Company, when I put down every last detail I could remember so they could feel even a small portion of what I felt, I tried my hardest to block out any image of her except for the one I knew before junior high.

She'll always be the young, excitable, exuberant girl with the big nose and the long hair who came over to my house to drink homemade milkshakes and play insane made-up games. The angry, bitter Megan of high school, the shadow version of her when she was possessed . . . those weren't her.

I sat there alone in the dark, wanting to remember the good times, but always ending up thinking about how messed up the lives of everyone around me had become.

Eventually I would give up, and I would creep back downstairs and join the others. We would resume talking and planning and pretending that all of us were fine with being a bunch of scared kids with an uncertain future, with no homes and no families to protect us except the flimsy building we slept in and the family of Deviants we'd been forced to become.

At the end of the third day, someone showed up at the model home.

Dalton was upstairs, sleeping. The rest of us were taking a break from pretending we had any plan other than "attack Vesper Company again and hope for the best." Spencer, Tracie, Evan, and I were halfheartedly playing a game of Clue, which we'd found laid out in the kids' room.

Amy was curled up in a recliner, head in hand, watching us.

And someone knocked at the door.

We all stiffened. My hand stopped, hovering over the little pad used to mark off suspects. We sat still, silent. Waiting.

Another knock. Then, a man's muffled voice shouting, "Hello?"

Meeting the others' eyes, I put a finger to my lip. Then, I crouch-walked as silently as I could toward the front door.

I heard the man on the other side let out a disgruntled sigh. There came a beep, and a few seconds later he began to speak.

"Yeah, it's James Chapman. I'm here to set up for a viewing. One of your people was supposed to meet me here with a key, but—" He stopped talking. A few more seconds of silence, then, "What do you mean next week? No one called to reschedule. I—" A pause. "Mm-hmm. Yeah. Yes, a Katrina does work for me." Another pause. The man sighed. "Fine. No, no need to apologize for the mix-up. It's not your fault everything is frozen. We'll just come back when it thaws."

Another beep as the man clicked off his phone. Muttering obscenities, he stomped off, his footsteps growing quieter and quieter.

Slowly I turned around to face my fellow Deviants, the

man's final words sparking the first real idea I had in weeks.

Quite suddenly, we had a deadline.

And just as suddenly, I had a plan.

"Hey, guys," I said as I walked back into the living room. "I know how we're going to take down Vesper Company and make sure they leave us alone."

Interested, Amy sat up straight in her seat. "And how's that?" she asked.

"You know that old cliché, 'The enemy of my enemy is my friend'?"

Everyone nodded.

I met their eyes one by one. "I say we go back to the plan we had before we were captured, only this time we're going to blow up Mr. Handler's portal. But with the powers he has, we're going to need a little help if we're going to face off with him."

I took in a steeling breath, knowing I had to go through with what I was about to say even though the idea of it made me deeply uneasy.

"We're going to unthaw ShadowMegan. And we're going to let her lead the attack."

28

I GUESS OUR REPUTATION
PRECEDES US

I expected them to, but no one questioned my plan to free ShadowMegan.

I could sense the tension among Spencer, Tracie, and Amy, who had all seen her in action in the parking lot of BioZenith before Vesper Company's forces sedated us, but not even Amy raised any doubts.

Probably because it was the only viable plan we had.

I didn't admit it to them, and I barely admitted it to myself, but part of me wondered if maybe I could still save Megan. She wasn't actually dead, just jailed within her own mind, kept prisoner by Rebel, who Dalton knew, and who we knew hated Mr. Handler.

Maybe there was a way to excise Rebel from Megan.

Maybe blowing up the portal would be enough to cut ties between worlds. Maybe . . .

But first things first.

Evan and Spencer snuck out to the local library to get online. We knew from our escape that Nikki and Patrick weren't at the Vesper Company campus, and neither was the portal that I'd seen on the monitors in Mr. Handler's office. Evan also told us that when he was scouting for us, he found the room where I'd been kept frozen, but Shadow-Megan's chamber was no longer there—she'd been moved.

Which meant there had to be some other location.

The two boys found it easily enough: a towering office building in downtown Volmond owned by Michael Handler. Spencer used his hacker mojo to access city planning files, in which he located the blueprints for the building. Blueprints that showed a cavernous basement beneath the building that had multiple design revisions so that the aboveground structure had enough support.

A basement big enough for a portal, perhaps?

The final step before we made our move was also up to Evan. Spencer, Amy, Tracie, Dalton, and I waited late into the night while Evan took a bus downtown to scout out the Vesper Company tower. We needed to know for certain that our hunches were right—and we hoped that our lost friends would also be found there.

My eyes ached, heavy, as the night drew on and on. I huddled beneath my blanket, vowing to stay awake, refusing to wonder if maybe Evan had been caught. Then, around four a.m., Evan appeared in the foyer.

We all leaped to our feet and ran to him.

"Nikki," Dalton said, grasping at the boy's arms, his eyes frantic. "Did you find her? Did they hurt her?"

Evan patted him on the back and gently pulled himself free. "I did," he said softly. "She's there and she's safe. She's not entirely comfortable, but she's safe."

Beside me, Amy let out a shaky breath. "Oh thank God," she whispered. "Thank you, thank you."

"Patrick too?" I asked.

Evan nodded. "They're being kept in separate rooms on the main floor, which are basically like the cells we were in."

The air in the foyer was chill, damp. The six of us walked back to the living room and huddled on the couches around the heater we'd set in front of the unusable fireplace.

Tracie tilted her head in thought. "How strange they were taken there. Especially Patrick. He's not even a vesper."

"He may not be a vesper," Spencer said, "but today he's an honorary Deviant. But do he and Nikki know why they're being held there and not at the facilities where we were kept?"

"Not really," Evan said with a shrug. "Nikki said they asked her a lot about her parents and yours, Amy. And Patrick said all they interrogated him about was Megan. They both talked directly to the guy in charge: Mr. Handler."

"Our good friend Michael Handler," I said. "He must have been really curious about everything related to Rebel's cult and Megan's possession."

"So why didn't they take me there, too?" Amy asked.

Tracie gave her a look. "You're kidding, right? You think they ever expected to get you to cooperate?"

Amy considered it, then smirked. "You're right. Nikki is much, much nicer than I am."

"We're going to get them, right?" Dalton asked me eagerly, his eyes opened wide, excited. "Please say we are, Emily."

"Of course," I said. Shedding the blanket, I got to my feet. "But we'll plan it out tomorrow—or, well, today. We need to sleep." I met Dalton's eyes. "Tomorrow. I promise."

He nodded at me.

We gathered our blankets and one by one shuffled up the stairs to our rooms. Soon, only Evan and I remained. He grabbed my sleeve as I started to carry my bundle of sheets to the staircase.

"Hey," he asked me softly. "How much do you know about that Patrick guy?"

I shrugged. "Not much, actually. He just sort of always ends up in the wrong place at the wrong time. Also, he's British." Tilting my head I asked, "Why? Did he seem shady to you? Do you think we can't trust him?"

Evan shook his head. "No! No, nothing like that. I was just curious. He seemed nice. Very . . . friendly."

I raised my eyebrows. "Oh yeah. Nice, if a little quiet. Also really hot."

Blushing, Evan turned from me and opened his mouth into an exaggerated yawn. "Oh man, I'm beat. Long day. Time for bed."

"Mm-hmm," I said, grinning at him.

What can I say? Even in the midst of hiding out and planning another jailbreak, sometimes we can't help being a bunch of teenagers.

The Vesper Company building was a glittering tower of steel and mirrors that rose ten stories above us. It was nestled downtown in a small corporate district that had ambitions to one day become a rival to Seattle. At least, that's what the sandal-clad tech CEOs hoped.

On ground level, there was a metal sign above the doors showing the logo and slogan I'd seen so often on letterhead:

THE VESPER COMPANY
"ENVISIONING THE BRIGHTEST STARS, TO LEAD OUR WAY."

They sure did envision something, all right.

The six of us were unwashed, in ratty clothes and stolen shoes. We looked like a gang of homeless kids, which meant the people walking down the streets in their designer frocks and business casual wear completely ignored us.

No one cares to look too long at the unfortunate deviants that roam city streets.

We strode purposefully down the sidewalk and right up to the double doors that opened into the lobby of the Vesper Company building. I was in the lead, so I was the one who grabbed the handles of both doors and yanked them wide open.

Flashbacks to the first time I went into BioZenith through the front door rushed through my mind. Every bit of me, down to my microscopic atoms, was ready to face off with whoever got in my way.

After all that had happened, all that had been done to me, I wanted to fight.

In front of us was an enclosed receptionist desk. She sat typing away behind a pane of glass, as though she was a movie-theater box-office attendant. Weird.

Weirder still: Upon seeing us, the woman went wide-eyed, jumped to her feet, and pulled down a metal shade. Like she'd been expecting us.

Not that I could blame her.

The lobby was covered in blood-red carpet. Emblazoned

in gold atop it was a giant *V* in a circle, a little star at the *V*'s top right corner. Leather chairs lined the walls on either side of us, with low black tables set in front. Beyond the receptionist's desk were doorways and elevators, plus signs that said which floor contained which offices.

"I guess our reputation precedes us," Amy said wryly as she came to my side.

"No kidding," Evan said, then laughed. "Man, who knew it'd be so badass to be a team of runaways."

"Now, now, Evan," Tracie said, patting his shoulder. "We're *Deviants*, remember?"

"Couldn't forget."

Gently grabbing Dalton's arm, I looked up into his sad eyes. "You ready?" I asked him. We'd been practicing going hybrid the past few days.

He nodded. "I've been waiting for this forever."

"All right," I said. Turning to face the entire group, I put my hands on my hips. "Evan, Tracie, you're on Patrick. Amy, Dalton—Nikki. Then we're all meeting in the basement. You remember the layouts?"

Amy rolled her eyes. "How many times you going to ask us that?"

I raised my brows at her. "That's not an answer."

Smirking at me, she said, "Yes, Miss Alpha. This floor. Straight, right, right, left—"

"She remembers," Tracie said, grabbing Evan's arm and pulling him toward an emergency stairwell. "Let's go before the guards come."

The teams went off, leaving me and Spencer alone.

"So, Em Dub," he said. "Where to first?"

I grabbed him by the hand and headed toward the elevator bays. "You and I are going to the offices Evan told me belong to an old friend of ours. Then we're going to find out where Megan is being held."

He met my eyes, concerned. "You mean Rebel, right? She's not Megan anymore."

I swallowed and looked away. I considered confiding in him that I still clung to the vague hope that I could save Megan, but I didn't want to make him worry. Or maybe I just didn't want anyone able to tell me the idea was a long-shot at best. I didn't need my hopes dashed. Yet.

"Yeah," I said. "Rebel."

We strode past the receptionist's fenced-in desk. I could hear her speaking quickly inside, calling somebody.

It didn't matter. If I was right, she was alerting the exact person I was hoping would join the fray.

Michael Handler, Vesper Company CEO.

I pressed the call button on the elevator and immediately a pair of doors whooshed open. We stepped in and I leaned back against the dark, wood-paneled walls while

Spencer pressed the button for the third floor.

One of the golden hand bars bit into my lower back. I crossed my feet at the ankles and smiled as Spencer whistled along to the classical tune playing from an unseen radio. I alternated looking at the lights change from floor to floor, to following the intricate patterns on the ornate oriental carpet beneath me.

Finally, with a ding, the elevator stopped its ascent. The silver doors opened once more, revealing an empty, carpeted hallway. We stepped out, looking both ways, but there didn't seem to be anyone about.

We passed plush chairs set against the walls, beneath paintings of modern art, reading the name plates on each office door until we found the exact one I wanted: the office of Mrs. Citrus Fruit. Otherwise known as Mrs. Limon.

She was in the midst of watching video footage of us storming through the halls of the other Vesper Company campus and transcribing all the details. She barely had time to gasp as Spencer and I busted through her office door, and even less time to react before I slammed her head against the keyboard and tossed her aside.

She wasn't knocked out. But Mrs. Limon didn't stick around to catch up—without saying a word, she crawled out of the door, then got to her feet and ran faster than I'd ever seen a woman run in heels. Well, other than myself that one time.

"Wow," Spencer said as he put his hands on his hips and took in the office. "All this over you, huh?" He grinned at me. "I'm impressed."

I grinned back. "Me too. Well, and a little creeped out. Mr. Handler is weirdly obsessed with me."

Something shiny caught Spencer's eye from a nearby counter and his face lit up. "Ooh, a tablet."

While he went over to steal Mrs. Limon's tablet, I focused on her desk. Papers were scattered all over it—my written accounts, marked up beyond recognition. There were small discs with dates written on them in blue marker, presumably DVDs of the security cameras. Earlier transcriptions of the videos lay nearby with notes from an *MH* written in the margins, scolding Mrs. Limon for not being entirely professional.

I decided then and there that I was no longer going to be an open book to Vesper Company.

On Limon's computer screen, the cursor blinked beneath the jumble of letters her forehead had typed. I couldn't help myself. Before searching the room further, I leaned over and typed in a message to my stalkers.

Something you probably learned about me
watching these tapes: I don't like to lose. So I think
I'm done letting you read what happened to me.
Done letting you watch me from the safety of your
observation rooms.

So I'm going to hit send and let this go where it's supposed to go. Just know, from now on, Vesper Co.? It's you who gets to be in the dark. Let's see how you like it.

See you soon!
Hugs and kisses,
Emily

Unable to wipe the grin off my face, I clicked save.

"Hey," Spencer said behind me. I turned to find him studying the tablet's screen, his finger swiping back and forth as he rotated through files.

"Did you find something?" I asked, coming to his side.

He tilted the tablet to show me streaming footage of a room that looked a lot like the lab I'd woken up in back at Vesper Company. Sitting opposite the door, next to a wall-size computer bay, was another of the glass coffins.

Inside was ShadowMegan.

He tilted the tablet back toward himself and continued tapping its screen. "This says she's on this floor. But there's something else I'm interested in down in the basement level. Something I think will help with the whole blowing-up-the-portal thing."

"What's that?" I asked.

Grinning, he tucked the tablet under his arm and then started to walk backward toward the door. "I think it'll be more fun if it's a surprise. Trust me, you'll like it."

"All right," I said, crossing my arms. "I'll trust you. Are you going straight there now?"

He nodded. "We're running short on time. That receptionist probably has the army on its way. You're good to free Rebel?"

"Yeah," I said, walking to join him at the door. "It's probably safer if only one of us talks to her anyway." Pulling him into a hug, I inhaled his calming, musky, wolf-hybrid scent. "I'll see you downstairs. Be safe, okay?"

"You too," he whispered.

Reluctantly, we parted. He pointed down the hallway to our left and gestured with his head that I should head that way. He went right, back to the elevator bays.

I stood and watched him until the elevator doors opened and he disappeared inside. Then, with a steeling breath, I turned and walked down the hallway to the door at the very end of the hall.

The door was innocuous enough—polished oak like all the others in the hall, with a gleaming brass handle. The etched black placard on the door read LAB 3A.

I opened the door slowly. The lights were on, sterile white fluorescents. The floor was marbled tile, and computer equipment lined the walls.

Directly across from me was the glass-front chamber that contained Megan.

The glass was frosted over, her body a shadow behind it, but I could make out her face. Still blue, frozen in place, though her expression had changed—her lip was curled up in a snarl, her eyebrows were scrunched in.

I shut the door quietly behind me, then walked across the tile to the computer bay next to Megan's high-tech tomb. It was a touch screen, and it showed a cross section of Megan's body—CGI representations of her heart, her lungs, her brain. Everything glowed in various shades of blue, and numbers streamed on the right side of the screen.

Taking a guess, I pressed a finger on the image of Megan's open head. A bubble popped up offering several options. One read: THAW: HEAD ONLY.

I pressed it.

The chamber buzzed and red light flared behind Megan's head. I watched as the ice crystals on the glass in front of her melted into beads of water that dripped down the door. Her skin faded to white and then gradually took on a healthier shade of pink.

Everything below her neck stayed blue.

For a moment, nothing seemed to change. She appeared thawed, but her expression was still that feral, angry snarl.

Then, slowly, her eyes blinked open.

They were not the pale blue eyes I had stupidly expected—no, her pupils were still dilated to the point that black overtook her irises. Her eyelids fluttered and then her gaze settled on me just beyond the glass.

And she smiled.

"Emily!" she cried, delighted. Her voice crackled from an unseen speaker. "Just a moment ago it was that fool Handler looking in on me. Megan is delighted to see you, as am I."

That sense of unease ran through me once again, and I had to swallow down the vomit that rose in my throat at once more seeing Megan's face controlled by another being.

I forced a smile. I noticed a button with a speaker symbol upon it set into the metal portion of the chamber near her head. I pressed it.

"Hi, Rebel," I said. "I have a proposition for you."

She raised a pale eyebrow at hearing my words piped through a speaker into her chamber. "I am listening, child. Speak your piece."

I laid it all out for her, starting with the words I'd used with my friends—"the enemy of my enemy is my friend." She nodded as much as she could, her smile growing broader and broader as I explained how we intended to bring down Vesper Company and the cult leader who convinced a bunch of scientists that merging with Akhakhu lords would ascend them to godhood.

I left out the part about how we planned to blow up the portal and how I intended to free Megan from her possession.

"This all sounds . . . agreeable," ShadowMegan said as I finished.

"So you'll work with us?" I asked.

She attempted to nod once more, then grimaced as the frozen skin of her neck bit into the thawed flesh.

"Yes," she said. "But I must be free of this containment cell."

"Oh yeah. Of course."

I went back to the touch screen and tapped again and again until the bubbles gave me the option for a full body thaw. Then I stood back and waited.

She was like some frozen corpse coming to life. The icy leaves on the door turned to warm condensation as the red light filled the chamber. Her skin softened and blossomed to life, and she wiggled her fingers and toes, laughing in delight.

Her laughter came out robotic and distorted through the speakers. I hugged myself to keep from shivering.

Finally the glass door slid open, revealing the girl who was not really a girl at all. Save for her eyes and the subtle differences in her expressions, she looked like regular Megan once more. Like I'd been inside my own chamber, she was dressed in flimsy blue pajama pants and shirt, and she was barefoot. Her white-blond hair hung long down to her waist.

ShadowMegan grinned as she came to stand in front of me. "Oh, Emily," she said. "You freed me just in time. I feared I was going to miss my own revolution."

Cradling my cheeks in her cold, clammy hands, Shadow-Megan brought my face close to hers. Despite her eerie blank black-and-white eyes, in that hectic moment all I could see was Megan.

"She wanted you to be here with us," ShadowMegan whispered, her breath a hot wind against my face. "I have spent much time in Megan's unconscious mind and have absorbed many of her memories. With each one I've come to feel her love for you that refuses to die."

Leaning in close, she gently pressed her lips against mine. A whisper of a kiss. A good-bye.

She smiled. It wasn't Megan's smile, not exactly.

My insides felt hollow, empty.

I grabbed her chilled hands from my face and tried to drag her toward the door. "We don't have time to talk about this now. We need to hurry."

Pulling free from my grasp, she crossed her hands across

her heart. ShadowMegan's pale skin seemed to swallow the flickering fluorescent light and transform it into a beatific glow off her skin.

"You are right," she said. "There is no time to waste. It is time for the true people of my world make their stand at long last."

And as I watched, stunned, she disappeared.

29

REBEL

I stood there gaping like an idiot.

She lied to my face. She didn't want to help me bring down Handler at all. She just wanted out of her chamber so she could go back to what she was doing before she was captured.

Of course. *Of course.* Why would I trust one of the things who'd been stalking me for months? Who'd stolen Dalton? If only she wasn't wearing the face of my former best friend. If only . . .

I had to pull it together. I gathered that Rebel was fighting her own battle against the upper-class Akhakhu, but their goals were still the same—take over humans.

I could only hope her next stop would be the downstairs

portal. And that even if she wasn't going to fall in line with me, she would be able to hold off Mr. Handler long enough for us to do some damage.

Sneakers squeaking against the tile, I spun in place and then wrenched open the lab door. I raced down the hallway to the elevators and pressed the down arrow.

Nothing happened.

The elevators had been locked down.

Like that would stop me. Pumping my arms once more, I raced down the hall until I saw a door with a stair symbol on it. There was a card reader next to the door to access the stairwell, but I didn't need it. Raising my foot, I kicked open the door. It slammed back against the concrete wall with a satisfyingly loud thud.

Sneakers clanged against metal as I bounded down the steps two at a time, rounding corner after corner as I descended past the doors leading onto the second and first floors. I didn't stop until I came to the very bottom step—and the door that led to the basement level.

This time I didn't kick the door open. Instead, I peered through the narrow window above the door handle and took in the scene.

Directly in front of me, deep in the cavernous space, was the Vesper Company portal. It was just as I'd seen it on the monitors in Mr. Handler's office: a giant metal ring with tubes and wires curling about its edges and writhing up toward the ceiling. Giant computer bays with blinking lights lined the walls.

A quick shift to my wolf eyes showed the portal was alive and active, the scene of the world beyond fading in and out of static.

A shift back to my Nighttime eyes and I looked to my left. Crouched behind a control console just past the door were six figures. I could barely see them, but I made out enough of their features to see that it was Amy, Tracie, Evan, Dalton, Nikki, and Patrick.

No Spencer.

Confused, I looked to the sides of the room. On one side, a few other scientists in lab coats sat at the computer bays, typing commands. Several armed guards watched over them.

And on the other side of the room, huddled on the floor, were five people I never expected to see: Mr. and Mrs. Delgado, Mr. Tate, and the remaining two triplets, Brittany and Casey.

The triplets' parents? And Nikki's dad? What were they doing there?

I didn't have time to think about it because one more person emerged from a doorway behind the cheerleaders and their parents.

Mr. Handler.

He looked as calm as ever, but his strides were quick, urgent, as he brushed past the huddled group and came to stand in front of the portal. He looked through it and I could hear him shouting something, but I couldn't quite make out his words.

I was just about to sneak through the door and join my friends when a hand fell on my shoulder.

I turned away from the door—and found Shadow-Megan standing behind me.

"We meet again," she said. "I see you found the portal as well. You shall have a front row seat!"

I'm ashamed to admit I froze. Even though I'd seen her just minutes before, I still instinctively saw *Megan*, and my brain ceased to work as it struggled to reconcile the past with the new reality.

Before I could speak, ShadowMegan brushed past me. The door behind me creaked open. I could hear Shadow-Megan step through, her footsteps echoing against the metal floor. With the door open, I could also hear Mr. Handler's loud shouting—something about holding "them" off.

Of course. The fight. I had to focus. I had to pull myself together. At least for a few more minutes. At least until this was finished.

Taking a deep breath, I became the hybrid.

I spun and grabbed the handle of the door before it closed. Yanking it open, I darted through, then skidded to a stop.

ShadowMegan strode purposefully, peacefully, toward the steel ring that surrounded the portal. No one noticed her. Yet.

"Why did you bring us here, Handler?" Mr. Delgado shouted. He stood in front of Brittany and Casey.

Mr. Handler ignored them. He raised his fists as he bellowed into the portal.

"You are gods among rats! Don't cower on the other side and beg for my help. Help yourselves and prove yourselves worthy of entering my new world! Beat back Rebel's forces!"

And ShadowMegan kept striding forward, black-and-white energy swirling around her.

"Emily!" Amy hissed.

Taking my eyes off the frantic scene ahead of me, I dove to the left to join my friends behind the control panel.

"Is she with us?" Tracie asked, jerking her head in the direction of ShadowMegan.

I shook my head. "I have no idea anymore. She left me behind, but when she saw me just now she acted like she's glad I'm here."

"Just as long as she causes a distraction," Amy said.

"Hey, where's Spencer?" Evan asked me.

"I was going to ask you the same thing. He left to go gather supplies, I think. He must still be on his way."

Nikki reached over and grasped my hand. The normally pretty cheerleader looked skinny, her eyes sunken, her hair matted.

"Thanks," she whispered to me. Reaching out with her other hand, she clasped Dalton's. "I thought I'd never get out of there."

"Yeah," Patrick said. "Same here. And sorry about the Megan thing again."

I smiled and nodded at both of them, but we didn't have time for thanks and hugs. Not yet. I peered over the console.

In the center of the vast room, beneath the catwalks and wires dangling above, ShadowMegan stood with her hands raised. The aura that swirled around her whipped into a twirling frenzy, becoming a pulsating ball of energy.

And just like in the parking lot outside of BioZenith, she rose into the air, a striking, angelic figure.

"That's Rebel," Dalton whispered. "She feels different." He met my eyes. "She feels stronger."

The cheerleaders' parents dropped to their knees, tears shimmering in their eyes. They raised their hands in the air. Noticing ShadowMegan now, the guards and scientists gasped, standing up from the terminals and lowering their weapons. One of the scientists clutched her heart.

Distracted by whatever was happening on the other side of the portal, Mr. Handler didn't notice her right away.

Which gave ShadowMegan just enough time to raise her hands and twist the energy around him. A small tornado whipped up from beneath his feet, catching his tie and jacket and swirling dust into his eyes. Hacking, Mr. Handler turned just in time to see ShadowMegan hovering above him.

And then he froze in place.

It wasn't quite the same thing he'd done to Shadow-Megan and to me. His skin didn't turn blue, ice crystals did not coat his body. I could see his eyes moving as he struggled to break free. He was in some kind of paralytic stasis—for now.

"Oh," ShadowMegan moaned, the ecstatic sound echoing through the cavernous room. "How I longed to do that. Oh, how I longed!"

"Rebel!" Mr. Tate called out. "We knew you would save us!"

She smiled down at them and gestured toward the portal. Beyond her, the open air at the center of the ring shimmered.

"Of course, my children," she said. "You have been so terribly faithful."

Focusing on my wolf eyes, I let my vision go gray. As I did, I could see the portal clearly—and finally see what was happening on the other side.

The image was clearer than any I'd seen through the rifts and portals before. Through the portal was some sort of vast great hall like one would see in an ancient palace. It was startlingly similar to paintings I'd seen in my ancient history textbooks—pillars gilded with gold, a sunken shallow pool filled with crystal clear water, statues of animal gods watching from the corners.

Only the designs were just different enough to seem wrong somehow. The angles of the pillars were unnatural, jagged in places, and they glowed with electricity. The water was a strange orange hue, and the statues were of no animal I'd ever seen, with triangle eyes and tentacles dangling from their mouths.

And then, shadowy figures began to appear, sketching in the same way I'd seen my mother and Tracie's father appear. These figures were humanoid, like the shadowmen who stalked us, but some wore suits of glimmering metal and giant, ornate masks that covered them from the top of their heads to where a human's navel would be.

And they were screaming.

Other people—*creatures*—stormed through the palatial space, carrying what looked like swords and guns and attacking the masked people. These ones were dressed in ragged, threadbare clothing. Their skin was matte gray and green and brown, and tumorous boils grew from every bit of exposed skin. Their mouths were jagged gashes exposing their rotting teeth, as though their lips had been chewed off.

All of these figures were the Akhakhu. The true form of the shadowmen who had partially breached our world, but had been unable to come further.

Until I'd led Megan directly to the portal, activated it, and let one come through.

In the moment it took me to take all of this in, back in our own world one of the guards stepped forward and raised his gun. ShadowMegan didn't even look at him, just flicked her wrist—and just like Mr. McKinney back at BioZenith, every bone in his body snapped.

"Oh God," Patrick said.

No one else made a move as ShadowMegan continued to spin, eyes open now as she studied the people below her.

"You don't need to fight me," she said warmly to the huddled scientists and remaining guards. "Mr. Handler must have been leading you on with the promise of ascendance for years now, but never delivered. Follow me and an Akhakhu *ka* shall be yours to share today. I will give you what you earned!"

The guards and scientists looked at one another. Then

the woman who clutched her chest upon seeing Shadow-Megan stepped forward. The one of the guards, and another and another until all of Handler's people were crowded at ShadowMegan's feet.

Legs trembling, Amy looked over at me. "What do you want to do, Miss Alpha? This chick is serious. She's going to start bringing over shadowmen."

Licking my lips, I said, "I know. I . . . I don't know yet. We can't just assault her outright. You saw what she did to that guard. Just . . . let me think."

Amy tsked and looked back to the scene in front of the portal. "Whatever. Just remember, this was all your idea."

Behind ShadowMegan, on the other side of the portal, I could see the violent revolt coming to an end. The masked Akhakhu must have been taken by surprise. They all lay dead on the tiled floor, slain by the ugly, boil-covered creatures. Brown-black blood drained from their lifeless bodies, flowing into the orange pool like an oil slick.

One by one, the mutated Akhakhu dropped the weapons they used to murder the masked Akhaku and came to stand in front of the portal. They stood still, waiting. Watching.

"There is no need to fight me," ShadowMegan said to the acolytes assembled at her feet. "Soon we will all be as one. And you will become more than you ever thought possible." Raising her arms, her energy bubble moved toward the cheerleaders' parents. "Please," she said to them. "Come to the portal. With the vespers here, we can interact with my former world, and we can merge."

Bowing their heads, Mr. and Mrs. Delgado and Mr. Tate left a bewildered Brittany and Casey behind and walked to the platform on which the portal device was installed.

Amy leaped up, mouth open as though ready to shout. Nikki and Tracie each grabbed an arm and hauled her down.

Frantic, Amy grabbed me by the wrist and yanked me toward her. "We have to do something," she hissed. "I know our parents went crazy, but that doesn't mean we should let them get possessed!"

I closed my eyes and nodded. Yes. I had to focus. I had to stop losing myself in the face of all . . . *this*. I wasn't just Emily Webb anymore. I was the alpha. They were counting on me.

"Nikki, Amy," I said, opening my eyes once more. "Brittany and Casey obviously sided with your parents back on the night we were going to attack BioZenith, right?"

Amy snorted. "Yes, the idiots. Casey was brainwashed by them the whole time, and Brit just got scared."

"Can you get them back on our side?" I asked.

Nikki and Amy looked at each other, nodded, then looked back at me.

"Dalton and Evan, I need you to hang back here and act as backup. I'm going to go in to talk to Megan alone. Megan—I mean, Rebel—seems to like me because Megan had memories of liking me. Just wait for my signal."

Licking my lips, I dared to poke my head back up. At the portal, the three adults held their hands up, waiting. I could see the first shadowy limbs of Akhakhu slipping through.

"What about me?" Tracie asked. "Should I be backup as well?"

I shook my head. "No, I need you to get Patrick out of here. He doesn't have powers, so he's useless to us." I leaned to the side to meet his eye. "No offense."

He raised his hands. "None taken. I am fine with getting the bloody hell out of here."

Tracie scowled. "Why can't I stay and fight? I have a knack for it."

I grinned at her and patted her shoulder. "I never said you wouldn't be fighting. There's bound to be guards upstairs by now. Try to convince them to evacuate the place with one of your presidential speeches. Or make them chase you. One of those."

She pursed her lips and ran her hands over her lap, patting the wrinkles out of her stretch pants. "I suppose I can do that."

Moans of ecstasy and pain echoed from beyond the

control panels. Just how Megan had sounded in the woods when I offered her up to the being that now possessed her.

The cheerleaders' parents were being taken over. Rebel was bringing over an army from the other side.

And once she was done, who knew what she would do next.

"Ready?" I asked.

Tracie, Nikki, Amy, Dalton, and Evan all nodded.

With a deep breath, I stood to my full height and looked up at the hovering creature that had once been Megan. Her back was to me now, and I could see her clapping in glee as the Delgados and Mr. Tate convulsed with dark energy.

Summoning up all the strength that Daytime, Nighttime, and the wolf could give me, I said, "Let's do this."

30

GO IN PEACE, CHILD

On my commanding wave, Nikki and Amy made a break across the room to Brittany and Casey. The determined redhead and the wild-haired triplet had their hands raised, preemptively blocking the other girls from using their powers. I could hear Brittany's and Casey's surprised shouts, but I couldn't worry about them.

ShadowMegan was still mostly aimed away from us. In front of her, on the platform, the Delgados and Mr. Tate lay on the floor, gyrating and running their hands over their abdomens, their chests. I could see the vaguest of auras around all three of them, the beginnings of the massive energy that ShadowMegan had summoned around her.

They were fully possessed.

Beckoning with her hands, ShadowMegan gestured toward the guards and scientists who now followed her. Enraptured, the five of them stepped over the fallen guard's broken body as though he wasn't there and took their place in front of the portal. Two of the guards and one of the scientists were full on crying, the tears making tracks to the corners of their upturned lips.

ShadowMegan followed the five men and women with her eyes, her energy orb moving to carry her closer to the portal.

"Yes," she sighed. "Yes, my children. Join with us. Become more than you ever dreamed. Lead yourselves to salvation!"

"Now," I whispered to Tracie once ShadowMegan's back was completely turned to us. She took Patrick by the arm and raced out through the stairwell door.

Behind us, a chorus of ecstatic wails rose up from the portal. The guards and the scientists had begun absorbing the Akhakhu's souls.

Dalton squeezed my shoulder. "Good luck," he whispered.

"Yeah," Evan said, nodding his blond head. "We'll be here when you need us."

I smiled at both of them. "Thanks. See you soon."

Slowly, I stalked around the computer bay, taking in

the scene in front of me. The swirling energy ball of white and black still carried ShadowMegan high above the floor. At the portal, the adults formerly known as the Delgados and Mr. Tate now stood to their full heights. Like Shadow-Megan, the color had seeped from their eyes. Their posture was unnaturally stiff, their every movement quick, jittery. Each one had an incredibly wide smile on his or her face.

The three guards and the scientists were just getting to their feet as well. As they did, they stretched out their limbs, their unnatural eyes wide with wonder as they felt and studied their new bodies.

Mr. Handler still stood frozen in front of the portal, forced to watch as his former employees became tools of the Rebel.

ShadowMegan gulped back sobs as she watched her followers rise. Shimmering black tears fell from her eyes, but they weren't real tears; as they reached her chin they swirled away from her skin like smoke.

"After so long," she intoned. "After all we have been through and all we have fought for, we are finally here. My generals, this is only the beginning. We must find more hosts. We must allow the true, honest Akhakhu the same chance to escape our world that we have been given.

"What did you do to my parents?" one of the triplets screamed.

I looked across the room to see one of them run from the other cheerleaders, bounding over grated steps to stand beneath ShadowMegan. Only when she got close could I tell who it was, and only by the waves in her hair: Brittany.

She was trembling all over, her chest heaving as though she was hyperventilating. "This isn't what they wanted!" she shouted up at ShadowMegan between gasps. "If I'd known this is what would happen, I'd never—" *Gasp. Gasp.* "I'd never have gone along with them."

ShadowMegan smiled down at the girl. Not saying a word, she gestured toward the possessed adults—the ShadowGenerals. The two who were formerly her parents came to stand on either side of Brittany. Her former father took her hand and squeezed it. Her mother caressed the cheerleader's cheek with the back of her hand. Both of them smiled at her lovingly.

"Your parents are not gone, child," ShadowMegan said. "They still love you. There is so much love in all of us."

The ShadowDelgados grasped Brittany by the arms in one swift, synchronized move. They yanked her arms behind her back.

"But," ShadowMegan said with a sigh and a shake of her head. "But, but, but. Our timeline is too delicate to risk dissidents from stopping us. Go in peace, child."

Before Brittany could even think about struggling,

ShadowMegan wiggled her fingers at the cheerleader.

I tensed to run, to leap and save her. But it all happened so fast.

The air shimmered around Brittany. Then it boiled.

Brittany howled.

"No!" I heard Amy scream.

And then the distortion in the air dissipated. Where Brittany had stood were now *two* Brittanys. One was the pristine, pale form of the girl, only she had gone entirely slack, the life drained from her. The other was an inky black facsimile.

Both Brittanys fell to the ground. The human version crumpled into a lifeless rag doll. The shadow figure exploded into a cloud of dust that swirled in the air.

Nikki, Amy, and Casey gaped from their corner. For a moment they didn't move—but I could see Amy's hands clenching, her lips curling into a snarl.

I had to stop her.

"Megan!" I shouted.

The pulsating sphere of energy sparked to life and ShadowMegan spun in the air to face me. Her eyes went wide and her smile broadened at seeing me.

"Emily!" she exclaimed with a delighted clap of her hands. "Oh, we were hoping you'd stay to bear witness. Megan is so very happy to see you."

Raising my hands to show I meant no harm, I took slow, purposeful steps toward her.

"And I'm happy to see her so happy," I said. "And . . . powerful. Tell her she looks as beautiful and amazing as she always wanted."

ShadowMegan laughed gently. "I don't need to tell her, child. She hears you."

Stopping just in front of and beneath the energy ball, I lowered my hands. Electricity crackled over my skin and I could feel the fine hairs on my arms rising.

"May I . . . may I hug her?" I asked. "I want to feel closer to her. Please. We've been apart too long."

The crackle of energy in the air faded as the pulsating ball began to fade and ShadowMegan drifted back to the ground. Her long white-blond hair whipped around her face and body, the girl caught in a windstorm only she could feel. Finally ShadowMegan was on even ground again and no longer shielded by her powers.

More of the glittering black, smoking tears made lines down ShadowMegan's face. Spreading her arms wide, she came to embrace me. I let her envelop me in her cold, inhuman arms, and I hugged her back, fighting back the revulsion and horror and immense sadness that swirled nauseously in my gut.

As ShadowMegan nuzzled her head into my neck, I

looked past the robotic forms of the Delgados still standing above Brittany's body to the three cheerleaders. Doing my best to speak with my face, my eyes darted between them and the stairwell door.

Amy had other ideas.

Arms straight out and palms aimed in front of her, she stomped down the grated stairs and directly toward her possessed parents standing before her. Nikki hesitated, then followed, raising her hands as well.

And the ShadowDelgados flew.

Neither made a sound as they flipped into the air, then slammed back down, head first, against the metal floor at the feet of frozen Mr. Handler. They met the ground with sickeningly loud thuds, and the two adults went unconscious.

The dark auras around them pulsated and I saw shadowy hands trying to pull free from their human limbs, but it was as though they were trapped in a tar-filled pit. Strands of inky blackness pulled the hands back inside their new bodies, which, it appeared had become prisons.

Amy and Nikki immediately turned their attention to the remaining six ShadowGenerals.

And as ShadowMegan realized something was happening, I turned my attention back to her.

Concentrating, I forced my fingers to elongate, for

my nails to stretch into the deadly black claws. With an anguished cry, I dug my claws into ShadowMegan's back, each daggerlike nail slicing through her flesh and between her ribs.

Gasping in surprise, ShadowMegan pulled away. The look of stunned betrayal on her face was all Megan, and inside I winced.

Couldn't think about it.

Snatching her arms by the wrists, I twisted them so that she couldn't aim her fingers at me, couldn't boil me alive or make all of my bones snap. Then, with a primal shout, I head-butted her in her chest.

The girl—the Akhakhu—barreled away from me, lost her footing, and fell to her back. Behind her, Nikki and Amy flipped and dodged killing blows from the Akhakhu possessed adults, flinging them aside like trash when they had the chance to focus and use their powers.

At my feet, Megan—Rebel! I had to remind myself—groaned. I had to be more than hybrid to finish this.

I had to be the wolf.

Deep breath. Eyes closed. *Change,* I commanded myself.

Like waves of grain, sleek brown-and-black fur rippled over my skin, covering my exposed flesh and disappearing beneath my sweater. As it did, my legs lengthened and my arms stretched longer, my muscles bulging and tightening, filling with animal strength. I kicked my shoes off just as my feet burst into claws.

The bones in my face came apart like a jigsaw puzzle, then the pieces rearranged. My mouth and nose pushed forward, becoming a long snout. My ears rose to the top of my head. My eyes shifted farther apart.

And sharp, rigid fangs filled my jaw.

The world went gray. The auras surrounding the fighting ShadowGenerals and Megan were clear now, like there was too much Akhakhu soul and it was overflowing from their human hosts. Through the portal I could see more of the disfigured Akhakhu standing, waiting, watching.

No time to worry about it. ShadowMegan was catching her bearings. I let the entirety of my Daytime and Nighttime personas fade away—except for the strength I needed to keep Wolf Me's primal fear of the shadowmen at bay.

Arching back and aiming my snout at the ceiling, I let out a long, loud howl that echoed throughout the cavernous room. The ShadowGenerals and the cheerleaders stopped fighting, momentarily stunned by my sudden transformation.

Out of the corner of my eye, I saw Casey Delgado taking the opportunity to slip toward the stairwell.

Didn't matter. We would worry about her later.

Filled with renewed energy, I focused on ShadowMegan.

Growling, I leaped. My clawed feet landed heavily on Shadow-Megan's thighs, digging into her flesh and pinning her to the ground. Crouching down, I held both of her arms down as well, then opened my jaws wide.

"Wait!" ShadowMegan screeched. "Emily, wait! You need me!"

I hesitated. For just a second, yeah, but still. I hesitated.

Nodding her head vigorously, ShadowMegan went on, her words spitting out rapid fire. "Look through the portal, Emily. We have your mother. Your flesh and blood. If you hurt me, my people are commanded to kill her. And I don't want that. No, no, Emily. I just want peace. I just want *love.*"

Snarling, I snapped my head up and looked through the portal.

And saw my mother, short and curvy and disarmingly young, held by the ragged-dressed Akhakhu holding sharp swords to her neck.

"You see her, yes?" she wheezed. "She can't come home, poor woman, but her life can be spared."

My mother—Caroline Webb. The one who had made me like this.

The one who'd made me an alpha, a leader.

I wanted to keep hating her. But white-haired, goateed Mr. Handler stood on our side of the portal, mere feet from her. The one who was truly behind this all. My mother had been manipulated just like all the others.

And even though I never expected that I'd see or speak to her again, I knew I could not stand by and watch her throat slit by an otherworldly being.

"Last chance, Emily," ShadowMegan said. "Will you let me go?"

Nodding my big, wolfish head, I slackened my grip on Megan's possessed arms. Rising to my full height, I stepped off of her.

"Good girl," ShadowMegan said. She stood and looked herself over. Blood gushed from her legs, and I could see it dripping on the floor behind her from the wounds in her back. But she seemed to think she was fine.

Beckoning me with her finger, she turned and said, "Come." Like I was a dog. And stupidly acting the part, I followed her past her fallen generals to step atop the platform. With each step I took, I willed myself to become human once more.

By the time I was face-to-face with my mother, all that remained of my wolf form were my eyes. She met my gaze, thankful. Her lip trembled. I merely nodded, then looked away.

ShadowMegan's back was momentarily to me. Meeting Nikki's face I mouthed, "Go." She gave me an exasperated, desperate look, but I shook my head and mouthed, "Trust me."

As quietly as they could, Nikki and Amy began to back off the platform.

Smiling at me, ShadowMegan waved at her tumored followers. With a flourish of her hand, she commanded her soldiers on the other side to let her go.

Behind me, I heard Dalton roar. I turned just in time to see him bound over the computer console and barrel through the room toward us. My eyes wide, I opened my mouth to shout at him to stop—I hadn't signaled for him, I was sure of it.

Before I could get a word out, he slammed into an unseen wall and flew wildly backward. His head thunked against the metal floor, hard, and he didn't move.

But it wasn't ShadowMegan who'd unleashed her powers on him.

Mr. Handler had broken free of his stasis.

BOOM

"Dalton!" Nikki cried.

ShadowMegan and I turned to see Amy and Nikki almost through the stairwell door. Even though Amy desperately tried to pull Nikki through, the auburn-haired girl yanked herself free and raced across the room. She skid to her knees as she came to Dalton's side.

"Dalton," she said. "Dalton! Oh God, are you all right?"

Wheezing, Dalton grabbed for her, and she ran her hands through his hair.

ShadowMegan raised her fingers.

"No!" I shouted, smacking her hand down.

The Akhakhu snapped her head to look at me. Her smiles, her kind eyes—both were gone now. Her dark pupils expanded, filling the entirety of her eyes with inky black-ness.

"This girl interfered with my soldiers!" ShadowMegan shouted. Gesturing at the fallen ShadowGenerals around us, she added, "And her boyfriend would try and attack me! I would grant both of them a quick death only because she did not kill anyone. Otherwise I would not grant such mercy."

"Now, now, Rebel," Mr. Handler said. Straightening his tie, he came to stand between us. "Always so quick to violence. And you wonder why we find your people so ter-ribly savage." He nodded to me. "Hello again, Emily."

Looking between the two possessed humans, confused, I said, "Hi. Sorry to bust in like this. We Deviants tend to be a nuisance."

Mr. Handler tsked. "I so hate that word. 'Deviants.' I don't know which of my scientists coined the term for you vespers, but I suspect Limon. I'll have to have a chat with her."

"I see you managed to break free of my bindings, Seth," ShadowMegan spat as she stepped toward us. "Oh, I'm sorry, you're going by Handler these days."

"I *am* Handler," the man said. "Seth and I share this body. It is not our way to possess as you do, Rebel."

She barked a laugh. "There's no need to lie, Handler.

None of your cultists is here to hear it."

I peered past Mr. Handler. Quietly, Nikki and Dalton crouched and ran back to the computer bay, where they joined a waiting Evan and Amy. Good. They were out of sight for now.

Arms behind his back, Mr. Handler began to pace. "There is no need for us to fight, Rebel. Your people clearly won the battle beyond my portal, and for that you have earned my respect. We have underestimated you. Perhaps you are worthy of sharing in our plan, after all."

ShadowMegan crossed her arms. "What are you saying?"

"I am proposing," Mr. Handler said, stopping to stand face-to-face with the possessed girl, "that we work together. Starting with ascending our good friend Emily."

I took a step back and raised my hands. "I'm sorry, what? No, I'm not here for that. You know this."

Mr. Handler turned to me now. "Oh, I know you think that's not why you're here. Perhaps you have some grand notion of destroying my building after your failed terrorist attack against BioZenith."

I didn't respond.

"I never told you why I held you in captivity for so long, did I?" he asked me. Not waiting for an answer, he went on. "Long ago, when I commissioned your creation,

I considered the vespers to be tools. Precious tools, yes, but nothing more—just a means to an end.

"But I got to know you through your pages, Emily. And through my own observations. Just as I feel I've come to know Megan and Rebel through my studies of them. Though once I considered the idea of further empowering a vesper body by allowing a *ka* inside, I have changed my mind. What more fitting a vessel could there be for our most well-regarded Akhakhu leaders than one so empowered as yours?"

"Oh!" ShadowMegan said, clapping her hands. "What a delightful idea! Emily, you can become a host!"

"No," I said.

"What?" Handler and ShadowMegan said at the same time.

Crossing my arms, I came to stand between the two possessed humans and the bay behind which my friends still hid.

"You heard me," I said. "No. I refuse. You were right, Mr. Handler, I came here for two reasons. First, to blow this portal the hell up." I glared into ShadowMegan's eyes. "And second, to tear you out of my friend's body and watch your soul die."

ShadowMegan's face twisted in rage. Her hand twitched as though she was fighting to raise it and was meeting resistance. I waited for her killing fingers to rise and for my bones to twist beneath my skin.

"This one begs for your life," ShadowMegan gasped after a moment. "And I cannot stand the screams. That is the only reason I let you live, the *only* reason I give you any concessions at all." Stepping closer, she lowered her voice to a terrifying hiss. "But don't test me, girl. I have been at the forefront of a civil war for decades. This budding alliance with the upper class is the culmination of my life's work. No *vesper*"—she snorted, the word disgusting to her—"will ruin this for me!"

"I'm sorry to hear that," a voice said behind me.

Spencer.

ShadowMegan, Handler, and I all turned to find the short, adorable guy I was in an awful lot of like with strutting toward us from an open doorway on the wall. Hovering above his head were two dozen of the spherical robots that had given us so much trouble. But when Spencer stopped walking midway through the room, the robots stopped with him.

He'd reprogrammed them.

Spencer flashed me a quick grin and a wink. I couldn't help but smile back.

"You," ShadowMegan spat.

"Now, now," Mr. Handler said, stepping forward and

placing a hand on her shoulder. "Remember, the vespers are to be prized."

ShadowMegan did not take her eyes off of him. "We don't like you."

Shrugging, Spencer crossed his arms. "There's not much I can do about that. But I do want you to know I'm really sorry about what you and your people had to go through. It sounds like you've been lorded over by powerful people who let you rot while they hid in palaces. And that's an awful way to live."

"Her people made their own choices," Mr. Handler said, his tone rising.

ShadowMegan pursed her lips, listening.

Spencer took a step forward, focused solely on the possessed girl. "As sorry as I feel for you, we can't let the Akhakhu's escape from your awful world come at the cost of possessing humans. We're individuals, and we have to fight for that. You would do the same."

Mr. Handler sighed in exasperation. "Do you think you would be standing there right now if you weren't granted gifts by our Akhakhu lords? Your individuality is an illusion. They have observed us through the veil between our worlds for thousands of years. Most humans do nothing of any importance, strive to do nothing but get through each day, until one day they die and in a few years are completely forgotten. Once, long ago, the Akhakhu even lorded over humankind—our silly, simple kind. It is time that we leave our dying world and come take our place back here once more. Only by giving yourselves over to our salvation will you be more than just one speck of dust among billions as the timeline of life continues ever forward."

His words hung in the rafters, echoing over and over until there was nothing but silence.

"Oh," Spencer finally said. "Heavy stuff. In the meantime, I'm going to blow your portal the hell up."

I don't know how he did it—a voice cue, maybe—but as soon as he said the words, all two dozen of the robotic orbs shot forward. They zipped over our heads in a blur, ShadowMegan, Handler, and I instinctively ducking. With loud, echoing clangs, the orbs attached themselves to the ring around the portal and to the computer bays.

"No," ShadowMegan roared, her hands raising, her fingers pointing at Spencer. "You will not do this! I need the portal!"

"Aaaargh!" someone screamed from the bays to my right.

I looked over just in time to see Evan, Amy behind him. While I'd distracted Handler and ShadowMegan, the two of them must have snuck around to our side.

His eyes narrowing into the purposeful glare I'd last

seen in the woods on the way to my house so long ago, Evan carried himself low like a linebacker and barreled toward ShadowMegan. He tackled her, his arms around her midsection. The two of them slammed down against the floor at Mr. Handler's feet.

"Nikki!" Amy shouted across the room. "Go already!"

From the bays near the stairwell, Nikki did as she was told. Standing to her full height, she motioned with her hands, and Dalton rose with the power of her telekinesis. Clutching his head, Dalton ran to Nikki's side and they took off through the doorway.

"You little vespers have *tricks*!" ShadowMegan shouted as she got the upper hand and slammed Evan bodily against the hard metal floor. He moaned, his eyes rolling into the back of his head.

Just as ShadowMegan raised a hand, I walked up behind her and backhanded her across the side of her face. The force of my blow sent her flying. She landed with an "Oof!" and lay facedown, perfectly still.

Mr. Handler stood above her, shaking his head. "Always so violent. So messy."

With one eye on Handler, I reached out and gave Evan a hand up. Groaning, he started to climb to his feet. "Thanks. She's stronger than she looks."

Spencer ran up to us. As he did, Mr. Handler stepped

over ShadowMegan, his hands behind his back once more. "I see you managed to reprogram my robots," he said to Spencer. "Impressive, especially considering the time frame you had to accomplish the task. Such a fine mind. Too bad it must go to waste."

"What—" he started to say.

Before any of us could move or think, ShadowMegan rose to her feet. "May I?" she asked Mr. Handler, wiping blood off her lip.

"You may."

"Spencer, watch out!" I cried as I spun to face him.

But I was too late. Enraged, ShadowMegan shot up to hover a foot off the ground, a tornado of energy surrounding her, tangling her hair around her like a tattered veil.

I saw her raised her hands and aim them at Spencer.

I found myself running to leap between him and Megan.

Too late.

The tablet he'd been carrying fell to the floor.

Shattered.

The air around Spencer shimmered.

Boiled.

Spencer screamed.

Spencer went still.

Silent.

And Spencer collapsed to the floor in a lifeless heap.

The world seemed to implode around me, to press against my body, so much pressure I could feel myself compressing into a small cube, unable to breathe.

I wobbled in place, my head swimming, my eyes unable to close, unable to look away.

A million thoughts raced through my brain.

Why did I bring back Megan?

Why didn't I make them run when I had the chance?

Why did I think I could plan anything?

Why are Evan and Amy calling my name?

ShadowMegan twisted away, her killing hands aimed at Evan. He froze in place and the air shimmered around him.

She was going to kill him too—she was going to kill every last person I loved.

One last question popped into my brain: *What is that roaring?*

The roaring. It was me. The wolf. I'd shifted without thinking, all fur and razor claws and shredding death. I burst forward at inhuman speeds, a monster of fury. ShadowMegan no longer looked like my childhood best friend. With my wolf eyes, all I could see was the shifting, shadowy blackness of the Akhakhu soul that wore the body like a suit.

She wasn't Megan, Shadow or otherwise. Megan was gone. All that was left was Rebel.

Memories flashed in my head as I leaped through the cavernous room.

Spencer and I, attacking Dr. Elliott, the man who tried to shoot us. It was me who went for the throat, I knew now. I was the one who made the killing blow.

Dalton and I, reassuring each other: *You are not a killer. We are not killers.*

But I am a killer. That's what they made me, even if it was just an accident of their true purpose.

In that last moment, Emily disappeared. I was an enraged alpha wolf that had just seen her pack member, her *mate*, go down at the hands of an enemy, while another pack member's life was about to be extinguished.

I burst through Rebel's swirling energy. It shredded my fur, tore it from my body in chunks. Blood oozed from my raw skin, pain shuddered through me.

I didn't care.

I slammed into Rebel's chest and she fell to the ground. She landed heavy, hard, half against the platform that contained the portal and half against the lower level. I heard a *snap* as her back cracked.

"Stop," she screamed. "Stop!"

She went silent as my jaws wrapped around her throat. My head yanked back and forth. Blood gushed, hot against my tongue, my snout. Inky, shadowy blackness, part of

Rebel's *ka*, stuck to my teeth. I pulled my snout back, dragging the creature's wispy head free from her chosen body.

For just a second, Megan's eyes were hers again. Pale blue and sad. She gurgled, blood seeping between her lips.

My body shifted from wolf to human again without my choosing to do so. The wolf faded away. So did Nighttime. It was just normal me. The me Megan had known before all this began.

Grabbing her by her bloodstained cheeks, I looked directly into her eyes. My vision was blurry, but not for lack of superpowered eyes. Hot tears dripped down my face.

"I'm sorry," I whispered. "I'm so sorry, Megan. I loved you too. I wish this had never happened to you. It's all my fault."

Then her eyes shifted back to those of the Akhakhu. The creature possessing Megan made one last try for air despite the blood choking her.

And then the human body in which Rebel lived died.

I collapsed back, my head spinning, my world hollow. Meaningless. In my peripheral vision, I saw Evan gasping for air on his hands and knees. Alive.

"No!" Mr. Handler roared, towering above me. His eyes glowed bright white, the fine hairs along the back of his hands rising on end. "Rebel was a nuisance, but she was an Akhakhu! No Akhakhu shall fall to a *human*!"

"Stop!" Amy shouted.

Eyes still glowing, Handler turned away from me and looked at the girl. "Do not interfere, Amy Delgado. I do not want to lose all of you vespers. These must be punished for killing one of my people!"

"I see," she said flatly. "So your gods or whatever can do that. They can decide on a whim who gets to live and who gets to die."

"Amy . . ." Mr. Handler said.

She raised both her hands and aimed them at the CEO. "Guess what, man," she spat. "If you get to do it, so can I."

Mr. Handler shot up into the air as though ejected from a jet. He hung there, stunned. Then, Amy flung her hands toward the floor, and the man flew down.

He landed heavy, hard against the concrete floor.

"Emily," Evan said, grabbing my shoulders and forcing me to look away from Handler, from the dead body of my old friend. "Wolf eyes. Wolf eyes!"

I let him aim me toward Spencer's fallen body. My vision went gray—and that's when I saw it.

The ghostly *ka* that belonged to Rebel had clawed its way out of Megan's dying body. Like some twisted shadow of a human spider, it crawled across the floor—and started to slip inside Spencer's body, starting with his hands.

No. Spencer would not be like one of them. I wouldn't allow it. I wouldn't!

Strength surged through my limbs. I crouched like a line-backer, then spread out my arms, letting claws burst from my nails. My teeth sharpened into fangs, but I didn't go full wolf—I didn't need to. All I needed was the gray vision that let me perceive the shadowwoman that was inside my sort-of boyfriend's body.

The aura hovered around him, just barely seeping out of Spencer's seams—a soul of a creature larger than the host in which it had climbed inside. Its head had yet to merge with Spencer's, but it was starting to seep in through his mouth, his nose.

I refused to let his body become another suit of meat for some alien being. And as had been made clear over and over lately—if I could perceive Rebel's *ka*, I could hurt it.

The creature inside Spencer twitched his limbs. His chest rose and fell and he started to climb up into a sitting position.

Half roaring and half screaming, I pounced.

I landed feetfirst against Spencer's chest, and he fell onto his back, hard, while I stood atop him. He gasped for air, the wind knocked out of him.

Meanwhile, Amy took out all her weeks of anger and rage out on Mr. Handler.

With a fling of her arm, he tumbled head over heels across the room before landing on a desk between computer bays. Paper flew everywhere, and a monitor crashed to the floor, where it thundered and sparked.

"Stop!" Handler gasped, his eyes flashing between normal and blazing white. "You don't know what you're doing! We are the future!"

Amy stalked forward, her wild hair an untamed mane around her face, her eyes filled with a fury I'd never seen.

"You don't get to have a future," she said.

Then, raising both hands, she flung Mr. Handler once more.

He flew off the desk—and directly into a computer bay. Glass exploded outward and blue bolts of electricity sparked through the air. Convulsing in pain, the man screamed louder and louder as Amy kept shoving him into the monitors. His skin reddened and bubbled, and smoke rose from his scalp.

Beneath me, ShadowSpencer struggled to toss me off. Turning away from Mr. Handler's gruesome demise, I jumped off Spencer's chest, landing with my feet on either side of his torso. Then, focusing on the edges of the shadowwoman, I fell to my knees, gripped its incorporeal limbs, and yanked as hard as I could.

Mr. Handler fell silent, but my screams took his place. Spencer thrashed and writhed, howling in pain, but I pulled with all of my strength. Gradually, bit by bit, Rebel's *ka* came free—first one arm, then another, and then the entire upper half of her body.

With one final primal scream, I flung myself backward.

And the shadowwoman came with me.

I held it in my hands, my claws penetrating its wispy, not-quite-there skin. It was a featureless shadow in the shape of a woman, but of course wasn't a woman at all. It tilted its head, studying me curiously.

And then I pulled my arms apart and tore the thing in half.

It shredded down the middle like a paper doll, complete with a satisfying rip.

Then it was gone.

No poof. No swirl of smoke. Just gone.

I stood there, chest having, looking at the empty spot in front of me where the creature had been.

"Perceive that?" I asked no one in particular.

Exhausted from the exertion, I let my wolf features recede, my Nighttime strength fade away, until I was just Emily again.

The cavernous room stank of burned meat and melted plastic. Trying not to gag, I turned to see Amy standing still, looking at the destroyed monitor bays. I couldn't see Mr. Handler from where I stood, but I could see the smoke rising from his body, could smell his remains.

"Holy . . ." Evan said, coming up to her side. "You've

got a lot of power, Amy. A whole lot of power."

"I did the right thing, right?" Amy asked me. She turned to me, her eyes momentarily soft, pleading.

I didn't know. She'd killed someone. Someone who had held us captive and wanted to give our bodies over to other souls. Someone who was definitely dangerous, and had definitely done a lot of evil.

But also a man who had become consumed with the promises of a devious, alien species. A normal, weak human who thought he was going to make the world a better place.

"You did," I lied.

"Yeah," Evan said, scrunching his nose as he turned away from the burned body. "He was going to kill Emily. You didn't have a choice."

Amy flashed me a smile, then her face hardened into the mask I'd seen her put on so often.

Coughing. Heaving, hacking coughing from the floor to my left.

I turned, expecting to see one of the possessed adults waking up. Instead, I saw something that made my heart leap and my hand fly to my mouth.

Spencer was sitting up, one hand on the floor. He looked dazed, confused.

But he was alive.

"Spencer!" I cried.

I ran over to him and flung myself to my knees at his

side. While he coughed into his fist, I put his head in my lap and brushed his hair with my hands.

"Oh God," I whispered. "Oh thank you. I thought you were dead. I thought I lost you like I lost . . ." I swallowed. "You're alive!"

Finally able to look into my eyes, he grinned. In a croaking voice he said, "Hey, Em Dub."

And I knew then it was really him.

I pulled him up and I put my hands on his cheeks, and I kissed him.

He was surprised at first. Hell, so was I. But soon his arms were wrapping around me and he was kissing me back.

Neither of us was any good at it. It was slobbery and kind of awkward.

I don't know about him, but I didn't care one bit.

Amy cleared her throat. Spencer and I pulled apart and looked up at her.

"I hate to break up the reunion," she said. "But we need to get out of here."

I stood, helping Spencer up along with me. He winced— moving so shortly after having an invading soul ripped out of you apparently hurt—and let me and Amy put our arms around him to keep him on his feet.

He looked between the both of us and smiled. "My heroes."

"Hey," Evan said, jerking his thumb toward the blinking

robot orbs still clinging to the portal and the computers. "What are those for, anyway?"

"Nothing yet," Spencer said. "Not until I activate them."

"Then, explosion?" Evan asked with wide eyes.

Spencer nodded. "Boom."

Nodding appreciatively, Evan said, "Sweet."

Boys.

"All right," I said, looking around at the unconscious people around me. Trying not to focus on Brittany's body.

Trying not to see Megan lying there, alone. Dead.

Tears stung my eyes. But I needed to focus. Needed to be the alpha.

"All right," I repeated, running my free hand through my hair. "Spencer, go ahead and set the bots to detonate. And, Amy . . . is it okay if Evan carries out Brittany?"

Amy's lip trembled. "No. Leave her here. She'll slow us down."

"Are you—" I started to ask.

"Yes!" Amy spat. "Drop it, okay? We can cry later. There's no crying now. None. Got it?"

I swallowed and met her eyes, apologetic. "Yeah. Later."

"What about all these other people?" Evan asked, gesturing at the fallen possessed parents, scientists, and guards.

"Leave them, too," Amy spat, glaring at her fallen

parents. "They betrayed all of us. And they're all possessed. Just leave them."

"Yeah," I said, though my gut twisted, hating this, hating all of it. "Let's go. Let's just go."

Spencer shouted, "Detonate!" and then a string of numbers. The bots blinked with red lights. They beeped, counting down the seconds to detonation.

Summoning the last of my strength, Amy and I helped carry Spencer out of the basement and back up the stairs, Evan behind us.

Just as we escaped the empty lobby and joined what looked like all of Vesper Company's employees on the street outside, the first of the explosions sounded below, and the first floor of Vesper Company began to collapse.

32

IT'S WHO I CHOSE TO BE

Megan was gone.

I had lost her weeks before, I know that, long before she was ever possessed by a creature from another world.

But I had hoped it was just a rough patch. That she would learn to be happy again, and I would learn how to handle a whole new life that could contain her, too.

I'd never get that chance now. And whenever I closed my eyes or was alone, all I saw was her face, and all I remembered was the way her eyes looked as I stood above her.

But, I guess, what's done was done.

After killing Rebel and Mr. Handler, we Deviants found one another and slipped away in the chaos on the streets as Vesper Company employees and others who worked nearby watched a cloud of concrete dust explode out of the shattered windows on the first floor of the Vesper Company building. Tracie had managed to convince the guards to evacuate, and we got lucky—the building didn't collapse to hurt anyone else.

We made it home—to our makeshift, freezing-cold, completely impractical model home-home, that is. But after all we'd been through, home was pretty much wherever me and my fellow Deviants were together.

I still couldn't believe Spencer was alive. When Rebel raised her hands with Mr. Handler's consent, I was certain he'd fall as dead as Brittany. But either her spell had faltered or Rebel's spirit trying to merge with Spencer had brought him back. I didn't know. I guess it didn't matter.

Spencer was next to me as I wrote the latest details down in my journal, his head resting on my lap with his eyes closed, his breaths shallow. He squirmed every now and again in his sleep, like a puppy chasing a dream rabbit, and I couldn't help but smile and feel sad all at once. Because I had him back, but everyone else was still gone, and I couldn't go back to my family again.

No. I wouldn't dwell on negatives, I decided. I mean, there was no point.

There was no going back. I wasn't Emily Webb anymore. I was the vesper Deviant alpha wolf girl. And even though I never asked for this, even though I'll never get over my resentment at those who did this to me, it's who I am.

It's who I chose to be.

We were all in the living room of the model home one last time, smelly and tired and alternately giddy at our success and devastated by the loss of Megan and Brittany, not to mention Nikki's and Amy's parents.

Evan and Patrick were sitting very close to each other, all shy smiles and furtive looks. There was definitely something happening there, and it was incredibly *cute*. I couldn't help but think of all the girls who'd lusted over our hot British exchange student when he'd first moved to town who'd never know he only had eyes for a blond wolf-human hybrid boy who could travel between worlds.

Nikki and Dalton were together too. He was staring into the distance, Nikki holding him and rocking him gently, her gaze similarly distant, her mind elsewhere. Seeing the two of them together, I was confident the fears Dalton had once confessed to me of becoming like his father, Mr. McKinney, wouldn't ever come true. Dalton was a good guy. I hoped one day he'd be his old self again. As much as any of us could be our old selves.

Amy and Tracie were playing checkers, another of the games we found in the designated child's bedroom upstairs. Amy was aggressive, Tracie calm and collected.

Tracie kept winning by taking the least-expected path. Something told me she was on better terms with the Nighttime part of herself that could see the world in ways the rest of us couldn't.

Amy was still hiding behind her mask. Maybe one day she would feel comfortable talking about what happened in that cavern of a basement when she lost her family, then took her anger out on Mr. Handler. I hoped she would come to me. I knew how it felt to be a . . . a killer.

That was us, I guess. Eight little Deviants squatting in a home on the outskirts of a city called Volmond with no clear idea where we were going to go next.

I felt a drive inside me, though. Twenty years before, Michael Handler and Vesper Company started something that put a lot of people in peril and changed the lives of dozens and dozens of unsuspecting children. Mr. Savage hinted about them to me that one time, and we read about them in the files we stole.

The vespers weren't just the wolves and the psychs. There were others like us. Kids and teens genetically enhanced all for the purpose of aiding an interdimensional invasion.

Maybe I would lead my team to find these kids. Though Mr. Handler was done for, surely other portals still existed, and so did the cult devoted to the shadowmen. Maybe together we could truly stomp out Vesper Company and its branches filled with acolytes of the dangerous, deadly Akhakhu, once and for all.

Big plans. Big danger.

I decided to sleep on it.

Right then, I was content to just rub my hand on Spencer's back, inhale his comforting scent, and try to forget all the horrible things I'd had to do over the past few months.

It was time to sleep.

One day, two months before, I went to bed as shy, geeky Emily Webb. The next, I woke up as something entirely new, and my life completely changed.

Who knew where life would take me tomorrow?